A SPELL TO DIE FOR

(Sonoma Witches Book 3)

GRETCHEN GALWAY

Eton Field

A Spell to Die For

Copyright © 2020 by Gretchen Galway

Eton Field, Publisher
www.gretchengalway.com

Cover design by Gretchen Galway
Illustrations: DepositPhotos

All characters in this book are fictitious. Any resemblance to actual persons, living or dead, is purely coincidental.

eBook ISBN-13: 978-1-939872-25-8
Paperback ISBN-13: 978-1-939872-26-5

v.20250723

Chapter One

I hadn't expected to find a demon in a hardware store on a Friday morning. It was mid-November, and I was just setting up a plastic display near the register to sell some of my handcrafted jewelry on consignment. Cypress Hardware was the biggest store in our remote forest town north of San Francisco and my best bet to make some rent money, but it was hardly the place I expected to sense the chilly prickle of demonic possession.

Looking up from my beaded necklaces, I scanned the store and saw two or three employees, all nonmagical humans, preparing for the day. I cast out a probing spell and recoiled as the rancid taste of Shadow magic filled my mouth.

The demon must've been drawn by the Silverpool Wellspring just down the river. On the winter solstice a month from now, the seasonal pool of magic would return, attracting vast numbers of mostly harmless fae, which demons loved to consume.

But why hadn't the witches at the Protectorate stopped

this demon from getting into town? That's what they were paid for.

Unlike me, which was why I was having a cash flow problem. Until a couple of years ago, I'd been a Protectorate agent, tracking and battling supernatural threats, and making jewelry had only been a fun hobby, not a financial lifeline. But I'd been cast out of that high-status life before my twenty-fifth birthday. Since then, every witch in the Protectorate had learned to sneer at the name Alma Bellrose: the first demon hunter to be fired for having an Incurable Inability to kill.

That's when I'd moved to Silverpool, seeking a fresh start.

Since then, however, one thing I'd been surprised to learn was that my infamous inability was limited to that one— albeit useful—skill. In other ways, I'd discovered I was quite… capable. More than most witches. For instance, the demon I'd just noticed was probably well disguised, sending out blinding magic to confuse me, but I'd sensed its presence immediately.

That still didn't mean I was eager to deal with the threat. Killing was as unappealing to me as ever, but who else could even try to stop it from hurting people and fae?

I looked around again and saw only Samantha, the teenager with too much makeup who used to work at the gas station, now wearing a Cypress apron and pushing a train of shopping carts back into the store.

But there, just behind her…

Icy, magical awareness pricked at my skin. An old man lumbered in wearing a khaki jacket, his sour expression scowling at Samantha, the ceiling lights, the customer service counter, the Christmas tree display, and anyone who'd have the misfortune of catching his eye.

The sense of Shadow intensified.

I shuddered and touched the strand of wood beads

hanging around my neck. Unlike the jewelry I was putting on public display, the necklace I wore was a focus string, an object infused with magic too powerful to hang on a plastic rack near jugs of windshield fluid and beef jerky.

I took a step back, shaken by the waves of power. A year ago, I hadn't thought a demon would ever dare to come within ten miles of Silverpool, which was supposed to be heavily guarded by the Protectorate. Dealing with supernatural threats to humanity worldwide was their job. But since a violent attack over the summer, new threats had come to town, and many of my assumptions had been shaken. I wasn't even sure what a demon was anymore, having learned not all possessing spirits were the same. Or possibly even evil.

But this one was—it reeked of Shadow, thick and nasty magic, making me use my beads to draw a bubble of protection around myself. Leaving my jewelry display and storage case at the counter, I turned and followed the man past the circular information desk, beyond the racks of paint swatches and aisles of wrenches and air compressors and roofing tiles, into the shadows behind a display of replacement doors and windows. Samantha was also with us, now pushing a cart of half-dead clearance shrubbery toward the garden center in the back of the store.

I loved my town and wasn't going to let the creature hurt anything or anyone here. Although my demon-killing career was over, I wasn't powerless.

I had to try to stop him.

He suddenly turned down the plumbing aisle. A dozen steps behind, I followed. But when he slowed ahead of me and turned to scowl at the display of toilet seats, I realized the blast of evil energy was weakening, not getting stronger, as I approached him.

I paused, put my hand on my necklace, and cast out my senses.

Demon's balls. He wasn't the source of the feeling. It was…

I backed up slowly into the main aisle and peered out at the teenager walking away with the cart of half-dead plants. Samantha? She was about ten feet away and her back was to me, but now that I focused my attention on her, I could see her posture was too rigid, her walk too wooden, her head tilted to one side as if she'd forgotten how to hold it up.

She released the cart and slowly turned around. Her eyes, unblinking, took in the sight of me and the aura of magic I'd woven around my head, chest, and limbs. Samantha must've been in charge of herself when she got ready that morning, because her makeup was as thick and flawless as always. The demon was moving the body clumsily now, suggesting the eyeliner had been applied before the possession with the real Samantha's excellent hand-eye coordination.

"Witch," the demon said, drawing out the *ch* sound in a long, low hiss.

Fear made me freeze. I didn't have a silver stake, but we were near the garden tools. Would any of the metal have the power to—?

No, no, no. I couldn't kill the demon—even if I were able—without killing Samantha. I didn't even know if she'd graduated from high school yet. But that's what the Protectorate would do if I called them in. It's what they always did.

Well… not always. Just last month I'd helped exorcise a demon from a child. But I'd only helped a stronger witch; I hadn't done it by myself. And that had been experimental, fully contained in a magic building, surrounded by other powerful witches.

I looked around, my heart pounding, afraid nonmagical humans might get hurt if the demon struck out. My protective spells were shimmering around me, buckling under the Shadow energy. I could protect myself, but how many others?

The demon lifted Samantha's arm and pointed at me with a fingernail painted a glittery bright blue. When it curled a finger, a surge of power lifted my feet and yanked them out from under me.

Pain shot up my spine as I landed on my back. I cursed, angry at myself for being careless. Feet were always a dangerously vulnerable spot. My wards had encompassed the rest of my body, but I must've left a spot on the sole of my boot open to attack.

I tried to roll over onto my hands and knees, but invisible force was dragging me along the floor on my back, toward the demon's outstretched hand. Legs paralyzed, I floundered on the floor, twisting and thrashing, clutching at my necklace for more power while the demon pulled me behind her into the garden-tool aisle.

For the first time, fear for my own safety struck me. What had I been thinking to go up against a demon without backup? Without a silver stake? Terror surged through me.

I flung a hand out to grab a shovel, but the demon jerked me forward, twisting my arm painfully beneath me. The space between us shrank another foot. Soon it would be able to touch me, and I had no idea what would happen then. For all my training, I'd never been alone with a demon on the offensive; I'd always been the predator, not the prey.

With that reminder of my place on the magical food chain, I tapped into my magic well of power and this time was able to break the demon's hold on me for a full second, just long enough to flip over and knock a shovel off the hook. When it fell to the floor beside me, I grabbed it.

It was stainless steel with a hickory handle. I bared my teeth in a wolfish smile. Perfect. Metal *and* wood. Before I took my next breath, I tapped into the innate power of the materials and used the surge of energy to lift myself off the ground and land on my feet. I braced my legs in a fighting stance.

"Leave her alone," I told the demon, brandishing the shovel in both hands.

The demon twisted Samantha's face with its matte ruby-red lipstick and winged eyeliner into a sneer. "We're happy together," the lips said. "Leave us alone." The voice was that of a young Northern California girl's mixed with ice and nightmares, and it crawled down my spine like a centipede.

I moved my right hand down over the hickory, drawing from the magic in the old roots, while my left hand, trembling, stroked the cold steel. I was in way over my head. Way, way over. I'd been kicked out of the Protectorate because of my Incurable Inability to kill demons—how could I stop this one?

But what else could I do? Let the monster take over an innocent young human who didn't even know magic existed?

"Leave her alone," I said again. This time, before it could speak, I tapped into the power of the shovel, my beaded focus string, my body, my very life, and channeled it into a well of magic as Bright—and human—as I could make it. It pooled in my hands like tap water in a latex balloon, and then—

I shot it at the figure before me.

And it laughed. Pale light swirled around Samantha's head, exaggerating the lavender tones of her highlighted hair. The magic shooting from my fingers didn't seem to hurt the demon at all, only improve the lighting, illuminating how perfectly Samantha had applied her eyeliner that morning.

For a split second I reflected on how it would take more magic than I possessed to make my own eyes look like that. I'd been quietly critical of Samantha's obsession with her makeup, but who was I to judge? She had real talent. A passionate skill for an art form she'd chosen.

And the demon was taking it all away.

Renewed anger sparked in me. *"Leave her alone."* This time I spoke in a whisper instilled with all the magic I had.

At first the demon's smile, those twisted ruby-red lips, didn't waver. But as my breath floated across the distance between us and was inhaled into her lungs—Samantha's lungs, still a human body with a human soul—the mouth went slack. The young eyes widened. And then the lids fluttered, and Samantha's body lurched forward.

Fearing a trick, I didn't move. She crumpled to the floor like a puppet without a hand.

My own eyes were hard to keep open. I realized I was swaying on my feet, and the shovel, suddenly too heavy for my weak fingers to hold, clattered to the floor. My vision went black at the edges and blurry in the center and then, with each rapid thump of my exhausted heart, faded completely.

The effort of attacking the demon had drained me.

I fell to the floor next to the shovel, next to Samantha. As my senses washed in and out, I noticed how cold the tile was against my cheek. I didn't have the strength to lift my head and see if by some miracle Samantha had survived; I couldn't even open my eyes.

What a disaster. Now the Protectorate was going to come to town, find the problematic Alma Bellrose unconscious next to a dead demon, and haul me in for questioning. Again. Over the past several months, I'd either been under arrest or forced to work for them. Sometimes both at the same time.

I wish I'd made it home in time to feed the dog first, I thought. Then I lost consciousness.

Chapter Two

I woke in my own bed with Random, my dog, curled against my hip. He was fussing at his paws, bumping me as he licked and gnawed, an annoying habit the vet suggested might be allergies. For all my witchy powers, I hadn't yet found a spell to make him stop.

"Leave it," I said with a yawn, pulling his snout away from his feet.

Random was a medium-sized mixed-breed, maybe part Lab, and I'd rescued him from my father, who had kept him enchanted as either a golden retriever or a dragon. Life with me was a lot easier, though lately I'd been making him wait until midmorning for his food to teach him to stop waking me up at dawn. "Wouldn't you rather have breakfast? Let's get—"

Only then did it all rush back to me. My sleepy good mood exploded, and I sat up with a start. My dark, wavy hair fell into my eyes, and I slapped it away, looking around the room to figure out what was going on. Random, taking my sudden move for enthusiasm to pour kibble into his bowl, leapt off the bed and galloped toward the kitchen in a clatter of claws on the old hardwood floors.

Pulse racing, I cast my magic around and tugged at the covers to make sure I wasn't dreaming. How had I made it home? Had I found the strength—?

No. Something was wrong. I looked at my arms, my hands; slapped my hands over my neck in a panic.

My jewelry was gone. *What had happened?*

Random reappeared in the doorway, head tilted, scrutinizing me for signs of breakfast delivery. Sun poured through the windows, looking more like afternoon than our usual foggy coastal mornings. How long had I been asleep? I looked at the clock: 12:34. Over four hours had passed since I'd been at Cypress, when the store manager had allowed me to set up my jewelry before the morning rush.

"All right, all right," I said, sucking in a calming breath. At least I was alive. Wiping the sweat off my forehead, I put my feet on the floor and stood up. My knees buckled before I straightened completely, and I had to fling a hand out to the nightstand for balance. Stars sparkled in my vision for a moment, then passed. I walked slowly to the kitchen, touching the wall for support, and served the kibble.

Blinking away stars in my vision, I pulled healing power from the hearth magic of my kitchen and tried to remember what had happened. Steady thinking was the only way to control the anxiety that still gripped me. My weakness and Random's hunger showed I hadn't dreamt about being at the store that morning. I'd fought the demon; I'd collapsed. Now I was home.

But how?

A knock on the door wasn't enough to distract Random from his delayed breakfast. He continued inhaling it even as the door opened and my friend Birdie's face appeared.

"Hi, Alma," she said. "Can I come in?"

Until recently, Elizabeth Crow, nicknamed Birdie, had been living in my second bedroom and taking magic lessons from me. A few months ago, she'd discovered she was a witch at the same time she'd inherited a fortune that included the Silverpool Winery. Now she was using some of that wealth to pursue her dream of owning a bookstore.

"Of course," I said. "You're always welcome here."

"That means a lot, coming from you," she said, stepping inside. She was in her early twenties, just a little younger than me, with long brown hair, big brown eyes, and a lanky figure. In her skinny jeans and flattering sweater, she was much more fashionable than I was—in part because of her normal, nonmagical upbringing in nearby Santa Rosa. With my messy hair and baggy clothes, I looked like a stereotypical witch next to her. "Can you believe I'm getting my last box?"

Just in the past few weeks she'd sold the winery and bought a storefront and second-floor apartment in Silverpool's tiny downtown. I'd urged her to test the magical aura of the property before closing the sale, but within only six days, she'd declared the aura perfect and put down her money. It was a done deal.

"It happened so fast," I said. My privacy was precious to me, but I'd already begun to miss her. And not just because she'd also been covering some of the household expenses.

"Turns out the old owner was on the hook for some permit violations," she said. "Guess that's why he was in such a hurry."

I sat down at the kitchen table and idly stroked my left wrist, still sore from the newest tattoo that had mysteriously appeared after a recent witch house party in Mendocino. The marks were thin, concentric arcs in black ink that radiated outward from the bend in my wrist. One had appeared that summer, and a second ring just over a month ago. I didn't know why or how they had appeared, but I suspected it had something to do with the first witch I had fought, a witch who died—

Something strange about the pain made me look down, and I stared in shock. A third ring had appeared, stretching out above the other two. The skin around it was bright red and inflamed.

I cupped my hand over it and sent a probing spell into my own skin, searching for answers. Was it a curse? The marks had appeared after I fought other witches.

It had to be something about magical confrontation. Had my fight with the demon left the mark, or had there been another witch, too?

If only I could remember.

Birdie continued to talk about her new store, the building, the code violations. "An electrician I knew from Cypress checked it out. He gave me a quote. It's not too bad."

Setting aside the mystery of my tattoos—for now—I gave Birdie a concerned look. "I hope you got a discount on the selling price." I tended to be overprotective of Birdie, even though we were about the same age, because she was so nice, so deeply kind, walking through the world with her heart open.

"I can afford it," she said. "Those witches at the Protectorate might be brilliant at magic, but they weren't very good at negotiating a deal. My lawyer said they way overpaid for the winery."

Birdie's inheritance was more complicated than a local lawyer could know. Until that summer, the winery's owner had been Tristan Price, who had been Birdie's biological father (and, to my embarrassment, briefly my boyfriend), although she'd never known him. He'd also been the Protector of Silverpool, assigned by the Protectorate to guard the wellspring. He'd loved wine and had cared as much about his vineyards as he had about demons and fae. After his murder, Birdie had inherited the winery, then promptly sold it to the Protectorate. Someday they would install a new Protector in town. For personal reasons, I wasn't eager for that to happen. I'd risked my life to find his murderer, but I'd also learned to distrust the Protectorate. They were too quick to kill creatures they didn't understand.

Birdie bent over to greet Random, who had finished eating and was now celebrating her return. He'd miss her when she stopped coming around so often. Our tiny town, magically hidden to avoid danger, was unlikely to have the foot traffic to support a bookstore, but she didn't actually need the income. She'd learned from me how important it was for a witch to establish a home base where she could centralize and grow her power. Living with me had made it increasingly difficult for her own magic to develop.

"Listen," I said, rubbing my temples, "did you happen to notice anything at Cypress while you were driving by?"

"At what?"

"Cypress Hardware," I said. "Was there anything strange in the parking lot, on the street, any Protectorate SUVs, anything unusual?"

"What's Cypress Hardware?" she asked, sitting across from me.

I stared at her. Demon's balls. More proof I hadn't imagined it. Protectorate agents, responding to the demonic emergency, must've set up confusion wards around the property. "The massive big-box store in the center of town that sells anything you might ever want," I said, my voice rising. "Your inspiration for opening your own store since they seem to do a good business even though hardly anybody lives here."

She blinked, furrowing her brow. "Right," she said slowly. "How could I forget?"

I pushed to my feet. "I need to go." Had Samantha

survived? Were they here to investigate a murder or a thwarted demonic invasion? "I might need to ask you a favor."

"Sure. If I can remember it."

I smiled weakly. "If I don't come home this afternoon, could you take care of Random until I get back?"

"Why— Oh no. What happened?" Birdie leaned over the table. "Was it something at Cypress? Why did I forget what it was? Is that why you're so weird-looking, all limp and splotchy? I thought maybe you were hungover, and now that you've given up coffee, it's impossible to recover, but of course it's not like you go out clubbing or having fun or anything, which you totally should, even though it makes you look sick the next day, it's actually good for you. I mean, it would be if you did it."

Because Birdie tended to ramble, I waited for the current of words to come to a complete stop before saying, "I'll explain later. Will you check on Random?"

"Of course, yes, of course. I'll put a note on my hand so I can't forget it." She took a marker out of her bra and made a wobbly X on her right index finger. "I was using it to label boxes. They can't erase Sharpie on my skin, can they? Protectorate agents?"

I didn't want to scare her by telling her how much of her they could erase, so I just nodded and went to the door, where my footwear was lined up under a coatrack. How had I taken off my shoes when I was unconscious? Or my jacket?

"I'll take him for a walk right now, if that's OK with you," she said. "I miss our jaunts around the neighborhood."

"That would be really great," I said. "Thanks, Birdie. Thanks so much."

"But you have to tell me everything when you get back. You're going to be sneaky and try to hide things from me, so promise me you won't."

I stared at her, biting my lip. There were things it was probably better she not know, at least not until she'd learned more. She'd only discovered she was a witch a few months ago.

But maybe I was being too protective. "I promise to tell you what I can," I said, pretending not to see the face she made.

MY JEEP, which I'd driven to Cypress that morning, was in the driveway.

Not good. How had it gotten there without my knowing?

Leaving it there, I set out on foot to return to the store, down the narrow lane where our three houses perched amid the trees on the hill overlooking the Vago River. The rest of Silverpool's business district fit within the next three blocks along Main Street, which also followed the river. And a couple of miles past that, on the way to the Pacific coast, was the magnet for all the demons, witches, and fae that come to town: the Silverpool Wellspring.

Once a year, a flood would coincide with the winter solstice, bringing water with magical properties to the surface. The fae found it irresistible and traveled great distances to enjoy it; the demons found the fae irresistible and so came to consume *them*; human witches, under the organizational umbrella of the Protectorate, stayed to prevent supernatural chaos. Weeks away from the solstice, the wellspring was still dry. Why had a demon risked coming so close?

And I didn't want to think about how my vehicle had returned to my house. Just the thought of having been carried and driven, without my awareness, sent a shiver through me. Why couldn't I remember? There should've been some magic residue on my body that gave me a clue what had happened, but I felt nothing.

I would have to find answers at Cypress Hardware.

As I'd expected, the parking lot in front of the wide, squat building was behind a blur of boring, misty air. But then I was overcome with a yawn and stood in place a moment, feeling my head swim. Maybe I was getting sick. I had a sudden, vivid, delicious craving for an almond-milk latte and pumpkin-spice scone from the café down the street. The taste of cloves and butter and cinnamon tingled on my tongue, luring me past the scene of the crime—and the trio of black Protectorate SUVs parked out front—to the warm, cozy café across from Birdie's planned bookstore.

The second I touched the crosswalk button to go to the café, I returned to my senses and snatched my hand away. Annoyed with myself, I pinched my arm to keep myself in line, then returned to the enchanted parking lot and strode through the spell.

I made it through, but I had to fight off a wave of nausea.

I was definitely not at my peak form.

When my stomach settled, I was able to get a good look at the faces of the Protectorate agents. With mixed feelings I saw Darius Ironford, my former partner. He was a serious-looking man in his late twenties, tall and lean, with his dark hair in twisted curls—a little fuller on top than when I'd last seen him. He wore his usual diamond earring and a generous amount of gold on his wrists and hands.

The five others, young men and women, all wearing silver-studded black leather jackets, were unfamiliar to me. Darius watched me approach as if he'd been waiting for me, which he probably had.

"You were seen here this morning," he said without greeting. That was typical for him and didn't necessarily mean he was angry, suspicious, or annoyed with me, though he usually was. I hadn't been the best partner, but recently I'd been able to make up for some of my limitations.

"I set up a jewelry display," I said. "For the holidays."

He raised a skeptical eyebrow and looked away. "Save it for Raynor when you give him your report."

Raynor was the director of the San Francisco office of the Protectorate. Until his promotion to management a few months ago, he'd been the most infamous demon hunter in the country. I'd never worked for him officially, but I'd been forced to do odd jobs for him off the record. My trip to a recent house party of murderous witches in Mendocino had been for him. Now he wanted me to take on more assignments, work as some kind of spy or off-the-record investigator, and I kept refusing. The house party had been a terrifying ordeal. Why would I want to repeat that kind of experience?

"I won't be giving him any *reports*," I said. "I don't work for—"

He held up a hand. "Not now. I've got to watch the new Flints." He nodded at the crew of agents. Flint was the entry-level position at the Protectorate. "A nonmagical human is attacked near a wellspring, and all they give me is a handful of Flints." He scowled.

I opened my mouth to say she was more than attacked—total demonic possession would trigger a high-level investigation involving New York and Emerald-level witches—but froze. How would I know about the demon if I'd only been setting up my jewelry display? Avoiding Protectorate entanglement in the demon's attack on Samantha was going to be complicated.

If I told Raynor about what I'd seen, there was a chance he would keep it a secret from the rest of the Protectorate. He'd already had me work off the record with Darius before in Mendocino—fairly successfully, although we hadn't prevented as much death as I would've liked—and he might want me to do it again. From the way Darius was acting, my old partner probably assumed I was still one of Raynor's secret agents.

But I didn't want to be. I wanted my privacy, my independence, my safe, peaceful life.

Not that I'd ever had a safe, peaceful life, but I could fight for one.

"Do you know the name of who was attacked?" I asked. It was a deceptive question, because I knew it already, but not technically a lie.

"Samantha Ashe," he said. "Eighteen. Female. Nonmagical."

"Is she...?" I began.

"What?"

I swallowed, bracing myself for tragedy, and spoke in a whisper. "Alive?"

He shot a hard look at me. "Yes," he said carefully. "She was found sitting on the floor in one of the aisles, saying she'd fainted."

"That's it?" I asked, feeling uneasy. Maybe the demon was still active inside her. "You talked to her?"

"We suspect she'd been attacked an hour earlier. The demon sign was all over her." He eyed me. "You must've felt it yourself, since you were here. It triggered one of our automatic wards, alerting us in San Francisco around seven o'clock this morning."

"I—"

He flung up a hand. "Please. Don't tell me anything. Raynor wants to keep you off the record, and anything you tell me will have to go in my report. An Emerald witch will be scanning me for memory and truth errors when I make it." He took out his notebook and began sketching the layout of the parking lot, the cart return corral, the sliding front doors. "I'm telling you what I know just because I figure you'll poke around to find out what you want to know anyway, and getting it from me keeps you from causing more trouble."

"You make it sound like I want trouble in my life," I said, "when that's the last thing I ever want."

He continued sketching.

"But since you're answering my questions," I continued, clearing my throat, "what does she remember happening this morning? Other than the fainting?"

"She felt light-headed while she was collecting the shopping carts from the parking lot, and the next thing she remembers was waking up inside on the floor next to the garden tools."

"And…" How could I ask if she'd said anything about me without admitting I'd been in the same aisle? "She was alone?"

He flipped back through his notebook. "An assistant manager, Carolyn Kemper, found her and called for help. She can barely walk, but declined an ambulance. Doesn't have insurance. Two of our people pretended to be off-duty EMTs and checked her out, confirmed the demon sign. Her mother just took her home."

"Who called the Protectorate?"

"We were already on the way after the ward was triggered," he said. "We have to conduct a complete sweep of the town, starting with this store and the wellspring. When a human being is affected by any Shadow presence, however briefly, we still have to make sure the threat is driven away or destroyed."

From the way he was talking, I feared they didn't realize just how serious the threat actually was. The demon hadn't brushed up against Samantha accidentally and then passed on; he'd completely possessed her. For him to be driven out —by me, apparently—was too unusual for Darius or the other agents to consider.

But if I told them what I'd seen, a horde of powerful, aggressive, intrusive Protectorate witches would descend on Silverpool and not only interfere in my own privacy, but uncover the existence of one of my neighbors—an individual who'd become important to me: the changeling Seth Dumont. Since in modern witch politics, Seth was technically a possessing spirit, that made him no different than a demon—a threat that needed to be destroyed.

Seth, however, was stuck in Silverpool. Years ago his mother, a lake fae, had put him in the body of a human baby, and Seth had grown up in Minnesota with loving, nonmagical human parents. This past summer, feeling guilty, Seth had tracked down the human spirit who now inhabited his fae body and offered a corrective exchange. But the former human, living as the fairy Launt, was an angry, violent creature, and had died in the ensuing conflict. Now Seth found he could only survive if he stayed near the grave of his dead twin, and so he'd bought the house nearest to it—next door to me. He'd discovered that any travel outside of town made him mortally weak.

He frequently annoyed me, but I didn't want the hardliners at the Protectorate to discover him. I'd helped him stay alive this long and had gotten rather attached to the idea of him continuing to live.

But if I didn't tell the Protectorate about the demon, other residents of Silverpool, also my friends and neighbors —could lose their bodily and spiritual autonomy if they were possessed and consumed by the evil spirit I battled that morning.

"I have to talk to R—" I began.

Darius strode away before I could finish my sentence.

Right. He didn't want to know. Always ambitious, Darius still played by the rules and hoped to climb the ranks to Emerald before he was forty. Associating with me wasn't good politically. Worse than having an infamous criminal as a father, I'd been canned from the Protectorate and now made a living with hearth magic, growing herbs and selling wooden beads out of a cottage in the woods for rent money. Very old-fashioned, and very uncool.

I watched him talk to the Flint agents near the row of SUVs, who were talking to a very tall woman with dark hair I'd seen around the store before. The Cypress employees were milling about, adjusting the early Christmas trees, collecting shopping carts in the lot, acting as if nothing had happened. None of them glanced at the agents. The ignore spell was strong, and fighting it had started to give me a headache.

There was nothing else for me to see here. Why had I even come? There was a load of laundry in my washing machine I needed to move over to the dryer. I turned around and left, stepping through the boundary spell with relief and hiking up the hill to my house. By the time I was walking past Seth's house next door to mine, I'd forgotten why I'd left home in the first place. I didn't even have Random with me —why was I walking around without my dog? He needed as much exercise as I could give him, and here I was leaving him at home.

But when I stepped over the wards at the end of my driveway, my memory returned with full force.

And I realized I'd learned nothing about how I'd gotten home that morning. I shook my head, disgusted with myself for being so easily stupefied by a crew of Protectorate agents, most of them Flint, when I should've been completely prepared to fight off their predictable spells. As I went into my house, feeling my head clear of intrusive magic on my own turf, I allowed myself the excuse that I had still been weak from the battle with the demon. And my necklace and bracelets had been taken. I had come to rely on those, perhaps too much, to focus and enhance my natural powers.

Who'd taken my jewelry? Who'd brought me and my car home?

Chapter Three

Because of my exhaustion, I didn't talk to Raynor until late that evening after I'd had a nap. I'd slept through Birdie bringing Random back from a walk, a Protectorate visit to my heavily warded front door, and three calls from the big man himself, whose message told me if I didn't call him back before moonrise, the agents would break through my boundary spells and haul me to San Francisco for questioning at dawn.

And so, when there was the faintest hint of moonglow on the horizon, I called him. A woman answered the phone.

"May I speak to Director Raynor, please?" I asked.

"He's retired to his private residence for the evening," she said.

I stifled a snort. She made it sound like the White House, but Raynor didn't live like other Emerald witches. Usually the upper ranks of the Protectorate demanded they be treated like kings and presidents, with housing and clothing and formalities to match, but Raynor had chosen to sleep in the Diamond Street office like a lowly Flint agent. His private residence was a pull-out bed next to his desk.

"Please put me through," I said.

"Code word?"

He'd left me one, but I felt silly using it. He was determined to make me into some kind of secret agent. I sighed. "It's about a female bear with young offspring."

The woman on the phone hesitated. "That's not exactly... Well, I guess that's close enough."

In a moment, Raynor picked up. "The code word is *mama bear*."

"I'm not a spy," I said.

"No, you're a mama bear," he said. "Fiercely protective of the vulnerable, underestimated at your enemy's peril."

I smiled. It was hard not to like Raynor, in spite of the way he liked to throw his weight around. Just recently I'd discovered we shared a dangerous secret in common—we each bore the mark of a demon ancestor. I'd had no idea until about a month ago when a witch had used an opal ring to expose the trait in other witches. The only clue I'd had before then was my ability to hear and see fairies, even when they didn't want to be seen, which was highly unusual. In fact, Raynor was the only other human I'd ever met who had the same ability. Apparently it indicated a demon possession somewhere in the family line, possibly generations ago. Because it was taboo, the trait hadn't been studied openly.

I was still struggling to come to terms with what this meant for me. I'd never known my mother, not even her name, and it was hard not to blame her, whoever she was, for the trait. Was I part demon? I didn't feel evil, but maybe it was lurking deep inside me, just waiting for the right moment. The thought woke me in a panic sometimes in the middle of the night, and I'd have to pet Random for comfort before I could go back to sleep. A good dog would know if I was a Shadow threat, right? I'd always felt different from other witches, but I'd thought it was just my lonely upbringing. Would I discover my great-grandmother had left a wake of terror and death, some of it lingering in my own DNA?

That seemed to be the opinion of hardliner witches in the Protectorate. They called the trait demon "stain," although I thought "print" was more polite. Whatever it was called, both Raynor and I had to keep it to ourselves. If anyone else found out, it could end our careers and possibly limit our freedoms within the witch world. Raynor would certainly lose his job as director. But even I would suffer because most of the jewelry I made was magical, priced much higher than my Cypress Hardware display, and sold to other witches. Prejudiced witch customers would be reluctant to buy "demon-stained" focus beads, bracelets, and other crafts. I couldn't pay my rent from only the cheaper nonmagical designs. My reasons for staying away from Raynor and the Protectorate weren't just to protect my ego from the embarrassment of being fired—it was to protect my life.

"If I keep my head down and stay away from the Protectorate," I told him, "I won't have any enemies." In fact, the events of the morning suggested I had a guardian angel.

Of course, sensible witches didn't believe in angels anymore. Modern life had convinced them there was no such thing as pure goodness—only gradations of Shadow. I'd thought the same thing until recently, when I'd met a demon with a heart of gold. What was an angel if not that? There was so much we didn't understand about the world, especially in the realms of the supernatural.

"You were at the site of the demon attack today," he said.

Flinching, I rubbed my hand over my face. He was counting on my telling him everything, precisely for the reasons his code word suggested. And since we'd bonded over the demon-print-secret thing, he seemed to expect me to share all my secrets with him.

But what if protecting some people meant leaving one of them exposed to imprisonment, torture, even death?

Samantha's young face with the perfect eyeliner flashed before me. What if the demon returned to claim her familiar body? The Protectorate had to know how vulnerable the town had become, even if that put Seth in danger.

Maybe Seth had figured out a way to travel by now, I thought frantically. It had been a couple of weeks since I'd talked to him. And ultimately I would have to accept that Seth was an adult—in a stolen body, but one he'd had since infancy—who would have to take care of himself.

"The demon fully possessed Samantha," I said finally. "I was able to drive it out of her. I'm not sure how, but I did."

Raynor was silent a moment. "You didn't alert me."

"The exorcism wiped me out. I slept most of the day."

"You were feeling strong enough to hike across town on foot a few hours later," he said. "Darius didn't mention you being insensible or otherwise unable to speak."

I rubbed my temples, wishing I could ask him what he thought had happened to me, how I'd transported home. Was it possible, in my delirium, I'd learned how to teleport like my father could? He'd worked for years to develop that skill. Could I have just learned it in my sleep?

Unlikely, in my weakened state. And it didn't explain what had happened to my Jeep and jewelry.

I had an obligation to tell Raynor about the demon possession, but not about what had happened to me afterward. The less I exposed of myself, the better. Raynor was somewhat benevolent, but he wasn't harmless. We shared one secret; that didn't mean we should share all of them.

"I'm afraid of what you'll do to Seth," I said quietly.

"Who, me?" Raynor asked. "I've left him alone this long."

"You know what I mean," I said. "When your bosses hear

there was a full possession, you'll have to order a complete magical sweep of the town. He might get caught in the dragnet."

Raynor was quiet.

"Can you at least give me a back-channel heads-up so I can warn him when the Sweep Team is on its way?" I asked. "He can survive a little while away from his death site. Then when the team goes—"

"There isn't going to be a Sweep Team," Raynor said.

Exhaling in relief, I sank back into my couch. Raynor would be taking a risk to limit the investigation. I'd been on a similar team when I was a trainee agent, sorting through the crime scenes of departed (executed) demons. A Sweep Team had the time, authority, and budget to comb through every inch within the designated area, every building, every square of land. If the Protectorate demanded it, they could catalog every strand of hair on a person's head. And then do their neighbors'.

"Thank you," I whispered. "Are you just going to set up wards around Samantha, maybe set a trap to—?"

"A new Protector is being assigned to Silverpool," he said. "Full-rank Emerald. More assistants than Tristan had. The Protectorate is tired of getting bad news from your neck of the woods."

I jumped to my feet. "No, now?" My breath caught in my throat. Of course it was inevitable they would eventually replace Tristan, but Raynor had been able to prevent it so far, using it as leverage to pressure me to work for him.

"I've been reprimanded for the delay," he said. "The assignment is being made by some Sapphires in New York. Out of my hands." Sapphire-rank witches were a step above Emerald.

"But Seth… He's never hurt anyone. I even think humans and fairies are safer with him here. If the Protectorate would just investigate more carefully before trying to kill things they didn't understand—"

"I'll do what I can to suggest they appoint a witch with a more nuanced view of suprahuman beings," he said, "but the decision won't be mine."

I moved through my living room to the windows overlooking the street. Seth's bungalow next door was snug and tiny under a redwood tree, like mine, and a faint yellow light glowed from its windows. "You know he doesn't deserve to die," I said. "Please tell them that."

"I'll do what I can, but you need to lie low," he said. "Things are about to get tricky."

❧

ALTHOUGH I RESPECTED Raynor's advice to lie low, going completely underground wasn't possible.

For one, I couldn't rest until I'd warned Seth, and as of Saturday afternoon, he wasn't answering his door. If he had a current cell phone, which I doubted, I didn't know the number. I called Birdie, who told me she'd seen him walking along the river, and then I talked to another neighbor, Madge Souter, who told me he'd mentioned going to the beach. Born a lake fairy in Minnesota, Seth liked the water. So I drove around until dark, looking for him, but no luck. The thought of him wandering around, not knowing the Protectorate might be sending an agent to kill him, made my stomach hurt. I didn't want to worry about him—I had no obligation to—but I did. I'd given up fighting it.

Sunday morning, I had to take a break from looking for him to drive the two hours south to San Francisco. My father was getting married in less than a week to a woman I'd never met and had booked a table for brunch at the Top of the Mark, a penthouse restaurant and bar in a hotel overlooking the city. As I hiked up Nob Hill from a distant parking spot, I told myself that I'd had to come, that I couldn't spend all my days looking for a reclusive changeling who wasn't my responsibility anyway. This unknown woman was going to become my stepmother on Wednesday. I had to size her up.

My father, Malcolm Bellrose, was a complicated figure in my life. Although he never talked about the past, I suspected that becoming a father had never been one of his plans—and as an infamous thief of magical antiquities and treasures, he was better at plans than anyone I'd ever met. He'd spend a year plotting a heist, and the fact that he'd never been convicted of any crime, in spite of everyone knowing he was a criminal, proved how brilliant his plans were.

But they'd never included me. I'd tagged along on his burglaries, occasionally helping when I was too young to know better, but for the most part I stayed in a hotel room, friend's cottage, or boarding school, waiting for him to show up again.

The last time he'd shown up, a few weeks ago, he'd handed me a wedding invitation. He'd dated all kinds of characters over the years, but none had been serious. The wedding was days away, and I still didn't know anything about the woman he was about to marry. But what had most disturbed me about his delivery of the invitation was how he'd dropped a hint about how his new bride reminded him of my mother.

My birth mother.

Nobody had ever been able to give me any details about her, and I'd been unable to find any on my own. And in all my years growing up, Malcolm had never once told me a thing about her, no matter how many times I'd begged to share the simplest of details.

So when he'd implied he'd finally tell me something, I'd been weak enough to fall for it—for a few minutes. A day at the most. But then I'd wised up, realizing he was just manipulating me, trying to get me to come to the wedding, betting my pathetic, childish need to know my mother would make it impossible to stay away.

He shouldn't have bothered, because I would've attended anyway. I had my safety to consider. Knowledge of all kinds was power, and I had to protect myself. That didn't mean I was going to expect to get anything from him.

I paused at the top of Mason Street to catch my breath, gazing around at the plunging, rolling streets, the stone and steel buildings, the white-capped and sailboat-dotted bay beyond.

Of all places, why had Malcolm chosen this restaurant? Didn't he remember what had happened the last time he'd brought me there? Granted, it had been sixteen years, more than half my life ago, but it had changed everything.

The cable car tracks rumbled along the base of California Street, and tourists took pictures from each corner. It was a stunningly clear day, blue and gleaming, and I could see for miles. I wondered if my father had cast a spell to chase the fog away for a few hours or if he'd just gotten lucky. Malcolm Bellrose had always been very, very lucky. An essential quality for a thief.

I myself didn't seem to have inherited that luck; never having known any other family, I'd had to rely on him and his erratic, felonious ways my entire life.

I brushed the hair out of my eyes and inhaled the chilly, sea-scented November breeze, reminding myself to let go of the past and be grateful for the present. I was alive and well. I didn't need him anymore. Whatever scheme he was hatching now had nothing to do with me. If he was planning a heist at the hotel, and the brunch with me and his fiancée was all a cover for him to slip away and break into one of the rooms and steal a magical valuable of some kind—as it had been on my tenth birthday—I was prepared. I'd learned to expect the worst from him. I'd learned to expect nothing.

Dodging tourists, I crossed the street and walked to the corner entrance. Nothing had been the same since that birthday over sixteen years ago. On that day, I'd thought the celebration at the cool restaurant with the three-sixty views was a treat for me, a genuine present to make me feel special. But at a key moment, when the waiter had brought out the cake and began to sing, my father was gone. The bill had been paid, but he'd vanished. I'd sat alone with my uneaten slice of cake until a witch named Bronze, one of his associates, had appeared and said he was driving me home. At our apartment the next morning, Malcolm had woken me to show off the amulet he'd stolen as if he fully expected me to be happy for him.

But I'd finally seen him for what he was. Before the sun had set on the first day of my eleventh year, I'd insisted on going to boarding school far away, and never again went "home" (we'd never really had one anyway) for breaks, instead staying at school or with friends.

Hauling myself back to the present, I looked up at the landmark hotel rising above me like a fortress tower and tapped into the new redwood necklace at my throat for strength. I needed to maintain my composure. I'd never forgive myself if I showed how much it hurt to return to this place, if he ever learned how much he'd hurt me and still had the power to hurt me.

I walked over the brick drive and up into the ornate lobby, past the gold and shimmering holiday decorations, and got in the elevator. As it rose to the nineteenth floor, I scanned the rooms for anything especially odd or dangerous. If my father was here to steal something, it would be valuable enough to require magical wards, perhaps a witch or two standing guard.

Although I'd made my new necklace twice as powerful as my old one, I wasn't able to detect anything unusual. A few witches here and there, that was to be expected, but none of the magic felt particularly strong, dangerous, or deceptive. But an advanced ward could fool me from this distance. There could be anything hiding in the hotel.

A hostess greeted me at the top and escorted me across the maroon carpet to a table in a far corner where my father sat with a surprisingly ordinary fortysomething woman in a turtleneck sweater. I pretended to admire the view of the city, the azure water of the bay, Alcatraz and the rest of the post-card panorama, but all my real attention was on the blondish, roundish woman smiling at me through her glasses. She looked like a woman in a laundry detergent commercial. I realized I'd been expecting someone sexy and sophisticated, a witch of the world—like Malcolm.

But he'd said she was like my mother. Had he meant she looked like her? Or was it her personality? Her magical talent?

"Alma, how lovely to see you," Malcolm said, as if meeting had been an accident, rising to greet me without moving his hand from the woman's shoulder. "Would you like to join Vera and me with a glass of champagne? Bottomless, they call it, but nonmagicals don't mean it the way we do. Our waiter has to fill it with a bottle." He turned to his fiancée and winked.

She smiled at him, then at me. "It's so nice to finally meet you," she said, her smile widening. Her unblinking stare suggested she'd been very curious about me too. She didn't extend her hand, which was good manners among witches who didn't want to invade another's personal space, unbalancing their personal wards or spells, but she did get up and lean toward me as if she wanted to hug.

I quickly sat down on the other side of the table and

grabbed a water glass, alarmed by the threat of contact. No hugs on my menu today. Too many emotions were swirling inside me—fear, curiosity, disgust, anger, longing. This woman was like the mother I'd never known? Was that why I felt drawn to her?

I looked away to clear my head, belatedly noticing the opulent spread on the buffet tables. I saw raw oysters and caviar, steak and eggs, pastries and pancakes, fruit and salad, desserts. On my fateful tenth birthday, it had seemed like a cartoon feast, thrilling me with its opulence, more food than I'd ever seen in my life. But today I wasn't sure I'd be able to swallow a single bite. Old memories were crowding in, pulling childish emotions to the surface.

My father signaled one of the many waiters, and in a few moments I had a flute of champagne in my hand.

"So tell me," I said, forcing a polite smile for Vera, who seemed quite nice. Really nice. "How did you meet?"

Chapter Four

"That's the funny thing," Vera said. "We think we met years ago."

"You think?" I asked.

"She remembers it," Malcolm said, giving Vera an amused look. "I don't. Of course I'm a little older. Memory isn't what it was." He sighed self-deprecatingly. Although he was at least a decade older, he looked the same age as his future bride. Magic was better than plastic surgery.

"I work in a library in Denver," she said, then caught herself, shooting a smile at Malcolm. "Worked. Past tense. I live here now, of course."

"Are you going to be working in a library here, too?" I asked. Could there be some angle for my father to steal something? Antiquities in a guarded collection, perhaps?

But Vera shook her head. "Your dad and I are launching a nonprofit. I've always wanted to work with disadvantaged youth," she said. "Young witches without the advantage of a family name or connections."

A nonprofit? My father? He himself had been born with all the advantages of our old family name, but had always acted repulsed by the idea of sharing those privileges with anyone else.

"Don't look so skeptical," Malcolm told me, smiling tightly. "Vera might get the wrong idea about what kind of people we are."

I stared at him. "*We?*" There had to be some kind of angle. Maybe not for Vera—it was possible she was sincere, but manners prevented me from using a truth spell on my future stepmother, at least while she would notice—but my father only acted for his own interests. "I'm all for helping out young witches who need it. But *you*, Dad—"

"Am going to get some of those oysters." He rose gracefully to his feet, holding out a hand to Vera. "There's caviar too, darling. We want to get our money's worth."

Our money? I wondered if that explained the match: she was rich. But then why would she have been working at a public library? And the jewelry she wore was modest, just a few pieces of gold here and there, a fine chain, hoop earrings, a topaz stone on her ring. Rich witches heavily adorned themselves with platinum and gemstones, usually as ancient as their illustrious family trees. Her jewelry was mass-produced and modern.

Their engagement made less sense to me now than when I'd received the surprise invitation less than a month ago.

We got up, Vera taking my father's hand, and walked a few steps together before I turned away and headed for the pastries and fruit. Raw oysters weren't appealing at the moment. My father was slippery enough for one gathering.

I filled my plate and hurried back to our table in time to do a quick scan of Vera's magical residue before she returned. Pretending to tidy up, I held her napkin, moved her water glass, and rested my palm on the tablecloth where hers had been.

Her magical fingerprints were faint but steady and

smooth, precisely what I'd expect from an average witch of her age in a nonmagical profession. A Protectorate agent might leave a concentrated taste of silver, which in its enchanted state was used to hunt demons, whereas the impression of a witch who drifted in the gray area between Bright and Shadow magic, like my father, might feel as rough and slightly damaged as a ragged fingernail.

Hers was as even as my own. There was a faint hint of silver, but she'd been wearing a few pieces, typical for middle-income witches who couldn't afford pure gold or platinum.

Malcolm and Vera returned with heavy plates, and as we ate, conversation turned away from dangerous topics like morality and life choices to the food, the view, and the weather. Reluctantly I told her about my brief career in the Protectorate, glossing over my dismissal for my Incurable Inability to kill demons, and how I was now happy making jewelry. She expressed interest and pleasant enthusiasm for my artistic choices.

My father seemed to genuinely adore her. The only enchantment I could detect was the natural haze that ensnared all humans, magical and not, when they were in the irrational fever of new love. My father's feelings were stronger than hers, I decided, but she seemed genuinely happy to be sitting at his side.

I'd brought a gift but had waited to give it to her until I'd had time to measure her up a little. Now I took the small, white cardboard box out of my pocket and held it out to her.

"It's nice to meet you," I said, intentionally not saying anything about us being a family because that would be misleading. Malcolm and I weren't like normal people. I wouldn't pretend we were.

Vera's eyes widened—were they actually shining?—and slowly reached out for the box. She stared at me a moment before opening the lid. "One of yours," she said, not a question, drawing out the necklace. Hung from a braided silk cord was an oval pendant about the size of a quarter I'd made from copper wire and polished redwood. The copper bore only its own innate magic, but I'd infused the redwood with some of mine.

"If you only want the natural energy, let me know and I can wipe out my fingerprints," I said. Some witches wouldn't want to wear an object that was created by a stranger unless it had been verified and certified by a Protectorate mage. I'd run into customers like that. They didn't trust their own powers to sniff out dangerous or ineffective amulets.

Vera, however, immediately clasped it around her neck and gave me a huge smile. "It's wonderful." She rested her open hand over the pendant, and I could feel her magic blending with mine like two voices in a song.

I smiled back until I saw the triumphant grin on my father's face. I sank back in my seat and dropped my gaze to my plate. Old memories of being emotionally manipulated made me tighten my grip on my fork and stab a chunk of watermelon.

"Such a lovely day," Vera said, still smiling as she looked out the window. "The water's so blue, like sapphires."

"Neither sea nor sapphire is as lovely as your eyes," Malcolm said, tilting his head toward her.

I suppressed the urge to grimace, turning my attention instead to a powdered-sugar-dusted waffle. As I chewed, I noticed a little girl standing at Vera's shoulder who was trying to see past her out the window. Other tables surrounded by occupied seats made getting close to the window difficult, especially for a little kid.

Before I could move aside and invite her to look out the window next to me, Vera stood and said to the little girl, "Isn't it beautiful? Sit here. You can get a better look."

The girl, about five or six, stayed on her feet but leaned

closer, pointing out the window to the northwest. "Is that the ocean over there?"

"On the other side of the Golden Gate Bridge," Vera said. "See that little orange thing poking up? That's the bridge."

"It doesn't look orange," the girl said. "Mommy said we're going there on a bus without a roof."

Suddenly a woman, presumably the mommy, appeared beside us and took the girl's arm. "Brianna, you can't just run away like that." She turned to us, flashing an embarrassed smile as she pulled the girl away. "Sorry. She's never seen the ocean before."

They returned to their table farther from the windows, and Vera sat back down, watching the girl and her family. "I'd offer them our table, but I think it's too late. See? They're already leaving."

I looked at my father, expecting him to scoff at the idea of giving their primo table to land-locked tourists, but an unflappable, dopey smile clung to his lips.

"Shame we didn't notice them earlier," he said.

I turned back to Vera, studying her more critically. Did she have him under a spell? The Malcolm Bellrose I knew would never allow a prize of his to be given away for nothing.

But maybe her goodwill was the prize.

"Shame," I muttered.

Vera got to her feet and picked up her small purse. "Excuse me. I need to use the ladies' room." She put her hand over her wineglass. "Don't let them give me any more champagne. My head's swimming." She smiled, tucking a strand of hair behind her ear, and walked away.

Malcolm's gaze followed her as she disappeared between the crowded tables. Touching a bead on my bracelet, I risked a quick scan of my father's hand on the table. If I tried anything closer to his chest or head, he might notice my probing, but the hand, caressing the water glass with his elegant, tapered fingers, was probably safe.

I detected nothing, not even a boundary spell. Was that in itself suspicious? No, there it was. It was simply weak under the alcohol; he'd been drinking the bottomless champagne as well. And blended in with the booze and the personal ward was a warm, golden thread of something I didn't associate with my thieving, amoral father.

Love.

How strange. I'd never sensed anything so Bright in him before, even when I'd been a cute kid. *His* cute kid.

I was almost jealous. How annoying of me. Why would I mind if he'd finally discovered how to care for another living thing? The world would be a better place if Malcolm's heart had grown a few sizes. It would be wrong to resent his personal growth. I, unlike him, always sought to be as Bright as I could be, which would mean wanting others to be Bright as well. Wishing he had a selfish, sinister reason for marrying a nice woman would make me as cynical as he was.

And yet…

"I need to pee too," I said.

Malcolm wrinkled his nose, probably because of my language, making me happy to see the man I knew again. I was smiling as I walked to the ladies' room.

I stopped, however, when I saw Vera had paused with a few other diners near the piano, where a tuxedoed man was playing what I thought was Mozart. Standing a few inches away from Vera was an older lady in a tailored navy suit, wearing more gold than I thought would be comfortable for such a petite, frail-looking woman. Her wrists were heavy with bangles and bracelets, and her throat was encircled with beads, chains, pendants, and lockets. A quick scan told me she had no magic, but she certainly wore enough precious metal to be a witch.

Vera hadn't seen me yet, and I stayed where I was, out of her line of sight, watching her. Maybe I'd been stupid. Maybe Vera had suddenly needed to use the restroom not because of the champagne, but because she'd sensed a vulnerable old nonmagical woman laden with gold.

While I watched, all my powers on alert for magic, Vera leaned over, picked something small off the ground—something gold—and handed it to the woman.

I couldn't hear what Vera said over the piano, but the lady suddenly reached for her earlobe, exclaimed "oh!" and took the object from Vera with a grateful, effusive smile.

I moved closer to hear better.

"Thank you, thank you," the woman said, clutching it in her fist. "It's a clip, you know. An antique. I wear it because it was my grandmother's—you can imagine how old that must be—but it's always falling off. I think I should just leave it in my jewelry box at home. I would be heartbroken to lose it."

"Then I'm so glad I noticed you dropped it," Vera said.

I squatted down, pretending to tie my shoe—though I was wearing boots without laces—and sent out a spell to probe Vera. Was she pretending to return one item so she could steal another? If so, I wasn't able to feel any magic coming from her. I touched my throat and increased the power as I—

As I probed the open air. Vera had walked away.

I stood and used my magic to feel around where she'd been standing, where the earring had fallen, where the old woman, now returning to her seat with a younger one, had stood as she listened to Mozart.

I felt nothing. Vera must've seen the earring by chance, without magic, and returned it to its owner like any good person would.

More confused than ever, I stood near the piano a few more minutes—the player, in a mood shift, was now playing

Seal's "Kiss from a Rose." I needed time to think, catch my breath, restore my magical equilibrium.

Every piece of evidence showed Vera Vanders to be a loving, decent human being.

So why in the big Bright world was she marrying my father?

Chapter Five

It was already twilight when I got back to Silverpool. The early sunset reminded me of how close we were getting to the winter solstice, the most dangerous and interesting time of the year for our tiny town. Any conflict that affected humanity gave the Protectorate its justification for imposing order through laws, magic, and violence.

The violence was what I had a problem with. Seth wasn't harmless—he had powers I didn't understand—but he was a sentient being who didn't deserve to be executed just because he hadn't been born into the body he currently possessed.

The Protectorate, unfortunately, had an uncompromising policy about possession. My own opinion was evolving. Seth's mother had stolen the human form, not Seth; and when Seth reached adulthood, he'd tried to give it back. It wasn't his fault the original owner of his body had fought him to the death, leaving Seth in the human body by default.

I stood beside the grave of his dead "twin" now, just outside Seth's house next to mine. It was impossible to tell if Seth was home; he borrowed a car if he needed one, and magic could hide or conjure lights in the window. He was cagey about what magic powers he had. I knew he could apparate, but how far and what else he could do, he wouldn't tell me.

Without warning, his voice boomed behind me. "Why'd you go to San Francisco?"

I rolled my eyes, accustomed to Seth's sneaking around but not liking it. I turned. "Can you smell it on my tires or something?"

Seth was absurdly handsome, tall with dark hair, blue eyes, and a dimple in his chin. He raised a pierced eyebrow. "I'm not a search-and-rescue dog," he said. "Birdie told me. I hear you were missing me desperately." He put a hand over his heart.

There was no time for his mock flirting. "Can we talk inside?"

"I'd ask 'My place or yours?' but since you've made your home inhospitable to my kind, let's say mine."

I followed him up the steps to his front door. A witch would need to give me permission to go into his domain, but he didn't seem to do anything other than turn a key and stand aside for me to enter before him.

It was a lovely, inviting home with soft lighting; fresh, natural scents; oversized furniture with lots of pillows; no drafts. The aura was so changed from when Birdie lived there, I knew fairy magic had to be involved. He'd put his essence into the place. He'd intended to stay.

I rubbed my face with both hands, suddenly reluctant to tell him the bad news.

"What happened?" he asked seriously.

I lowered my hands and looked at him. "They're sending a new Protector to Silverpool."

He relaxed. "Is that it?" He waved a hand. "That was inevitable. You knew they would eventually."

"They aren't just sending anybody," I said. "Raynor can't

control who gets the job. New York is going to assign an Emerald."

"Ooh," he said. "Not pyrite? Or peridot? At least they aren't sending that nasty coal guy. He's the worst."

"An Emerald is a very powerful witch," I said. "And worse —an ambitious one. It's one of the top levels of the Protectorate food chain."

He shrugged. "You're doing that thing you do again."

His nonchalance annoyed me. "Keeping you alive?"

"Suffering in a future that may never come." He kicked off his shoes and unzipped his fleece hoodie. I noticed both showed signs of outdoor adventure—sand and mud on the lug soles, sand and bits of leaf on the jacket. The hems of his jeans were wet.

"Where were you, by the way?" I asked, even more annoyed. "I drove all over looking for you yesterday. Birdie said she saw you walking along the river. Were you going to the wellspring?"

"If only I had the means to acquire meaningful amounts of wellspring water this time of year," he said, resting a hand over his heart. "Too bad I gave you the little torc thing that made that possible. I've had to start rationing my stash."

Seth had indeed returned to me a magic amulet of great value. The torc was a thick, C-shaped band of gold, designed to be worn around the neck, that gave year-round access to the water of the wellspring, even when the ground was dry. It had caused significant trouble over the past year, and I felt that keeping it in my possession was a fair trade for the suffering I'd endured. It had changed hands many times and was only mine now because Seth had, at last, bought it from Malcolm and given it to me.

"Please don't mention that particular item," I said. If the Protectorate found out I had it, I'd be dragged into San Francisco for questioning or worse.

"I'll try not to let it slip when me and your agent friends are playing pickle ball next weekend," he said.

"Stop making jokes! I'm worried about you. A new Protector might kill you."

"Stop worrying," he said. "I can take care of myself."

"Like you did—"

He held up a hand. "I know I can't repay my debt to you, but I refuse to add to it."

I rubbed my face again. "You don't owe me as much as you think. I told them about a demon attack on Friday, which is why they're sending the Emerald. If I hadn't, they—"

"They would've found out about it anyway," he said. "They have agents here, I'm sure, or wards and sensors at the very least."

"They knew about the attack," I said. "They didn't know it was a full-blown possession until I told them."

He looked thoughtful a moment. "And how did you know, but they didn't?"

I glanced at the door behind me, thinking I could leave now. I'd told him about the Protector; he'd rejected my warning; I was off the hook. "I was there."

"Cypress Hardware?" he asked.

"You heard?"

"Kind of hard to miss your old friends setting up a zone of witchy forgetfulness in the middle half of town."

"That's the idea," I said. "Are you immune to hiding spells?"

"Only bad ones," he said. "*Those* wouldn't fool a baby bridge troll."

"They fooled me," I admitted. Then, for my pride, I added, "I was a little weak from the fight."

His flippant attitude vanished. "Fight?"

Pleased by his alarmed expression, I said, "It was just a little exorcism. No biggie."

"You exorcised a demon?" He looked me up and down. "Have you been scanned for hitchhikers?"

"Excuse me?"

"When you kicked it out of its host, it might've climbed into you," he said.

"It didn't."

He raised an eyebrow. "How do you know for sure? Different spirits have different methods."

I thought about the mysterious journey back to my house that I couldn't remember. Doubt struck me. "I don't feel anything."

He gestured at the square wooden table in his little kitchen near the front door. "Sit. I need to make sure you're all right." Three tea candles were arranged around a small Zen garden, and he lit them with a naked fingertip.

Impressed with his trick—it was magic I couldn't feel or understand—I paused. "You're allowed to worry about me, but I'm not allowed to worry about you?"

"Yes," he said. "As long as that debt is hanging around my neck, I've got a free pass to interfere in your life to ensure your well-being."

"Like Shadow you do," I said. "You have no pass. Not a free one, not a paid one."

"Sit," he repeated. "I saw that look in your face. You're not sure if you're alone in there. I'll take a look to ease your mind."

"I'm sure—" I cut myself off. He was right; I wasn't sure. "Fine," I snapped, striding over to the table and plopping down.

Seth sat across from me, reached over the table, and put his hand on mine, flinching as our skin made contact. "Turn those off, will you? The wards?"

I hesitated, reluctant to expose myself to him, but did as he asked. After everything we'd been through, I trusted him as much as I trusted anyone. Maybe that wasn't saying much, but would it be crazy to fight for his life if I didn't trust him enough to lower my boundary spells in his own home?

"Feel better?" I asked, closing my eyes to confirm the threads of power snaking out from my body and jewelry were no longer coming between us. We were in a cocoon now, wrapped inside my spells. I wondered if he could feel them.

He raised an eyebrow. "You can't turn them off completely?"

"Not without taking everything off," I said.

He grinned. "Everything?"

I began to get to my feet.

"Hold on," he said, holding my wrist. "Sorry. Just kidding. Sit your butt down and let me give you a quick once-over."

Unsure, I sank back in the chair. If I hadn't been so worried about what had happened to me after fighting the demon, I never would've let him probe me. But I *was* worried. "Fine. Do it."

Leaning forward on his elbows, he took my other hand and closed his eyes. If he were a witch, I would've been able to feel something that told me about his spell—hunting for truth, probing for secrets, seeking weakness, distorting a memory. But with Seth, whose changeling status was unique in my experience, I felt nothing.

After a full minute, I asked, "Well?"

He shook his head. I took that as instruction to wait, so I did, taking a deep breath and taking the moment to dwell upon Vera Vanders, who that morning had sent me a smiling photo of her wearing the necklace I'd given her.

Had my father bewitched her? Nobody that good would *want* to be with my father.

Another minute went by, and I began to get suspicious. I stared at Seth's lowered eyelids. "You're still working?" I expected a smirk and a joke that he'd just wanted to hold hands for a while.

But he frowned, kept his eyes closed, and gripped my hands tighter. Then I felt a hint of magic, not from him but from the room around us: the candles flickered in a sudden draft, and the spa-friendly, lavender-scented air became acrid and unpleasant.

"Seth, what's—?"

"Wait," he said, opening his eyes. "Did you get really close to that demon?"

"Pretty close. A few feet away."

He tilted his head and gave me an inquisitive look. "You had a silver stake?"

"I wish," I said. "No, just my jewelry."

His gaze dropped to my necklace. "What you're wearing now?"

I hesitated. My plan was to keep my mysterious journey home a secret. "No, different pieces. Same general idea though. Redwood. Handcrafted by myself. And a quality shovel."

"And the spirit just... left the body without a fight?" he asked.

"I told you. There was a fight. I fell down, wiped out," I said.

"But you seem alive and well now."

I still didn't want to tell him about my lost memory. Overprotective, he might jump to conclusions. "Did you sense anything?" I asked, pulling my hands away. "The aura around you changed."

"I'm not sure. You've been messed with somehow, but I don't feel anything that suggests there's a possession now, or ever was one, within you."

My stomach clenched as I again imagined my unconscious body being transported through space. "Messed with how?"

"I don't know. The thing is…" He got up and poured himself a glass of springwater at the counter.

"What?"

He drank the entire glass and sighed extravagantly before turning to me. "You only remember one demon?"

I stared, my heart thudding in my chest. "Of course. It's not like they travel in pairs." Demons were a secretive, stand-offish lot. "Did you feel two?"

"No, of course not," he said.

I let out my breath. One had been bad enough. "Don't scare me like that."

"I felt three," he said.

I got to my feet. "Three? Are you crazy?"

He set down the empty glass. "Of course they weren't really demons."

"Seth—"

"One of them was. But your Protectorate friends would call all of them that. I'm not sure what they were, but they've got their supernatural spirit cooties all over you."

I was too shocked—too afraid—to argue with him. Reeling with the idea I'd been violated in some way and didn't even remember, I moved to the door, suddenly intent on getting home as soon as possible.

"I don't think they meant you harm," he said to my back.

Hand shaking, I turned the knob. I needed to cast some spells of my own, see if I could find what he'd seen, protect myself from letting whatever they were from touching me, or whatever they did, again. Could the demon have had allies of some kind who sought revenge for casting her out of Samantha? Or had my display of power drawn them to me out of curiosity? Seth said they hadn't tried to hurt me. What then?

The fae were curious, but demons were arrogant monsters who thought they knew everything already.

The fresh air from outside cleared my head a little, and I turned to him. "If they weren't demons, what else could they be?" A question struck me, one I'd never thought to ask before. "Are there others like you in Silverpool? Changelings?"

A familiar mocking smile appeared on his face. "If I told you, I'd have to kill you."

I didn't think he was joking, but I still wanted to know. "Then just give me a hint."

"I don't think they were changelings. I don't even think they were the same thing, each creature. It's like you... I don't know, like you were mixed up with a bunch of energies all at once. Like you've picked up a few different scents, but now that they've mixed together with your own innate spirit, I can't identify them or tell them apart."

I had to get home. My own spells might guide me, might give me an answer or a clue. I stepped outside, inhaling the fresh forest air deeply into my lungs. The acrid odor in his kitchen had given me a headache.

I turned back to him one last time. "Watch out for yourself, Seth. Something's up. Something bad."

He gave me an unconcerned smile and shrug of his shoulder. "Live in the moment, human. The future never comes. There's only now."

I rolled my eyes at his wannabe Zen ways and went home to find answers of my own.

Chapter Six

The November evening was foggy and cold, but I took my herbs, copper, a jar of blackberry jam, and a pint-sized bottle of wellspring water to the backyard, where I liked to sit beneath the redwood tree as I cast my spells. Inside my house, the magical wards I'd woven between the walls might make detecting any lingering spirit impossible. I didn't know what I was looking for, but if Seth had been able to detect something when I was at his house, then I should be able to find something under my favorite tree.

And maybe Willy the Gnome, who lived beneath it, would get curious and help me. He had more powers than I'd assumed when I'd first met him, but I didn't know the extent of what he could do. He'd helped me in the past, however, as had others of his mysterious, underrated kind. The jam and wellspring water was for him. He loved sweets, and like all fae, coveted the water. Willy appreciated gifts. Calling it payment would insult him. His manners were very particular.

It was important to me that I not offend him. He'd been

here when I moved in, and we'd developed a powerful, although unpredictable, friendship. Up until this year, I'd thought it was my job, as the resident witch, to keep him protected from malicious humans and demons. He'd accepted my help with polite grace.

But he'd also interfered to help me. He might have saved my life. And he looked after Random when I was away, sometimes breaking through the boundary spells of my house, which I would've thought was impossible.

And so Willy, my little neighbor, was a big mystery, and I worked hard to keep him happy.

I sat cross-legged in the damp, weedy grass and set the bottle and bags of herbs on a concrete stepping-stone. The copper wire was wrapped around my forearm, with the curving lines of the enchanted tattoo on my skin, above the beaded bracelets I always wore. The old magic in wood was hard to measure or predict, but copper, a metal, was a sure thing. Unlike silver, it wouldn't kill or frighten the other-worldly but could still give me a steady boost of power. Most modern witches, and all the Protectorate, preferred stone and metal to magnify their power, and it was how I'd been origi-nally trained. Silver for killing, silver for protection, silver for investigation. Gold for everything. Platinum had the same power as gold but was expensive, so the rich preferred it to flaunt their status. At least that was my cynical theory—I'd never owned platinum of my own to experiment with. My father had stolen plenty over the years, but that was different.

But copper, what I wore tonight, was a practical witch's metal. Like steel and iron, it was easily attainable at any home-improvement store—such as Cypress Hardware, where I'd bought this particular spool of copper wire. As the only big retailer in town to fulfill the wishes of a diverse, eccentric group of residents, the store sold all kinds of weird odds and ends, even many of the little crafts I used to bead my jewelry.

If a demon or other creature had messed with me, I might have better luck finding evidence if I used copper that had been nearby when it happened.

"Pleasant evening to you, Alma Bellrose."

I turned to see Willy at my left elbow, smoking his pipe. He was just over a foot high and wore the old-fashioned velvet jacket of his long-ago European youth.

"Good evening, Gnome Willy," I said, smiling. "It's very nice to see you. I hope you don't mind me sitting so close to your front door."

He bowed slightly and shook his head, making his pointed cap wobble. The little door between the trunk's base and the roots of the tree appeared, a shimmering red, just behind him. "I was worried you were doing more of your magic, that which is most unpleasant to me, and I feared for your safety, as I know you would not willingly offend me without a good reason, such as being in danger."

I flinched inwardly, not knowing which of my herbs was particularly offensive to him. I never could tell. "I appreciate your understanding, Willy. Would you share a sip of springwater with me? In fact, if you were able to store the bottle beneath your tree, in your home, I would really appreciate it. I've run out of room in my house."

"Of course, dear Alma. You humans are like birds in spring, collecting the worst pieces of garbage and stuffing them in your nests."

"Guilty as charged. I've got way too much stuff. Will you take it?"

"It would please me to be doing this favor for you." He lumbered over and put both arms around the bottle, which was almost as tall as he was, and dragged it along a surface tree root to his door. "Just be giving me a moment, please, most happily." Never touching the door, he disappeared with the bottle, then reappeared a second later with two thimble-sized cups. He offered one to me, and I took it between my thumb and forefinger.

He lifted his in a toast. "To the health of your devoted animal, who is wishing I would bring him fresh grass to nibble"—he nodded at Random, curled up on a cushioned lawn chair—"and also to your human life, which is precarious, most sadly for me and your other friends who enjoy your company and thus are not wanting it to end for all time."

I was used to him talking about the precariousness of all mortal beings, but his tone made me nervous. "Thank you." I held up my cup, then we drank together. It was barely enough to wet my tongue, but good manners were essential. "Is my health precarious in any particular way you might feel inclined to mention, dear friend?" I asked carefully.

He shuddered and sighed as the springwater hit his system. "Alas I cannot speak of it. You are really needing to be staying home with your animal. The reasons for going away from your safe dwelling are always fooling you with their lies. Why risk yourself with the worst beings the magical fires of the world have created when you can stay in your box of food and bedding until your life comes to a natural end?"

With a shudder at the second reference to my death, I looked up at my bungalow. The candle I'd lit in the kitchen was a faint, flickering glow through the window. "I'd get bored if I stayed in my box all day and night until I died."

"Surely not. The sad day of your death is not very long from now."

My breath caught. "It isn't?"

"The lives of you humankind are very short, which sometimes I enjoy very much, quite a great many times in the old days, but other times, as with you, your brisk expiration can bring sadness."

Although my heart was pounding, I kept my voice level. "Willy, do you have any premonition or information that tells you I'll die in the next few, uh, turns of the earth or moon?"

"I am having no information, but I fear a great many things, especially, as I said, when you bring me the precious water from the spring, which has no value to you, peculiar but enjoyable human. You seek me out when you are in distress."

"But other than me acting suspicious by coming out here with gifts for you and my magic, has anything else happened to make you fear for my safety?" I asked. "I fought a demon, Willy. I'm worried another… something, maybe another demon… did something to me. Did you notice or can you say if—?"

He clapped his hands, sending sparks of light into the air. "Oh, how that springwater gets stronger every year. Is this the broken ring of metal that you have that is to thank for the powerful, delicious beverage you've shared with me?" The broken ring he referred to was the torc. Willy put his hand to his forehead, knocking the cap off. Then he bent over and stumbled to pick it up again. "I am feeling too dizzy to talk to you, friend. Heed my warning, stay in the nice box of your home."

"There has to be something you can tell me—"

He held up a finger. "Neighbors do not be pressuring neighbors," he said. "You know my ways. I have told them to you. I thought you learned them."

"Yes, but—"

He scowled at me, shook his head roughly, and disappeared in a flash of light.

I stared in surprise. If it had been demons he'd felt on me, he would've said so. They didn't scare him as much as they scared other fae. Something he sensed in me, however, had made him both angry and afraid.

Or was I exaggerating his feelings? He was a gnome. They had all kinds of odd pet peeves that could quickly turn a friendly conversation into an affronted falling-out.

I looked at Random, who generally ignored Willy's coming and going unless he had food in his hand. My smart dog wasn't acting as if he was afraid of me, and he'd had good training—my father had once kept him enchanted as a dragon, making him commit crimes—so how contaminated could I be? And although the demon attack the other day was the most obvious supernatural event I'd experienced recently, it was possible Seth and Willy were feeling something that had happened weeks or months ago. I'd had quite a busy year, after all.

But I didn't really believe it was something older than the past few days. They were only noticing it now, and they'd spent time with me since my earlier adventures.

I reached into my pocket and pulled out a heavy cloth napkin from the brunch in San Francisco. Since the demon attack, the only stranger I'd spent time with had been my father's fiancée. I'd hoped to ask Willy to scan the napkin, but he'd run away too soon.

Or maybe he *had* scanned it, which was why he'd taken off.

Worried that was the answer, I opened the drawstring on my bag of herbs and spread it open on a flagstone. Mixed in with a handful of dried rose hips was a stick of cedar incense, which I lit with a plastic lighter—not traditional, but effective—and then blew out the flame and set it back down. My backyard became very quiet as the magic began to weave through the air. I draped the napkin over the herbs and smoke, then rested my hands on my heart and throat, closed my eyes, and sent my senses into the white cloth.

Bright, beautiful images flashed before my eyes: platters of delicious food, smiling people in groups and in pairs, a sparkling view of white-capped sea, rolling hills, blue sky. It was pleasant, but I wanted to focus on the woman who had touched the napkin I'd pocketed, not see a slideshow of promotional images I could find on any travel website.

Deepening my focus, I touched the edge of the napkin, inviting its secrets to unfold. Vera had seemed nice. Was she really? She'd told my father she loved him. Was that possible?

Another vision of the panoramic San Francisco cityscape flashed before me, this time streaked with warm, inviting sunshine, a few fluffy white clouds, and only a distant blanket of fog outside the Golden Gate. Involuntarily I smiled, felt my shoulders relax, the tension in my neck release, my breath grow deeper.

I opened my eyes and pulled my hand away, more suspicious than ever. My father was in deep trouble if he was marrying a witch with the power to hide her nature so effectively on an object she'd only touched once, days after the contact and under my most intense scrutiny.

The copper wire around my arm grew warmer. Drawing upon it for strength and focus, I stopped scanning the napkin and moved my attention to my body and the thin layer of spirit in the air around me.

I found a hint of Willy, who had brushed a fragment of his spirit against mine when he'd given me the cup of springwater. It felt playful, intelligent, and very, very old. No surprises there. Then I noticed how the copper wire around my arm bore no trace of Willy, repelling his spirit like water off a duck.

But... maybe... *there*. I sensed a foreign magic on the metal, just a sparkle of something, like a single fragment of glitter on a woman's cheek.

I frowned, wondering at my analogy. What had made me

imagine a woman's cheek? I chased down the thought. Some lotion and makeup had tiny pieces of glitter in it. Samantha wore makeup. Had I seen glitter on her face? Likely. The contoured eye shadow had shimmered a bit. And the copper wire was from Cypress. I turned my full attention to the wire snaking around my arm, digging deeper into my well of power to see what was hidden.

A thread. A trail of faint but connected sparkles that led from my arm, over the yard, the patio, along the driveway at the side of the house.

Hopeful, I got to my feet and followed the trail. It sloped upward from my arm toward the sky. Holding my arm up above my shoulder, I walked around my house, watching the trail of magic extending upward. Could fae be living in the overhanging branches? I thought they'd all departed when I'd moved in, but dryads could be very small, and I was no expert on the fae. Perhaps it was time I worked on that.

Or could it be one of the other demon-like creatures Seth had mentioned? I scowled at the dark shadows in the trees overhead, worried about the effectiveness of the sweep I'd done when I'd moved in. I had faith in the wards I'd set up that summer around the perimeter, but maybe I'd missed a spot. Witches often forgot the feet as a point of vulnerability on their bodies; maybe a house was vulnerable on the roof.

I squinted helplessly—it was dark—at the old chimney. Sparing some of my strength for an illumination spell, I pointed my finger at the roof and watched intently as the trail of sparkles linked the copper wire around my arm to the brick chimney top.

My stomach clenched. Was it worth getting a ladder? My house was small, but tall enough to dread climbing in the dark.

Playing with my hair, I tried to think of other options.

If only I weren't allergic to cats. And if only my ability to transform myself into a cat—a rare gift but one that came with a price that was usually too high to pay—had included the ability to think like a human the entire time I was in my cat shape. Unfortunately, however, my human brain would fail me for hours after the shift, rendering investigation impossible, and then, adding insult to injury, my cat self might refuse to come down from the roof until somebody came to help me down, at which time I would be naked and in the throes of an allergic attack.

And so tonight, as usual, shape-shifting into a cat had too many limitations to be practical.

I'd have to do my investigation from inside the house. That's where something had transported me on Friday, after all. With Random leading the way, I went back inside with my herbs—the napkin, which I didn't trust, I left outside— and set up a probing spell around the hearth in my living room. Nobody should be coming through my chimney without permission, not even Santa, and it was weeks too early for him anyway.

Staying on my feet, I spread out my fingers and felt the air above the mantel. When I detected nothing, I used the matches I'd made myself, stored in a walnut box, to light the candles. There were five candles around the room, each hand-made with native Californian nettle leaves and a strand of my hair—at the bottom, where it wouldn't burn and stink up the house. I wasn't at Seth's level, but I did have some domestic skills.

The burning candles enhanced my probing spell, and I squatted down and opened the flue as I focused, alert for any sign of the sparkling lights I'd seen outside. A cold draft swept down, but other than dust and leaf fragments, I saw nothing.

Stepping back for a broader view, I looked around the room for any sign of disturbance, anything at all. The candles flickered, but their brightness was steady. When I snuffed out the one on the mantel, the smoke that rose from the extinguished wick was pale white, nothing strange about it.

I bent over and closed the flue.

Nothing. I couldn't feel anything.

I sighed, and Random, next to me, sighed as well.

Something or somebody had made it as far as the roof, but there was no trace of them inside, so I should've been relieved, but…

It only raised more questions.

Chapter Seven

"Why aren't you here yet?" demanded my father's text on Wednesday night, the third I'd received in the past hour.

Hiking up a hill in San Francisco with a priceless view of Alcatraz, I ignored his message and shoved my phone in my bra. The wedding invitation specified ten p.m., and it had just struck 10:01. The binding rites happened at midnight. I was taking my time, wanting to minimize the time spent mingling. I hated mingling.

The wedding was at my father's new house, a Pacific Heights mansion that used to belong to a now-disgraced tech bro. I'd never been there and was nervous about where Malcolm had found the millions to buy it. Seth had admitted to me that he'd bought the torc from my father before giving it to me for nothing—but could Seth have possibly paid him enough to buy real estate worth eight figures? And then just casually gifted me something worth that much?

Short of breath from climbing up Broderick Street, where I'd parked at a lower altitude with quicker access to the freeway, I bent over to tie the laces in my stacked-heel, knee-high black boots. They were closer to witch cosplay than I usually liked to get, but a wedding called for something more upscale than the flat, scuffed pair I usually wore.

I was procrastinating again. Parties were not my thing, even with people I liked. Malcolm Bellrose was an infamous criminal, but a popular, graceful, rich, fashionable, and connected one. There would be a lot of guests who would tell the Protectorate they hadn't been there, then brag to their friends and enemies that they had. My father had a way about him.

Or he *had*. Would marriage put an end to his exploits? The humble librarian from Denver didn't seem like she'd be comfortable with my father's dozens of illustrious acquaintances. I wondered how many of her friends were coming to the wedding. She hadn't mentioned any family.

Yes, I was definitely procrastinating. I pulled out my phone and checked the address again. Movie stars lived around here. Senators. Billionaires. My dress was new, but purchased online at a business probably founded by one of the guests. Would Malcolm tell them I was his daughter, or could I slink about and pretend I was somebody's date? One of the caterers?

I noticed a homeless man sitting beside a construction sign across the street. A blue tarp and a pile of dirty blankets were spread out beneath him. He wasn't watching me, but I could feel his attention.

Without letting on that I'd noticed him, I continued my unenthusiastic meander up the street, but my heart was pounding.

I should've been prepared for the Protectorate to assign agents to stakeout the event, but I'd been preoccupied with my own problems. Malcolm was popular, but several powerful witches would love to have him arrested. I imagined some would personally hex him into Shadow. If there was one agent I could see, there would be more I couldn't.

There was a woman in a green scarf, sitting on a scooter, pretending to take a selfie. I tapped into my focus string of redwood beads, lightly probed the messenger bag slung over her shoulder, sensed the sharp tang of a silver stake inside.

Startled, I stumbled over an uneven crack in the sidewalk. They weren't fooling around. I retracted my current of power and used it to build up the wards around my head and heart. If the agent wanted to know everything about me, she'd have to get permission from Raynor to force through my spells. An agent carrying silver probably wasn't as good at subtle defensive magic as I was. She'd been trained to kill, not spy.

When she was a block and a corner behind me, I let out the breath I was holding and released some of the power I was focusing on my defensive spells. Temporarily drained, a wave of dizziness overcame me. It took me several long moments to regain my senses enough to realize I was standing beside the side entrance of my father's new house.

The building took up half the block. I really, really hoped he was only renting, otherwise that torc was worth more than I thought and would attract thieves much worse than my dad. Maybe Malcolm had simply stolen ten or twenty million dollars in cash from some absentminded billionaire. The thought gave me some comfort.

I walked around the corner to the main entrance, climbed the marble steps, and waited without bothering to ring the doorbell. His wards would be special today, allowing some witches to enter that he might not otherwise. He'd have erected a magic screen to feel for any arrival he would greet personally. In spite of his many acquaintances, he was solitary at heart and had always lived alone. Well, except for me. And maybe my mother.

The door opened, and my father stood there in a tuxedo, dashing and gleaming. His new beard, dark without a single gray hair, was trimmed in a subtle point below his chin. Thick waves swept away from his forehead, his hazel eyes lined with dark eyeliner, just a touch of makeup to emphasize his best feature. He'd never been afraid to express himself.

His jewelry was extensive, in honor of the occasion, his status, and his profession: diamond studs, gold chains, platinum cuff links, ruby and sapphire lapel pins, a stainless steel watch, silver belt buckle, and platinum tie bar. Those were just what I could see at first glance. Like most of the powerful players in our world, he was a metal witch.

He welcomed me with a handshake. "Alma," he said, holding my hand between both of his, scanning me as if I were a stranger, head to toe, just like he'd taught me.

His gaze darted over my shoulder to the street, his eyes narrowing when they fixed on a distant object, probably one of the agents. Smiling, he pulled me inside. "No date?" he asked.

"Did you really think I'd bring one?"

"Ironic," he said, glancing again at the street. "So many want to come who aren't invited."

A young female servant in black and white stood in the foyer nearby, but he closed the door himself. I gave the woman a quick scan, discovered a poorly hidden Protectorate fingerprint, and looked curiously at my father.

He shrugged. "I've made a deal with them. If I allow a select few inside, the others will respect the occasion."

A twinge of irritation went through me. What right did they have to harass him? If they had evidence of a crime, they could arrest him. Otherwise they should leave him alone.

My sudden familial loyalty surprised me, and I shook it off. He'd chosen this life; he could take care of himself. I wouldn't let my own well-being depend on his again.

"Are you afraid they might try to arrest you again tonight?" I asked, taking off my jacket and handing it to the undercover agent, staring directly at her until she broke her gaze, dipped her head, and hurried away.

I regretted giving it to her; if I needed to leave suddenly, I wouldn't know where to find it. It was my favorite, a burgundy leather jacket that didn't collect dog fur like my fleece or cotton.

"They're always prone to terrible misunderstandings. It's in their nature." He gestured at another servant with a tray of champagne flutes, this one an older man without any Protectorate aura, and rubbed his hands together. "Have a drink and celebrate my happiness, daughter! This is a wonderful day. A wonderful transition. A new life for both of us."

"Us?" I asked, taking a half step backward.

"Vera has lived far below her merits for much too long. She deserves the finest things in life." He took two glasses and handed me one. "She deserves me." He smiled without a hint of irony and sipped the champagne without waiting for me to join him.

I wondered if he was right about that. Did she know what she was getting into? Did he?

"Where did the agent take my jacket, Dad? I don't want to lose it."

"Have you forgotten everything already?" he asked, shooting me a disappointed look. "Can't you track your own garment only moments after it was taken? And the individual who has it is hardly an Emerald. Surely your meager—"

"Never mind. I'll find it myself." I gulped a mouthful of bubbly and turned away. "Good luck screening out your enemies," I said, striding through an archway. I could feel the magical hum of a large number of other guests gathered somewhere deeper inside the house. A few witches walked quickly past, holding drinks, commenting on the decor.

The place was in an overly classical style, reminding me of Golden-Age-of-Hollywood opulence: white marble floors, giant potted palms, indoor columns, twin curving staircases with gold-plated banisters, and a chandelier as big as a Prius, hanging from a vaulted ceiling painted with winged cherubs flying amid a baby-blue sky.

I drained my drink. What in Shadow had attracted him to this monstrosity? His taste was usually more subtle. He coveted valuable objects, but had never been the type to flaunt his treasures. Wise. It would've been impossible for him to enjoy his freedom so long if he'd lived ostentatiously, so close to a Protectorate office, with a big wedding to show-case the fruits of his crimes.

Using the tracking spell Malcolm had taught me as a toddler, I followed the agent/servant to a small room behind the left staircase, then waited behind a column until she'd hung it up and returned to the front door.

The small room was lined with coatracks already laden with the outerwear of dozens of witch guests. The agent had hung mine with the other leather jackets, most of those heavy with silver and steel hardware and ornamentation, and I took a moment to scan each one for criminal intent, illegal magic, hidden identities, and—out of habit—demon sign.

I found everything but the demon sign. The proliferation of Shadow didn't worry me; I would've been more afraid if I hadn't found any. Malcolm wasn't a kindergarten teacher, after all.

My jacket had a Protectorate tracking spell on the collar, which I removed with a snort. Did she think I was incompe-tent? Well, maybe she did. Everyone at the Protectorate knew I'd been fired for an Incurable Inability to do the job.

I decided to wear the jacket all night. The marble monstrosity was cold, and my cheap black cocktail dress, from what I'd glimpsed of the elaborate formal wear on the other guests, would draw attention to my poverty. At least in my leather, I looked like I'd underdressed on purpose.

The magical energy coming from the other witches was giving me a headache. I had no interest in joining them, wherever they were. I looked at my watch, disappointed to see it was only ten fifteen.

Witch weddings happened in reverse order to a traditional nonmagical one. First was the party, usually beginning at sunset or evening; then, at midnight, preferably at a full or new moon, depending on the mood of the couple, the rites were held outside. Standing inside a Circle with guests around them, the couple shared their vows. Most were unspoken, an enchantment. Only a dedicated few stayed all night to see if the couple lasted until dawn. That wouldn't be me, I thought, sliding my arms into my jacket.

Malcolm had taught me to always case out any unfamiliar place, and so instead of following the noise and magic to the heart of the party, I climbed the stairs to the second floor, casting a spell to make my outfit look like the black-and-white uniforms of the servants so nobody took any interest in me. I wanted to find the spot for the ceremony to see how they'd equipped the marriage Circle for their night under the stars. Traditions varied on if bedding was allowed. Soft green grass was popular, but some stayed on flagstone, earth, or—the very rich—in a pool of springwater. Cold, but prestigious.

Would Malcolm go for status or comfort tonight?

"Excuse me, Alma Bellrose?"

An older woman appeared at the top of the stairs. She wore a dark pantsuit and a few simple pieces of gold jewelry.

She had to be a witch, given her ease in seeing me, but an unthreatening one.

"Yes?" I asked, dropping my attempt at magical shielding. Maybe my father had blocked any disguise spells under his roof.

"The bride would love to see you," the woman said, slightly bowing her head.

Chapter Eight

I hesitated, reluctant to get swept into Vera's personal space. We'd only met once, and a lot of magic was gathering to enforce her union with my father. "I don't know...," I began.

"She told me to assure you she is alone. She's in the master suite at the end of the west wing." The woman gestured to her right.

Curious. A bride would usually surround herself with family, friends, and a mentor in the hours before midnight. The nightly rituals were intimidating, and most kept trusted advisors at their side to prepare them, comfort them, and in some cases I'd heard, stop them from bolting out of nerves.

If that's what Vera hoped to get from me, she'd be disappointed. "All right," I said. "Of course."

I walked past the woman, who didn't follow, and turned down the hallway. The second floor seemed more comfortable than below, with lower ceilings, wood floors, earthtoned walls. Vera, in a flowing white dress, was waiting for me in the doorway at the end.

"Alma!" she called, waving me forward. "Come in, come in."

The bedroom was huge, taking up the entire northwest corner of the house, and smelled like roses, probably because of the countless bouquets around the room—red, apricot, pink, white, cream. They were unusually diverse in shape and scent, suggesting they were picked in a private English garden in May, not a commercial greenhouse in November. I smiled at the creative use of magic.

The lights of the Bay Area glittered through floor-to-ceiling windows. I'd seen the view a million times before, but somehow, seeing it like this, from the Pacific to the East Bay hills without any traffic or crowds to share it with, enjoyed from a secluded, rose-scented bedroom, made me forget to breathe for a moment. "Enchanting view," I said softly.

"I'm so glad you're here." Holding out her arms, Vera stepped toward me, then stopped politely before making contact and put her hands over her heart. "My best friend back home got in a car accident on Monday. Two broken legs. I feel guilty for thinking of myself, given how much pain she's in, but I never thought I'd be alone on my wedding night."

"She's— You didn't have— Isn't there someone—" I stumbled. There was no polite way to ask if there was only one person in her entire life she was close to.

"No, it's just me," she said.

I suppressed my suspicion. Who was I to judge? I'd isolated myself for years. I'd only become friends with Birdie by unavoidable circumstance. "Is there anything I can do for you?" I asked.

"What do you think of my dress?"

I was forcing a smile on my face, but her dress confused me. It was as if she'd wrapped a bedsheet around her torso, pinned the corners at each shoulder, then cinched the waist with a gold satin sash.

"It's lovely."

"I know, I know, it's not at all traditional, but it called to me." She turned, shaking out the long skirts around her ankles. Her bare feet peeked out from beneath an asymmetrical hem. "I had to respect the magic that drew me to it. That's what they say, isn't it? The dress chooses the witch."

"I've heard that too," I said. "That's probably why I'm wearing this." Smiling weakly, I patted my leather jacket.

Her smile didn't falter as she looked me over and nodded. "I wanted you to put on the final touch." She held out the redwood pendant I'd given her when we met.

"Wood for your wedding?" I asked, my voice rising. "No, please, you don't have to do that."

"What do you mean? I don't *have* to do anything. I want to." She lifted the hair off her shoulders and turned her back. "It's lovely old magic. It reminds me of... of stories my grandmother would tell me."

"You don't have to wear it around your neck," I said. "How about I double it around your ankle? Or you could stick it in your bra. Nobody will see it there, but you'll still feel—"

"I want people to see it," she said sharply, lifting her hair higher. Then her tone softened. "Please. That's all I want. Then you can go and enjoy the festivities."

Although I'd dreaded the idea of supporting her before the ceremony, now I felt guilty about my selfishness. I clasped the silk cord holding the pendant at the nape of her neck, careful not to touch her skin. "No, I'll stay. I can cast an extra warming spell around you so you don't freeze tonight."

"We won't need to rely on magic to stay warm," she said, turning to me, patting the pendant under her chin.

Just as a mental image of them consummating their union struck me, so did a tickle of power. She'd allowed my spell to remain inside the redwood, and now, if I concentrated, I could feel her heart beating. Neither sensation was pleasant, and I flinched.

"I beg your pardon." She touched my arm and squeezed, doing something to the power link between us, easing my discomfort. "I meant that your father has had workmen prepare nonmagical heating for the rooftop."

I studied her hand, still on my arm, not recognizing the spell she'd used. Whatever it was had been faint. Her magic didn't seem very strong, which given my father's ego was probably better for their chance of happiness. "Well, that's good," I said, feeling awkward. Would we share years of uncomfortable dinners and holidays together, or would they drift out of my life, happy in each other's company?

"Let me show you so you don't have to give it another thought." With a gentle tug, she guided me through a pair of french doors out onto a balcony facing the Golden Gate Bridge. Below us the noises of the party spilled into a ground-floor terrace, but she led me up a staircase to a higher level. The house was in tiers, stacked on the hillside, and the uppermost portion, above her bedroom, was a wooden deck (redwood, which hummed to me) laid out in grand style for a wedding ceremony. There were urns, garlands, and bowls of flowers; strands of enchanted floating lights; a rose on each guest's seat; a black velvet carpet for the couple; even a golden harp.

As elaborate as it was, I felt like something was missing, something I really shouldn't forget...

"Tell me what you think of the Circle," Vera said, drawing my attention to the centerpiece of the marriage rites. "I wanted you to see everything before all the guests arrive and spoil the effect."

Seven feet across, its perimeter was marked with white pillar candles set a foot apart that would burn until dawn. Inside was a pile of something botanical to form a soft bed; yellow and white, it was wide as the Circle and at least knee-high in the center. I cast out a quick probing spell to identify the plants, but the magic of the Circle blocked me. It was a powerful force, buzzing in the center of the deck. I wondered if Vera could feel how the redwood was enhancing the Circle's magic.

"What's making up the bed?" I asked.

"Milkweed floss and California buttercup," she said. "Malcolm knows a witch who specializes in out-of-season wildflowers."

"Should be soft," I said, impressed. Buttercup petals were tiny. It must've taken thousands. "It's beautiful."

"Malcolm did ask for memory foam," she replied, "but I told him we needed the old magic with us tonight."

I smirked. "Yeah, foam wouldn't quite fill the same role. I'm surprised he didn't insist on an air mattress at least."

"Perhaps he has hidden one under the petals."

I laughed.

She flashed a quick smile, then sighed and put her hand over her stomach. "Butterflies. Let's go back to my room, and you can rejoin the party." She inhaled deeply. "It's a perfect night."

As we left the rooftop, I felt the pull of the delicious magic behind me, inviting me to stay. In spite of my lack of enthusiasm for the marriage, I smiled, tempted to go back, only able to think Bright, optimistic thoughts about their union. How beautiful that they'd found each other after so many, many years alone, how perfect that we were all here now to witness destiny.

Witness *what*?

I stopped walking. That didn't sound right. Digging all

ten fingernails into the redwood railing, I focused my power on wiping away the matrimonial enchantment. It took a full minute, drawing sweat out of my armpits and dampening my brow.

Demon's balls, what a spell. If anyone should've been able to resist that particular conjuring, it was me, but I hadn't felt a hint of it coming on. Good show. Malcolm must've paid an excellent performing witch for that level of creative deception. I'd met a witch recently during a trip to Mendocino whose magic was in entertainment and illusion. She could make some extra money doing weddings.

After a cleansing breath, I went down the stairs and caught up to Vera in her bedroom, where she stood in front of a mirror, adjusting her hair. "You can get springwater punch downstairs in the Pacific dining room," she said, pointing at the floor. "That's the one on this corner. The one on the other side of the house is the Alcatraz room, where the banquet has been set up. I'll walk with you to the stairs. This house is easy to get lost in."

Still fighting the residual romance spell from the rooftop, I might benefit from springwater if it wasn't laced with more enchantments. "Sure you don't need me for anything?"

She studied me with an inscrutable smile on her face. "Just that you enjoy yourself," she said. "Be happy."

I managed to nod, maybe even smile faintly in return, and we walked out of the bedroom together. My mental sharpness was returning, and I suddenly understood what had been missing on the rooftop.

The fae. All the beautiful decorations—the magical lights, the powerful Circle, bouquets of enchanted flowers—even in a crowded city, should've attracted some fairies.

But I'd seen none. Maybe I was wrong to expect them, though. Maybe the dozens, maybe hundreds of witches gathering together at the house could act as a deterring blaze of disagreeably human magic.

But there hadn't even been any wood sprites. The hillside gardens and rooftop patios of the well-tended residences in Pacific Heights would surely attract many of those, and they could fly away in an instant if they sensed danger.

Perhaps they had.

I cast my senses down the hallway, detecting an unpleasant but inactive threat nearby. Very nearby.

"I'm sure you'll have a nice time," Vera said. "Your father has invited an old friend of yours. He said you would be lonely and bored without somebody you already knew to talk to."

Touching the beads on my bracelet for protection, I turned to her with my pulse picking up. The odds of my father worrying about my happiness, let alone taking advanced measures to ensure it, were extremely low. Anyone he invited would be to benefit himself. "What old friend?" I asked carefully.

"I'm sorry, I don't remember her name. I believe she arrived before you did. Malcolm mentioned he'd seen her."

She. Her. A female friend. *Old.* Did she mean chronologically old, like Helen, or a friend I'd had a long time? "Someone from school?" I asked.

"Yes, that sounds right," she said, smiling. "An old friend. From school. I'm sure you'll find her downstairs and have a nice time catching up."

I nodded and continued walking down the hall onto the landing. A string quartet had begun playing in the foyer downstairs, and the sounds of Bach floated up the marble steps, filling the air with a light, playful melody.

And then I saw the profile of a man standing at the railing overlooking the quartet, and my lungs lost the ability to breathe air at all.

Kurt Bosko. The infamous Protectorate agent known for being almost as good as Raynor at killing demons, but without his grace and twice his fanaticism. Bosko was known for killing demons but also for capturing witch fugitives. In a controversial case we'd discussed in our last year at school, one witch had died en route to the Protectorate office before she'd been formally charged. Bosko had claimed self-defense, that she'd resisted with Shadow magic.

In his early fifties (or appearing to be), Bosko was lean, muscular, and scarred, with short blond hair cut in a trendy style. The full beard was new, but his long, pointy nose, backlit by the celebratory pillar candles on display behind him at the top of the stairs, was unmistakable.

I risked a step forward to see what he was looking at so intently. His probing spell was active, aimed directly at somebody downstairs. Perhaps the cellist was a demon.

No such luck. The object of Bosko's penetrating interest was the man standing in the foyer, greeting and screening the wedding guests.

My father.

Chapter Nine

Stomach tensing, I retreated back into the hallway, never breaking my gaze from Bosko's profile.

"Your father isn't the only one with an old acquaintance here," Vera said in my ear, nodding at the infamous agent. "They went to school together," she added.

I touched my beads for calm. I'd had no idea my father knew Kurt Bosko socially. But why had he allowed a vicious hardliner under his roof, even if they were old classmates?

Next to me, Vera seemed unconcerned, suggesting she didn't know about the man's reputation. It would be typical of my father to hide that little detail and to derive pleasure from the thrill of a secret, of danger, with so much at stake on his wedding day.

I clenched my teeth. Malcolm always had to play the daredevil. It was his reason to live. Having an agent at his own wedding known for killing fugitive witches must make it seem all the more exciting. I hoped that if my father really feared arrest, he wouldn't have let him in, and if Bosko was going to arrest him, he would've done so already.

The panic eased, but it was wise to remain cautious. "Is there another way to get downstairs?"

"Just wait a moment," she said, squeezing my shoulder. A wave of harmless energy washed over me. "I'd like to get to know Malcolm's old friends anyway."

While I waited in the sanctuary of the dim hallway, Vera strode out in her voluminous white gown and greeted Bosko at the top of the stairs with a cheerful hello.

He turned, took her hand in his, and kissed her on both cheeks. The intimate contact would be rude in a professional setting, but at a witch wedding the bride had to put up with a few kisses, which were known for their good luck.

"We meet again," Bosko said, his voice booming over the marble. "I was just taking myself on a little tour. I'm sure you don't mind."

"No need to take one alone. Let me show you…" Vera's voice trailed off as she led him down another hallway.

I waited a minute and then scurried onto the landing down the stairs to find the bar. Wine sounded good, more attractive than springwater right now. My nerves were shot. Seeing agents, even famous ones, shouldn't upset me so much. The ceremony was still over an hour from now, and I couldn't afford to burn myself out early. Watching my father go through wedding rites when I didn't know if he'd ever done the same with my mother was going to be painful.

When I had a glass of wine in my hand, I took a long sip, appreciating the expensive cabernet and pretending not to notice how the other guests stared at me. The red carpet for a British royal delegation would have had fewer people taking an obsessive interest in their appearance than were now mingling in my father's home. Some of the fashions were trendy in the nonmagical world; most were ostentatious in a magical way, with pounds of silver, gold, platinum, and precious gems on display. The men next to me wore long, hanging chains over their tuxedos that made them glitter like department-store Christmas trees under the enchanted floating candles.

I drained my glass, plucked a second glass off a tray, and went searching for the source of distant harp and piano music. The string quartet was taking a break. My father had always loved live music. He himself was a trained ballroom dancer, and I expected a luxurious dance floor had been set up somewhere in the house for the party.

The harp and piano were in yet another room with a view, this one with a moss-green velvet sofa, overstuffed leather chairs, and walls of bookcases. A cozy library, the only space I'd seen yet in the house that I would actually like to spend time in.

Bent over the piano keys was a familiar helmet-shaped head marked with a distinctive floppy bow. I stared, my stomach tightening.

No, not Florence Werner. I watched in dismay as the woman lifted her head and looked around the room with a big toothy smile. She'd had them magically enhanced when we were teenagers.

Brightness, it really was Flor. I'd wondered how my father could've known any of my old friends; there was my answer. He hadn't. He'd invited somebody he'd known by chance, a former classmate who'd invited me to her house for summer break nearly a decade ago. Flor had been an ambitious, self-centered, competitive witch without many friends, which is probably why we'd ended up spending so much time together. I was the new kid—I was always the new kid—and she liked my last name. Old family connections were still valued in the witch world, and her parents pretended to be ignorant of my father's reputation while at the same time trying to get to more prestigious connections for their daughter through me.

The music stopped. Flor jumped up and walked directly to me, her white teeth gleaming. "Alma! Congratulations and all that. Or should I offer my condolences?" She held out her arms for a hug.

Surprised, I almost let it happen. But then, just in time, I brought my glass to my lips and nodded at her over the rim, turning slightly to prevent her invasion. "Florence."

"Is something wrong?" She held up her hands, showing naked wrists, wriggling bare fingers. "I couldn't hex a fly. Metal's at home. My granny said that's proper for weddings. Of course, nobody else seems to know that. I've seen more metal in the past hour than I have all year."

I remembered Flor's family being obsessed with what was proper. It had made for uncomfortable dinner conversations, given the gossip about Malcolm Bellrose stealing a pair of ruby earrings from a powerful Emerald's wife that summer.

"It's been a long time," I said, staring at her. The last time we'd spoken, I'd told her about my letter from the Protectorate that had invited me to join the organization for training after my seventeenth birthday. She'd ghosted me after that.

Later I'd learned from one of our teachers that Flor hadn't received a letter—which was more typical at our age, since most had to apply a year or two before breaking in—and was disgusted with me for getting something she hadn't thought I deserved. Also, the Protectorate had arrested my father around that time, if I recalled. He was released without charges, but I'd assumed our family disgrace was at last too costly for the Werners.

"I'm sorry I dropped off the face of the Bright green earth," Flor said. "I got so stressed out in school that I had to spend a year in a Swedish health facility. The witches there were really good at healing my spirit. I was really a mess back then."

Compassion reluctantly stirred inside me. "You spent a year in the hospital?"

"Lots of saunas, lots of coffee, lots of candy," she said. "The fae were amazing, and the spells were fine, mostly old hearth magic you'd probably appreciate, but it was the nonmagical culture that did the trick."

"I had no idea," I said. "I thought…"

"Thought I was jealous?"

"Sorry," I said. "You weren't the only one. It wasn't fair, and I knew it too. Merit should be all that matters."

"But you're out of the Protectorate now, aren't you?" she asked with a smile, as if she didn't judge me at all for my failings. In fact, they seemed to make me more appealing.

"I'm out," I said. "You must've heard. Incurable Inability."

"And you'd had no idea?" she went on. "You went up against the demon, thinking you could drive the stake through his heart, but then… Pfft? Just couldn't do it?"

I didn't want to talk about it, but I felt an obligation to say something since she'd told me about her breakdown. Maybe the experience had mellowed her. "Turns out I'm not cut out to be an assassin," I said. "I don't know why that came as a surprise, but it did."

She frowned and gave me a puzzled smile. "It's not assassination. We're acting in self-defense for all of humankind."

The harp player began to strum another tune, and I gestured at the piano, eager for a distraction. "Don't let me interrupt your playing. I had no idea you were so good."

She shook her head. Her blunt-cut bangs barely moved. "Now I know why they called you Incurable. You're actually squeamish about killing demons."

"That's basically it," I said, forcing a smile. Unless a witch had met the supernatural beings I had, who were not all bloodthirsty monsters, she was unlikely to agree with my radical ideas about supernatural justice. "How about you? What are you doing with yourself?"

There. Safer topic. Anything other than me.

"I'm working toward my doctorate in Fae Studies, looking for a mentor," she said. "I need to apprentice for two years to get my degree. I don't suppose you know any mages looking for an app?"

This was the Flor I knew. Fae Studies was a popular degree, like Political Science for nonmagical people, very common among witches wanting to get ahead in the Protectorate. "No, sorry. I live up in Sonoma County now, middle of nowhere. I don't know any powerful mages."

Her dark eyebrows rose. "Middle of nowhere?" She glanced around, a smile curving one corner of her lips, and lowered her voice. "Right. It's supposed to be a secret. Don't worry, I've known for years."

"I don't know what—"

"Fae Studies. My year in Sweden sparked my childhood interest in the fae into a lifelong passion." She put her lips near my ear. "You're so incredibly lucky to be living near a wellspring."

Her warm breath on my neck sent a shiver through me. I stiffened. "Why?"

She regarded me unblinking through the round lenses of her glasses. The floppy bow rested just above her right ear in the smooth perfection of her auburn bob. As much as when she was younger, she reminded me of a doll. "For the fairies, of course," she said.

"To study?"

"Of course! I live in San Francisco. Look around! There are simply not enough fae in a big city to get the data I need to make a dissertation."

"Not even in the park? Or at the beach?" Although I could see the fae who didn't want to be seen, plenty did make themselves visible, especially in the city.

"Everyone studies *them*. The same dryad, the same troll, putting on a show for students year after year to get their vial of springwater—it's an industry. Nobody will be impressed with that."

She had a point. "But you'll get the degree," I said, "and it's what you do with it that matters. The Protectorate will hire you—"

"Oh, I'm already hired. I'm an archivist's assistant at Diamond Street. That's how I got the invitation to the party, that and my connection to you." She smiled. "I am glad to see you, though. It's not just for the networking opportunities. I've wanted you to know for years that I didn't hold a grudge about your advantages. They helped me work through that in Sweden."

I shifted my weight from foot to foot, unsure how to reply. "Uh, well, good—"

"If I could find a mage who lives near a protected forest or wilderness, I'd be able to find enough authentic, unusual, *wild* fairies to use in my research. I need to write something that makes an impact. I need to stand out."

"Why?" I asked, honestly confused.

"What do you mean?"

"Why do you need to stand out? If they'll hire you anyway, why not just take the job and… live?" I asked.

We stared at each other. The harpist continued playing without her piano accompaniment.

"Because I don't want to just do what's *easy*," she said. "I want to look back on my life and know I did my best. I want to know I took advantage of the one gift I do have—life itself."

The little stabbing feeling in my gut was probably my ego

taking a direct hit. Since I'd left—er, been fired from—the Protectorate, I'd felt defensive about my more humble, low-status path.

For as much as Flor had always annoyed me, I had to admire her too for the strength of her spirit. She was a fighter. She was the type of witch the Protectorate should be recruiting, inviting, nurturing, promoting. "Good for you," I said. "I wish you the best."

"Thanks." She looked around the room, scanning faces and power with a probing spell. "If you run into anybody tonight who's looking for an app—"

"I'll be sure to tell them about you."

She flashed her perfect teeth in thanks and went back to the piano.

The two drinks on an empty stomach had gone to my head, so I went to look for some food. I should've brought snacks. Eating the food here would be risky, if the rooftop was a clue of the magic pressed into service for the evening. Brightness only knew what would be in the clam dip. Modern witches scorned hearth magic, but they weren't above putting sorcerer's violet or juniper berries in the refreshments as a way of putting their finger on the scale. Love was a subtle thing, perfect for the old magics.

I found the buffet in another room, wiggled past a trio of Emerald mages wearing enough silver to kill a city of demons, enough platinum to guarantee their invitation to a party like this one, and enough gems for Malcolm to figure they wouldn't notice if he stole one or two while they were in his home.

The dip seemed to be infused with nothing worse than dill and garlic, so I scooped a puddle of it on my plate with a crust of sourdough bread and ate it standing near the window, admiring the view of Alcatraz. What fae lived there? I wondered. Sad rock fairies, still feeding off the misery of the imprisoned men, or gleeful trolls, enjoying the daily influx of tourists with their germs, voices, and smells from all over the world?

"This property is exorbitant, but no replacement for the exceptional item your father stole from us," a man's low voice said behind me.

Belatedly, my defensive spells sent a cloud of protection to the back of my body, enveloping me from head to toe. I held myself still, glaring at Bosko's angular face in the window's reflection.

The Protectorate knew Malcolm had stolen the torc from them but had been unable to prove it. Now, unknown to them, it belonged to me. They had given up on believing I might have it, the only reason I still did.

"Don't pretend the Protectorate is any better," I said, giving no demon's balls, as it were, for whatever he thought of me. I didn't work for anyone; I didn't have to suck up like Flor. My hands shook with the risk I was taking, but I was stressed and kept going. "I doubt the agents who found that torc paid its owner a fraction of what it was worth before they confiscated it."

"You aren't even going to pretend you don't know what I'm talking about," he said with a snort. "Raynor told me you were better than your father. I didn't believe him. Time always proves me right."

I turned around and looked up at him, noticing he still wore his heavy coat and that the drink in his hand was tap water, not springwater, not wine, not champagne. He wasn't here to have a good time. He was on duty.

"Men like you only see what you want to see," I said. "You're an ignorant bully." I braced my knees to stop them from buckling.

"You've had too much to drink, failed little Flint." He turned and walked away before I could hex a pair of horns onto his head, which was really for the best, but I did regret my slowness.

So Bosko hadn't forgiven Malcolm for stealing the torc. The house was filled with undercover agents. The fairies were missing. And a call was going out, inviting everyone upstairs to the rooftop.

The ceremony was about to start.

Chapter Ten

I broke into a jog to find my father and warn him about Bosko before the ceremony. He probably didn't need me to tell him the agent was on the hunt, but I knew how he would discount danger, especially when his blood was rich with dopamine. One of these days his love of thrills was going to kill him—but I wasn't going to stand by and let it happen without a brief word.

It was eleven thirty-three, a powerful number. He wasn't at the front door anymore; it was locked to all passage now, with a handsome South Asian man wearing a five-strand gold-and-emerald necklace standing guard. I remembered his face from my teenage years, but not his name. My father had trusted him enough to introduce him to me.

"Brightness be upon you. Where's my father?" I asked him, hearing the urgency in my own voice.

He scanned me for a moment with a probing spell. "Upstairs with his bride," he said. "But you shouldn't—"

I broke away before he finished and took the stairs two at a time, pushing past guests making their way up to the rooftop. I took a left turn at the top and strode down the hallway to the master bedroom. When I reached out to knock on the door, a blast of energy sent my fist back, jerking my arm backward at a painful angle. Rubbing my shoulder, I paused and drew from my necklace for focus, then reached my senses through the door to see if anyone was hurt.

Two people. A significant amount of movement. And moaning, but not the kind that comes from pain.

Ew.

I sighed, dropping my hand from my throbbing shoulder. The pain had cleared my head. I wasn't his guardian. He could obviously protect himself. Maybe Bosko had left his coat on because he had the body temperature of a kingsnake.

I left and joined the flow of people walking up the main stairs to the roof. I caught sight of Flor, who waved and pushed through the throng to reach me.

"You should wait a few minutes," she said. "Your seat's reserved. No need to hurry for a good view."

"I don't have a reserved seat," I said.

She rolled her eyes. "Of course you do. That's protocol."

We reached the top and walked slowly with the others out onto the deck. The candles around the Circle were blazing, and many seats were already filled with witches sitting with hands clasped around small copper bowls filled with dried flower petals: rose, gardenia, hibiscus, chamomile.

"Come on," Flor said, hooking her arm through mine. More of my boundary spells were up now, and I barely felt her. "Facing east in the front row is the best spot."

The best spot for me would've been in my Jeep heading home, but that wouldn't be possible for another hour, so I let her drag me along. When we reached the front row of chairs only inches from the glowing edge of the Circle, she tapped a young couple on the shoulder and told them to move.

"These seats are reserved," she said, jerking her head in my direction. "Daughter of the groom."

They frowned but got up without a word and took seats behind us.

"See?" Flor asked, sitting down.

I scanned the crowd for Bosko or the other agents before I took the seat next to her. Suddenly she slapped my knee, laughing, and I decided she was drunk. My own head wasn't as clear as I would like, so I reached below my chair for one of the copper bowls and pinched some of the mixed flower petals and dropped them on my tongue. The world around me became sharp, clear, exceptionally real. The past and future dropped away—no, it was never here, time was an illusion, there was only now.

Flor lifted the bowl under her chair, sniffed it, made a face, and put it back. "The old magic doesn't do anything for me."

"It's not for you. It's for the couple," I said.

She took a flask out of her skirt pocket. I knew it was springwater even inside the spell-blocking stainless steel. "Now *this* will clear our heads nicely for the big moment." She offered it to me.

I shook my head. "No, thanks."

"I don't get why some witches get so addicted to it"—she took a long swig, wiped her lips, then drank again—"but it does help me sober up."

When she put the flask away, her demeanor became serious, the springwater having boosted her metabolism. She adjusted the bow over her ear, smoothed her hair, and sat up straight in her chair, one hand idly caressing her bare wrists.

I looked up at the sky, at the stars I couldn't see through the city lights, wondering about my mother. Would she be jealous? Maybe she'd loved my father so much, she'd put a spell on him to forget her. That was the sort of romantic, foolish explanation I'd come up with as a child.

The couple suddenly appeared at the edge of the circle. My father had the rare skill of apparating over short distances, advantageous for a thief. Vera was smiling, hugging his arm, the fabric of her dress sliding off one shoulder. The witches around us began throwing the flower petals overhead into the Circle, casting Bright spells of happiness, fortune, beauty, health, and power. Some of the petals landed in my hair—one of the perks of sitting in the front row—and I didn't brush it away. It had been a rough year. I welcomed all the good luck I could get.

Malcolm and Vera kissed each other on the lips, then broke apart. At the same moment, every guest silently stood; the harpist rested her hands over her strings; and the scent of orange blossoms and baked bread wafted over the crowd, filling our minds with images of pleasure, love, and domestic bliss.

As part of the tradition of entering from opposite directions, Malcolm walked to one side of the Circle, Vera to the side near me. Right and left, up and down, yin and yang, two parts of a whole.

The moment they stepped over the candles to enter the outer perimeter of the Circle, I looked for Bosko again. Surely he was here to watch the critical moment when they joined in the middle.

There. I saw his pointy nose six or seven rows back to the left. Then he dropped out of sight. Malcolm and Vera took their first step into the bed of flower petals, and suddenly Bosko appeared closer, only three rows back, his gaze, bright with malice, locked on the Circle. Surely he wouldn't interfere now. Why take a man into custody in the midst of a wedding ceremony, in front of so many witches, with so much magic woven into the air we were breathing?

I stopped doubting myself and stood up. He was going to interfere. I could feel it. I didn't know why, but my body was sure of it.

I moved to get around Flor, but she put a hand out to block me. "Hey, don't go. I worked hard to get you that spot."

Her interruption broke my focus, and I lost sight of Bosko. Vera, only a few paces in front of me, lifted the hem of her dress and took a big step into the petals. A sigh of pleasure went through the rows of observing witches. As Flor sighed with the others, she lowered her arm. I pushed past her, searching the crowd for Bosko's pointy nose.

There were too many faces, too many witches, and too many shadows. The candles were low around the Circle, and the fairy lights bobbing overhead had dimmed for the ceremony. A violin began to play a nameless, unearthly tune, sending a shiver through me.

I spun and looked to my right, then behind me. Bosko was going to grab my father. Some sick revenge fantasy had inspired him to humiliate my father at his happiest, proudest moment.

There! He was on the opposite side of the Circle, approaching my father. The large candles around the base of Circle cast hard shadows upward across his face, making him look like the Grim Reaper.

No, surely not Death—

Again, I shoved my doubt aside and acted on instinct. When your guts told you something, you should listen. When they shouted, you had to act. Quickly.

Bosko wasn't here to arrest; he was here to *kill*.

I held my breath, pausing just a moment to touch my sixth sense again. I had to make sure I was right.

Yes, it was Death. I felt *Death*.

Fewer than five feet from my father, Bosko lifted his arm

and pointed at the Circle, muttering a spell as he crossed the blazing perimeter. The light reflected off a large, pale stone he wore on his right hand.

An opal ring.

My breath caught. It was supposed to be locked up at the Protectorate. How could they have trusted such a dangerous object with a witch like Kurt Bosko?

The ring was the same one that had caused so much trouble at the house party in Mendocino. The opal exposed demonic possession in an otherwise innocent-seeming witch. But, as I'd learned the hard way, it also exposed demon *print* —the long-ago possession in a human's background, suggesting he or she was demonic in some way. The Protectorate didn't care that it was an inherited trait that might mean nothing—maybe the possession had occurred centuries ago and today's humans knew nothing of it. There was nuance to consider, but the ring didn't explain what it saw, just responded or did not. It was just the sort of magical object that would be used for evil by a ruthless hunter like Kurt Bosko.

I'd thought it was my mysterious mother's line that held the demon print, but what if it was my *father*? Had I inherited the mark from him? Bosko might've shaken his hand, discovered the hint of demon energy, and was now going to use it as an excuse to execute him.

Flooded with adrenaline, I jumped over the candles and charged through the bed of flower petals. I believed the stories about Bosko; I believed he'd done far worse. Perhaps he'd been carrying a grudge against my father since they were children, and now he had his excuse, his stature as an agent, to act without consequence.

I wouldn't let him. If I caught him by surprise, I could give my father and Vera time to run away. They wouldn't have the powerful bond of the Circle, but they'd have each other, unmarried but happy and free. Unmarried but alive.

Launching myself between Bosko and Malcolm, I lifted my arms in a protective *X*, muttering a spell under my breath —probably useless inside the enchanted Circle but worth a try. Other than magic, I only had my body to slow him down. It might be enough.

But Bosko strode past me without a glance. I spun, seeing the glint of a knife in the air above my father's shocked face.

Bosko plowed past Malcolm.

And charged Vera.

Oh Brightness, I'd misjudged everything. It wasn't my father, it was his bride. Of course a Protectorate agent couldn't kill a Bellrose witch on his wedding day in front of so many witnesses, no matter what the opal ring had revealed. But an outsider had no protection.

I lunged forward, reaching for something I could grab on Bosko's body, the hem of his jacket, an elbow, but I was too slow. Too slow.

Alone at her side of the Circle, eyes wide and unblinking, Vera watched Bosko drive the silver blade into her chest.

Chapter Eleven

I screamed. The magic of the Circle blended my voice with the piercing cry of the violin, and every witch on the rooftop slapped their hands over their ears to block out the sound.

Vera collapsed into the bed of flower petals. Apparently satisfied with his work, Bosko stepped aside, crossed his arms over his chest, and looked down at her.

I dropped to my knees to help her, try to seal the wound, at least prevent Bosko from getting in another blow. Malcolm fell to her other side and pulled her up into his arms.

"Vera, Vera, Vera…," he said.

Her eyes were open, her expression slack as she watched Malcolm sob. Then a sigh ran through her, seeming to give her a second wind. She smiled at her groom before turning her head over to me, where I knelt in the blood-spattered petals. Holding my gaze, she slowly reached out her hand.

I took it without thinking. A dying woman wanted comfort; how could I deny her? But the second her skin touched mine, I felt a sucking drain on my power as if the cork on a bottle had been popped. While I froze helplessly, my energy poured onto the ground. A wave of nausea choked me. My abdominal muscles cramped, and I slumped to one side, braced my weight on my hand, then slid to my elbow. The flower petals were soft, fragrant, seductive. I began to black out. Chaos was erupting around me—Malcolm shouting now as he held Vera.

The other witches didn't enter the Circle. It was bad luck, or worse, to interrupt the matrimonial enchantment. Perhaps that was why I was about to lose consciousness: more bad luck. I couldn't see Bosko, but I felt a dark, angry figure standing above me. He was the one who deserved bad luck. A lifetime of it. Yet he was standing tall, and I could hear him laughing.

Why did the very worst people always seem to win?

My strength continued to fade. Absently, I noticed my hand had gone numb, as if I'd dunked it in ice water. Then I realized it was actually hot, that it was in agonizing pain. I yanked it out of Vera's grip and brought it to my mouth, whispering a cooling spell into my flesh.

As sensation returned to my hand, a tendril of smoke began to rise from Vera's body. I blinked quickly, commanding myself to stay awake. I had to witness this for myself. The only eyes I could trust were my own.

The skin on Vera's arms shimmered like white flame and then, in spots and patches, began to char. Face breaking with a different kind of shock, Malcolm let her fall from his embrace. Vera's rigid body cut a path through the petals like a knife through wedding cake. The white and yellow flowers, so beautiful and fragrant a moment ago, disintegrated into a boundary of stinking gray ash around her body.

Bright moon and stars. How could she have fooled me? How could I have missed the demon sign?

Bosko was wearing the opal ring. As soon as he'd shaken

her hand, he must've discovered she had the demon mark. With that clue, he could've used stronger magic to uncover her full-blown demonic possession. I hadn't detected Vera's true nature, but I wasn't Kurt Bosko, famous demon killer. He hadn't hesitated to kill Vera only hours after meeting her. What would he do to me if I ever let him shake *my* hand?

Vera's limbs, torso, and face began to hiss.

Witnessing the unmistakable signs of demon corporeal death, the guests erupted in panic. Some shouted, some cried out in fear; others bolted for the exits, sweeping weaker witches aside. But every one of them cast a defensive spell as they looked out for their own interests, terrified the recently bodiless demon might select one of them as its next host, its next victim.

I hugged my body, too weak to run. The Circle prevented me from casting any wards of my own even if I'd had the strength to use one.

Somebody grabbed my arms and pulled me away from Vera's smoldering form, dragging me between the ring of candles marking the perimeter of the Circle. Idly I noticed the wax pillars didn't move even as my elbow raked across one of the wicks, and my foot another; the magic flames blazed as strong as ever without burning me or my clothes.

My vision hazy, I clung weakly to consciousness. Bosko stood above the corpse, gesturing at witches—no doubt more Protectorate agents—to control the crowd.

The killer had taken command of the crime scene.

No, not a crime, though, was it? She was a demon. Did I really want such a creature to marry my father? Malcolm couldn't have known what she was.

I looked up and saw it was Flor who had dragged me out of the Circle. Freed from its enchantment, I felt stronger, enough to sit up and make eye contact with my father. He shook his head imperceptibly and reached up to his left ear, where he'd always kept a powerful platinum-and-diamond cuff. It would focus his power as my beads did mine.

I'd never seen him look so forlorn. My eyes burned with unexpected tears. *Hurry, Dad. Get out of here. Apparate while you can.*

But Flor, my old classmate and rescuer, jumped into the Circle with a cry, her hands formed into fists, and tackled him. They fell, the herbs in her hands flying into the air around them, and I felt Flor's arrest spell pierce the Circle's wards and ensnare my father.

I staggered to my feet, horrified and disgusted that she'd used the herbs gifted to the wedding guests as a weapon to shatter the protection of the matrimonial bubble.

"I've got him," Flor told Bosko, casting another spell around my father's head.

"Dad!" I shouted. "I'll get you an advocate!"

He looked as drowsy as I felt; his eyes were fluttering shut, and he sagged into Flor's arms. Five agents in silver jackets appeared amid the crowd—at the top of the stairs and at each corner of the rooftop, calling for calm, demanding everyone stay where they were for questioning.

"Nobody leaves this property without an interview," Bosko shouted.

I glared at Flor. She met my angry gaze with a shrug. "I didn't know," she said.

Malcolm had lost consciousness. Flor bent over him and began removing his jewelry, beginning with the ear cuff.

Feeling hollow, I looked over at Vera, now a rapidly decomposing husk with gaping eyeballs and a hideous, toothy smile. The last corpse I'd seen like this hadn't been a bad guy in my opinion, and maybe not even a demon, but it wasn't my opinion that mattered.

I thought of Seth, another creature the Protectorate wanted to kill in the name of peace, safety, and justice, and wondered why it was that I couldn't seem to form lasting bonds with human beings.

Bosko, Flor, and two of the silver-jacketed agents hauled Malcolm away. I stopped myself from begging, fighting, or arguing with them; it would make no difference. I'd have to talk to Raynor. And if he didn't listen, I'd hire the nastiest advocate witch in the country to come down on Diamond Street and free my father from this travesty of justice.

My head spun. I was too weak to get so upset. The front-door agent and one of the silver-jacket women lifted me and helped me down the steps to an unfurnished bedroom on the second floor. Somebody brought a cushion, another brought a glass of springwater, and they propped me in a carpeted corner and told me to drink.

"My father is innocent," I said. "He never would've... He didn't know."

"What happened?" a voice demanded. There were at least six agents now in the room.

"I have no idea." I looked into my glass and frowned. "Could I have a real drink, please? One of you was probably pretending to be a bartender. How about a Manhattan?"

"How long did you know the demon?" another voice asked. I felt the truth spell pierce my weakened defenses and wrap around my mouth.

"I met her on Sunday," I said stiffly.

"Four days ago?"

There was no reason to fight the spell. The truth was my friend. "Yes."

"Had you been in contact with her any other way? Through glass or water, paper or speech?" asked another witch.

It was a formal interrogation phrase that went back centuries. Glass would be an enchanted crystal globe, used in the old days to communicate; water was probably also a similar, archaic form of communication, but I'd never seen it described in detail.

"I received a wedding invitation from my father listing her name," I said. "That was the first time I'd ever heard of her."

"How many times have you met with her since your meeting at the hotel on Sunday?" the woman from the front door asked.

So, they'd been following us. I shouldn't have been surprised.

"The only other time was just before the ceremony tonight," I said. Swamped with exhaustion, I closed my eyes and rested my head against the wall. I felt another magical probe scrape over my boundary spells, then another. They were searching for any sign of subterfuge. I let them.

They spoke among themselves, and then all but two of them left the room. They had to interview dozens of guests before letting them leave, and some of them were powerful enough to complain to high places if they were kept too long. When I opened my eyes, I saw two young, unfamiliar agents—Flints, the entry level—standing guard. I was a little offended Bosko thought I didn't need higher level witches to contain me.

They looked bored. Probably felt like they were missing out. I was just a half-conscious, botanical-wearing witch with an Incurable Inability, but just a few steps above us was a (literally) smoking-hot demon.

I dozed until I heard Raynor himself speaking in the doorway. At his side was Darius. They cut an impressive pair, especially in their black leather jackets heavily adorned with silver. Raynor had light-brown skin, a shaved head, and the massive build of a movie-star superhero. Darius, a decade younger and slighter of build, looked less likely to crush his enemies with sheer force, but looks were deceiving; when we'd worked together, he was quick, clever, and fierce.

Raynor dismissed the bored Flint agents and came over to me with a glass in his hand. I climbed to my feet, bracing my hand on the wall for balance, and blinked away the waves of dizziness before I met his gaze. He could scan me better than any witch alive, and I didn't want him to see anything I didn't mean to expose, such as the fact that the missing torc was at my house in a filing cabinet.

"Here, this might help," he said, offering the glass.

"Springwater doesn't fix me the way it fixes the rest of you," I said.

"It's not springwater." He pushed the glass into my hand, brushing his fingers against mine. I felt concern… anger…

Fear.

Both of us needed to avoid shaking Bosko's hand tonight. I'd been safe so far—Bosko had been busy with the scene upstairs—but my luck might run out. How would Raynor avoid detection?

I lifted the glass, sniffed it, and smiled as I took an eager sip. The whiskey burned a path down my throat and reignited the dwindling fire inside my belly.

"Darius couldn't find a cherry," Raynor said. "He'll do better next time."

"I'm not a bartender," Darius said with a sniff, taking out his notebook. He licked the tip of his pencil and gave me an irritated-but-concerned look. "You all right? They told me the demon burned your hand."

I lifted my glass with the hand to let him see. "It's fine. Thanks." Whatever Vera had done to draw energy from me hadn't left permanent damage, although I still felt weak, even with the booze.

"Wrap it anyway," Raynor said to Darius. "White gauze, half-inch thick, with a layer of blocking wards."

"It's fine—" I began, then cut myself off. Bosko couldn't shake my hand if it was injured. "Good idea. Thanks." I drained my glass and set it down on a table.

Darius stared at both of us a moment, then put the notebook in one pocket, took gauze out of another, and wrapped both my hands. He knew about the ring and our secret.

"I need to get to Diamond Street. My father needs an advocate." I leaned against the wall, trying to look casual about it, but my head was spinning. I wasn't sure I could stand up on my own.

"It'll only make it look worse." Raynor ran a hand over his bald head. "You're lucky they didn't bring you in as well."

I closed my eyes as if to show annoyance, but really I needed the moment to rest. "For what? I met her Sunday."

"That's what you claim," Darius said.

I opened my eyes to glare at him. "They probed me. It's the truth. Ask them."

"Relax," Raynor said. "Darius believes you. He's just explaining why you're lucky."

"Yeah, I'm real lucky." I held up my bandaged hands. This wedding was supposed to be a diversion from my real problems, but it had turned into a fresh, juicy one all its own.

"Go home," Raynor said. "Rest. You're in shock. You can barely stand up."

I brought my burned hand to my lips and cast a cooling spell around it—then frowned when the ward Darius had put around the gauze prevented my spell from getting through. "My father needs an advo—"

"He'll get one," Raynor said.

"You won't want any lawyer from San Francisco," Darius said. "They'll be too connected. You'll want an outsider. Try to reach somebody in New York."

I was surprised Darius cared enough to offer an opinion. I gave him a grateful nod.

"She won't need to reach anybody," Raynor said. "Her father already has advocates. I didn't have the pleasure of meeting them personally, but they negotiated the agent presence here tonight."

"But if he doesn't have the freedom to call for them—" I began.

"Every witch in Protectorate orbit will know what happened here before dawn tomorrow," Raynor said. "And his advocates were probably here in person to witness it for themselves."

"Which means they won't be able to represent him," Darius pointed out. "They'll be tied up for questioning themselves. She'll have to find a witch who wasn't here."

Their argument had become too hard for me to follow. The air around Raynor's head was cloudy. And around Darius, too. The whole room was filled with some kind of mist. Was it just fog? I hadn't lived in San Francisco for a couple of years, but I didn't remember the fog actually coming inside...

"She's about to pass out," Raynor said. "You and your sister can bring her home."

"I'm fine," I said. "It's just an unusual weather pattern." The wall began to fall over, and with it, me.

"I got her," Darius said, his voice loud in my ear. "Can you tell Rochelle to come up here? I can't carry her by myself."

Carry me? How ridiculous. I didn't need anyone to carry...

"Her car is on Broderick..."

It was the last thing I heard before the darkness took me.

Chapter Twelve

"Alma, wake up. Alma! You'll have to let yourself in."

I opened my eyes and looked into Darius's serious eyes. He seemed to be holding me. Remembering something about his sister, I looked to my right and found Rochelle Ironford, younger and even more serious than her brother, supporting my other side.

"Your wards are too strong," she said. "We can't get through."

I heard barking. Random, inside the house, scratching at the door. I closed my eyes, glad I was home. Honestly, why did I ever leave?

"She's out again," Darius said.

"No, I'm fine." My voice sounded far away. "Thanks for the ride. You can go now."

"We're not leaving you just lying here," Darius said.

Rochelle pulled my head toward hers and spoke loudly in my ear. "There's a gnome watching us from under that big tree. Is he dangerous?"

Last year, I might have laughed. But I'd seen gnomes do some powerful things since then. Rochelle must've had some experience of her own. "No," I said, yawning. "Let go. I'll manage."

"We'll leave when you're inside," Darius said. "OK, Rochelle. Go ahead. Do it."

"Do what?" I asked, forcing one eyelid open.

"He wants me to smack you," Rochelle said. "That's why I asked about the gnome. Will he retaliate if I slap your face?"

I forced my other eye open and managed to put a hand on my front door. They'd removed the bandages, and I'd been too wiped out to notice. "Maybe. Don't do it." The contact with the wood of the house gave me a jolt of clarifying energy, and I was able to stand up on my own. If Willy hurt Rochelle for obeying Darius, who was obeying Raynor, I'd never forgive myself. "He looks out for me. And Random. Good neighbor." Head spinning, I opened the door, already unlocked by the key they'd probably found in my pocket, and stumbled inside.

To my surprise, Random didn't scramble out the door to greet the guests as he normally would. He stayed near me instead, sniffing and looking up at me.

I braced my knees to stay upright and told my two favorite Protectorate agents with as steady a voice as I could manage, "All right, mission accomplished. Please go. I'm sorry you had to drive all the way up here."

Darius looked past me into the dark house. "You're still weak. Let us come in and—"

"No," I said firmly. "I'm fine. You both need to go home and sleep. Tomorrow will be a big day for all of us."

Darius made a frustrated sound. "Remember what I said about finding an advocate in New York."

I was already closing the door. My vision was going dark again, and I didn't want them to have any excuse to stay. "I will. Thank you so much. You're awesome. Really great. Best partner I ever had."

Just before I shut the door completely, I heard Darius tell his sister, "She's delirious."

I locked the dead bolt, cast a boundary spell, and rested my forehead against the wall for a second. Or maybe it was a few minutes, because Random began to bark and nip at my fingers.

I pushed away from the wall and wobbled through the house to my bathroom—took another little nap on the toilet until Random bothered me again—and finally made it the rest of the way to my bed.

The dream began before my head hit the pillow.

I was in Cypress Hardware again. The demon inside Samantha was talking to me over a table in a cozy café, a slice of vegan banana bread split between us. I couldn't understand what she was saying, but it didn't matter; we were just chatting like any two friends meeting for coffee on a rainy afternoon.

Rain. It was pouring outside, really pouring. So heavily that the glass was coated with a curtain of water, the way it would look if the café had been dropped into a clear lake.

We were in a lake, and Seth, born lake fae, swam by outside in a pair of red-white-and-blue swim trunks. He pounded on the glass, shouting at me through the water in words I couldn't hear.

The demon looked at me and asked (in words I somehow understood) if she could eat Seth for lunch.

"I wish you wouldn't," I said.

Suddenly I was on the rooftop of my father's house, dancing a waltz in Vera's arms, both of us in identical white gowns. We danced in perfect harmony until I looked down and saw the blood on our chests, like strawberry jam between two slices of white bread.

I screamed, the scream became violin, the blood became rose petals, and Vera floated away.

I woke up to Random licking my face. If I'd been wearing a heart monitor, it probably would've sent a worried notification to my doctor. Gasping for breath, I pushed Random's snout away and felt how wet my face was. Had I been crying?

After a few minutes to catch my breath, I felt my forehead. I wasn't sure, but it seemed a little warm. The rest of me, however, was freezing. Hands shaking, I pulled the quilt over myself.

My hands shouldn't have been shaking. Something was wrong with me.

"Random, call Birdie, will you?" My voice came out in a croak.

Random licked me and panted into my face. It was probably time for his breakfast. He was a wonderful dog, but even with so much experience with magic, having been enchanted by my father, he was still only a dog. He couldn't call anyone for me. I'd have to do that myself.

If I called Raynor, he'd get mad at Darius and Rochelle for leaving me alone. The dream about Seth made me reluctant to drag him into any trouble of mine—he was in enough danger as it was.

That left Birdie. She was close, she was trustworthy, she had a key, she could get through the wards, she kept her text notifications on at all times. I really, really, really wanted to see Birdie. The more I thought about it, the more urgent my need became to talk to her.

I was still wearing the leather jacket, thank Brightness, and my phone was in the left pocket. The effort of drawing it out made me short of breath, but I got it in hand, typed her a quick message, and collapsed onto the bed.

Then I slept without dreaming until she arrived. She

stood over the bed and, after I didn't move to greet her, said, "I'm getting Seth."

"No. I want you, Birdie," I whispered. "You're the only one who can help me."

"Me? No, I'm just a beginner. You need—"

"I need you. You're the one I need." I paused to catch my breath. "First get me my phone. Help me see if there are any messages."

She found it under my hip and held it in front of my face to unlock the screen. "You need to see a doctor."

"Magic," I whispered. "Need magic cure."

"Seth then—"

"Do I have any messages?" I asked.

"Raynor says your father is… under house arrest! Oh my God, what happened?"

I relaxed against the pillow, managing a weak smile. House arrest sounded bad, but it was just for show. He was free. "They let him out," I said. "That's great." They must've proven with probes that he hadn't known about Vera, which meant they'd formally drop any charges as soon as the publicity died down.

"Alma, are you asleep?"

I swam up out of the warm blackness. Birdie was talking to me, and I needed her to do something. "I just don't know what. If I could just remember…"

The world went dark again. Birdie had to shake me awake and shout in my ear. "Remember what?"

"My dream," I said. "It's in my dream. The clue. I was having banana bread with a demon in a café. Did you turn your bookstore into a café?"

"I haven't even opened it yet," Birdie said. She rested her hand on my forehead. "Oh my God, Alma. You're burning up!"

I thought about the dream. "The demon wanted to eat Seth." I tried to get up. "He's hurt! We have to—"

"He's fine. I just brought him some leftover pumpkin pie. Yesterday was Thanksgiving, remember?"

I went limp, relieved but confused. I'd slept through an entire day? No wonder Random had been hungry. "Right. Sorry."

"What happened to Seth in the dream?" Birdie asked.

"I told the demon not to eat him," I said weakly. Then I heard my words and came fully awake. "No, I *wished*. I made a *wish*. Demon's balls, Birdie! Cypress Hardware. That's it! You need to take me there. Right now."

"But you're sick—"

"Take me. Now." I grabbed her arm and hauled myself up to sitting. "Now, Birdie."

Chapter Thirteen

Ten minutes later, Birdie parked in a spot near the entrance of Cypress Hardware, and I lifted my head away from the passenger window where I'd propped it for the ride. The mouthful of peppermint, a cup of springwater, and two capsules of ibuprofen hadn't done much for me. My fever was still raging, making it difficult for me to keep my head upright.

Seth had said he'd felt three supernatural fingerprints on me. One had to have been the demon who'd possessed Samantha. The second, I now realized, must've been Vera. And the third—

I thought of the copper wire I'd wrapped around my arm. It had come from Cypress Hardware, from the creature who had helped me get home after the demon exorcism. That creature was still there.

It had to be a genie. It explained so much.

"You should be in bed," Birdie said.

"Did you notice anything strange when you worked at Cypress?" I asked.

"Strange like magic?"

I nodded, then flinched from the pain. "The store always manages to have just what people want."

"Jen's a workaholic," she said. "She's always asking people about their lives, what they want, what they need."

"Jen?"

"The owner. I think her mom owned it before her. It's been in the family a long time."

Jen. Cute name. Bit on the nose, though. "How long?" I asked. "Another generation or two?"

"Why do you—"

"Just tell me what you remember."

"At least her grandmother," she said. "Or great-grand-mother? There's a black-and-white photo of somebody from that generation welcoming the soldiers home from World War II. They had a party in the parking lot."

"You worked the customer service desk. Was there ever an issue with things being out of stock? Having to get things from other stores, other suppliers?"

"No, never. Management was really aggressive about in-stocks. Contractors usually shopped for lumber in Santa Rosa," she said. "But we kept some here, just in case."

"And in those cases, you had what they wanted, even though Cypress isn't usually known as a lumber yard?"

"Sure, like a few two by fours or a sheet of plywood. We kept those—"

She didn't see what I was getting at, and I was too tired to explain. "I'm going to need your help." I opened the door and blinked at the ground, which seemed very far away in my weak state.

Birdie got out on her side. "We should've called Seth—"

"No. Just you." Seth might inadvertently expose my plan. "I need you to put something in an employee-only area. Did you have a lounge or something?"

She hurried around to my side and gave me her arm. "The break room—"

"Perfect." I reached into my pocket and clasped my fingers around a black velvet bag holding an expensive gold necklace I used to wear when I was trying to get ahead in the Protectorate. I slipped it into Birdie's hands. "Set it anywhere and then get back out here as soon as you can. And don't touch what's inside the bag." She was too involved already.

"But you—"

"I need to be alone. Just wait here." I squeezed her arm. "Thanks."

We went into the store together, but separated near the entrance. She went through a door behind the customer service counter, and I weaved through the aisles to the patio seating, now on clearance, and collapsed into a padded lawn chair. After a few minutes, I made a silent but specific wish for regained health. It was a wild thought—I'd never met a genie before, but if my suspicions were true, it would explain a lot.

I waited, gripping the arms of the chair.

It happened all at once. One breath I was sweaty and weak; the next, better. In fact, I'd never felt so good. The fever and weakness were gone. The crick in my neck I'd had ever since my father had announced his engagement was gone. The hangnail on my left thumb was gone.

The necklace had done the job. I'd probably overpaid, but it wasn't worth the risk to be cheap.

I sprang to my feet and inhaled deeply, my sinuses clear, no hint of allergies. Scanning my body, I could find no bruise, no scab. My lower back didn't ache. All my worries about my life, my father, my friends—gone. My soul was overflowing with optimism and peace. It was a miracle.

A miracle with a price. Unbeknownst to them, people had been paying the genie's prices for generations. So far as I knew, the Protectorate had no idea she was here, which meant she was powerful. I'd have to be careful.

I strode out of the store to reassure Birdie. Now that my mind was clear from fever, I remembered she'd expected me for Thanksgiving dinner the day before. What a good friend she was to come today and help me, never complaining I'd stood her up.

"I'm really sorry about yesterday," I said as I got into the car. Now that I was stronger, I could cast a spell around her SUV, shielding us from most observation. "What did you do when I didn't show up, other than hate me?"

"I'd never hate you. You warned me you might be too tired after your dad's wedding," she said. "I figured that was it."

"But I didn't even call."

"You were sick— Hey! What happened? You're better!"

"You didn't know I was sick yesterday," I said. "You had every right to be annoyed. Don't let me walk all over you."

"A few minutes ago, you could barely walk at all." She lowered her voice, asking eagerly, "What kind of magic is hidden at Cypress? I never suspected a thing. Is it a healing charm? Herbs in the garden center?"

"Let's get to my house first," I said. "It's not safe to talk here."

"I noticed you put a boundary spell around my car," she said.

"Good job noticing. You're getting stronger." Maybe too strong. It could get her into trouble if she learned things before she had the skill to protect herself.

She drove out of the potholed parking lot, up through the wooded slope to my house, and parked behind my Jeep in the driveway. I'd have to thank Rochelle for driving my wheels home for me. First, however, I had to clean up the local situation.

Birdie came inside with me and sat at the kitchen table, the spot where she'd received most of my magic lessons over the past few months. At the counter, I opened a tin of home-made oatmeal-raisin cookies, her favorite, and set a dozen on a daisy-patterned plate she'd given me.

I was already feeling guilty. Leaving the cookies on the counter, I went over to the table and sat across from her. "Remember when you said you'd never hate me?"

She nodded, her brow creasing.

"Hold that thought. Because I can't tell you what's at Cypress."

"I promise I won't—"

"I'm so sorry, Birdie." I reached out my arm and snapped my fingers in front of her face. When she flinched, I sent a forgetting spell through the momentary gap in her defenses. It would only cover the past hour, but that might be enough.

Then I got up, filled the kettle with springwater, and put it on the burner for tea. There was a thud as Birdie's head struck the table.

Whoops. I hadn't thought it would be that bad—I should've put some dish towels down to soften the blow. When the kettle whistled, I poured it over the peppermint tea bags I'd put in mugs, brought them over with the cookies. Then I set a cork on the floor, sat across from her, and waited until she came to.

It took one and a half minutes, which meant she'd forget the previous hour and a half. I'd gotten pretty close. Aside from hitting her head, she'd feel fine, especially after she had the tea and cookies.

She lifted her head, pushed away from the table, and stared, blinking in confusion at the floor.

"Do you see it?" I asked, sending a gentle suggestion spell. "I dropped it over here."

She blinked again. "What—? No, not yet. What color is it?"

"Beige. The usual cork color. It's all right, I'll get another—"

Suddenly she lunged down and lifted it from the floor. "Got it!" She handed it to me, smiling, and reached for her mug of tea. "It's too bad you don't get the springwater buzz like everyone else. You're really missing out."

"Thanks." I fitted the cork into the bottle and picked up a cookie. "As long as I can eat these, I'm fine." I took a big bite and chewed slowly, watching her carefully. She sipped her tea, ate a cookie, and gazed blissfully off into the distance. When the tea was gone, I sent one last spell her way.

"What time is it?" she asked.

I turned around to look at the wall clock. "Five to two."

She slammed the mug down. "Already?" she asked, standing up. "I promised to bring Random to the beach today. I better get going. I've only got a few hours before the sun goes down."

"I really appreciate it," I said. "He really needs to get off leash."

"Of course. I love bringing him." Two minutes later, she had Random on his leash and was walking out the door. "Come on, buddy, it's tennis ball time."

I followed her out and stood in the driveway, watching her back out into the road.

I stood there until Jen the jinn showed up a few minutes later.

Chapter Fourteen

S he arrived on foot, appearing on the side of the road as if she'd just walked into view, as if I simply hadn't been paying attention.

But I *had* been watching carefully—with my hand wrapped around my most powerful redwood bead—and saw the instant she flashed into existence next to the hedge beyond my driveway.

She was middle-aged in the manner of a witch or a movie star, without any wrinkles or gray hair to give away her exact decade. Forty? Fifty? Her dark, curly hair was cut short, emphasizing her long neck, which was heavily adorned with gold chains, pendants, and beads. The necklace I'd put in the velvet bag hung there among the others. She also wore an oversized wool cape in a geometric pattern of purple and white over dark jeans and…

A pair of hummingbird-print waterproof clogs from the gardening department at Cypress Hardware. I'd almost bought them for myself once but had ended up ordering them online. I wondered if those were the same pair and she was making a point about knowing everything—and collecting on debts.

Without hesitating, she strode over the boundary between the road and my driveway where I'd cast the first ring of boundary spells and then walked directly to me.

Yes, she was definitely making a point. She wanted me to respect her power.

I did. I very much did.

When she was just out of arm's length, she stopped. I realized how tall she was, at least six feet, and could feel the chilly, ancient indifference in her demeanor. It was hard to hold her gaze, but I was still refreshed from the health wish she herself had granted me and so had the strength to manage a few long, awkward seconds.

"Welcome," I said. "Would you like to come in, uh…? Forgive me, I don't know your real name." She'd managed to break through my chimney once, but I'd been unconscious. She wouldn't be able to enter again without my formal invitation. Genie magic was much stronger than any witch's, but I had a better chance of surviving a confrontation inside the walls of my warded home.

"The name Jennifer Bardak is real enough."

I bowed my head politely. "I'm Alma Bellrose."

As she stared at me, her face showed no expression at all, but her hands were busy twisting the rings on her fingers. "All right, we can go inside." She glanced behind me at the redwood tree. "It's probably for the best if Decorum Salix and I don't run into each other."

I looked behind me. One of my favorite books when I was little had been about a genie and a gnome trying to dunk each other in a well. "Do you mean Willy?"

"Our names adapt to human years," she said. "He was Willow in the old country."

"And you?" I asked impulsively.

"Too many years, too many countries to remember," she said. "Let's get this over with." She nodded at my back door.

Avoiding having her behind me, I held out my hand in a polite, sweeping gesture, and we walked awkwardly side by side together. I opened the door to the kitchen and looked back at the redwood tree. If Willy was watching, he didn't want to be seen, for which I was grateful. One proud, unpredictable, and powerful semi-immortal creature was enough for me at the moment.

She walked inside with her head high, showing no sign of feeling any of my wards.

"Can I get you anything to drink?" I asked.

"A glass of the wellspring water, please. But nothing in it." She made a face at the mugs of peppermint tea still on the table.

I filled a shot glass, removed the tea mugs, and we sat across from each other.

"I'm a businesswoman," she said, taking a sip. "I make deals. This is an offer I rarely make, but you'll have to admit it's a steal. For your silence about my existence, I will give you a wish of equal value."

I'd been expecting something like it, but my heart began to pound anyway. A genie's wish was thrilling, even for a witch. "Who determines what the value of my silence is?"

"I do," she said.

"That hardly seems fair."

She raised an eyebrow. Her eyelids were heavily made up with black eyeliner, even more precisely than Samantha's. "You must know I'm capable of keeping you quiet in worse ways."

I clasped my hands together under the table so she couldn't see them shaking. The magic in my focus beads kept my arms from trembling right off my shoulders, but it wasn't enough to calm me completely. "I do know. But there's a risk in that. I'm a witch with Protectorate connections. Directors have been to this house."

"To berate or employ you," she said. "You have no power over those witches."

"But they'd listen to me if I said a genie had set up a power anchor in Silverpool and has been feeding off the wellspring for—what, centuries?"

"I'm not originally from this land," she said. "I arrived on the ships of gold hunters."

"Almost two centuries, then."

She shrugged. "It doesn't matter what you know. When I grant your wish, you won't be able to speak of it."

"Only if I agree to your offer."

"Why wouldn't you? If I wanted to harm the humans or fae here, I would've done so already. Are you so spiteful you want to expose me just for the fun of it?"

"I'm not going to expose you if I can help it. I promise you that."

"Your promise is meaningless without an equal exchange," she said. "I need it to be binding."

"This kind of wish would be different than what you give to customers at Cypress, though, wouldn't it?" I asked.

She sipped the springwater. "It would be better," she said. "It would be much more powerful. It's your chance to think big, Alma."

"When people go into the store and wish for things, they maintain some level of control." I put my hands on the table and showed her how they were trembling. "But I've got no control over you, even here in my own house. Your magic is stronger than mine. It would be too dangerous to accept your offer. It would be insane."

"You have to."

I swallowed over the lump in my throat. "I don't. I can still say no."

"You've accepted my wishes bef—"

"I paid for them with my jewelry," I said.

When I'd fought the demon, she'd taken my focus strings as well as the retail display of necklaces as payment for granting my wish to get home before the Protectorate arrived. Less than an hour ago, she'd taken the gold necklace to grant me my wish for renewed health. The velvet bag had also contained an invitation to meet me, including my promise to hide her existence from my friend, Birdie.

"The price for my health was defined upfront," I continued. "But I don't know what my silence might cost me."

It was dangerous to make deals with genies, especially if you were desperate. If you promised something you couldn't deliver, they could take the ultimate price from you: your life.

"I swear to you," she said, "it would be a wish of *equal value*."

The hair rose on the back of my neck. A colorful array of wishes paraded through my mind, but I clenched my teeth, remembering all the cautionary tales, and fought them off. "I can't see the future. I don't know what that value might be," I said. "For all I know, hiding you might cost me my life."

"I can't let you expose me." Her voice dropped. "I'm prepared to offer you a gift most mortals would kill for."

To break the tension, I joked, "Too bad for both of us then that I have an Incurable Inability to kill."

Her face broke into a wicked grin. "I can cure the incurable!"

"No!" I said quickly, regretting my joke.

"I've noticed your father can come and go in the genie fashion," she said. "I can grant you that ability. But with a little more flair, perhaps? A nice puff of smoke for dramatic impact?"

I walked to the door and pulled it open. It was getting

harder to resist her, not easier. Dreams of popping in and out of existence as I pleased, teleporting with the ease of a genie —how lovely that would be.

"It was a pleasure to finally meet you, Jennifer Bardak, but I won't be accepting any more of your wishes." I filled my words with the power of a magical vow, although I did add a silent *at this time* just in case. "I'll do my absolute best not to reveal your existence. I've already hidden it from Birdie, as you saw. You have my promise."

"Your promise is weak." She glared at me, then emptied the glass of springwater. It seemed to soothe her, as it did for so many, and she gave me a smile as she stood up. "Sorry, maybe I came on a little strong. Tell you what, I'll give you time to think about it. Don't give me an answer now."

Knowing it was wise not to argue, I remained silent. All I wanted now was to get her out of the house. My curiosity had been sated. Now that I was certain of the three beings Seth had detected on me, I could sleep at night.

As the wise witch Helen Mendoza liked to remind me, witches craved knowledge above all other fortunes. I was as greedy as any of us.

Jen walked out of my house, flicked a rude human gesture at the redwood tree, and strode off down the driveway. "You know where to find me, witch," she called out. "When you think of that one thing you can't live without, come to Cypress Hardware."

She disappeared in a puff of smoke.

❧

BIRDIE RETURNED with Random just as the sun was going down. Still preoccupied by my interaction with the genie, I didn't notice her car parked out front until she honked. I'd been sitting in my living room, which faced the street, and took the unusual route out the front door to greet her, kicking aside fallen leaves and sprawling rosemary from the path.

Random leapt out of the passenger seat and galloped over the overgrown shrubs to celebrate his return with me, but Birdie stayed in behind the wheel with the engine running.

Smiling at me, she reached over to pull the passenger door shut. "We had a great time, but I can't stay. I love what you've done with your hair!"

I lifted my hand away from Random to touch my head. I'd done one of those absentminded updos that held only half my hair off to one side in a messy bun. "Thanks," I called out. My spell must not have worn off yet. "How do you feel—?"

Not hearing me, she slammed the door and turned around in the street. In a moment, she was tearing away down the road. I turned my attention to Random and was grateful for how clean he was after a trip to the beach. Sometimes I had to hose him down outside before I could let him into the house.

Reunited with my dog, I locked up the house, put on my pajamas, and curled up on the couch to watch a movie with microwaved lasagna and a glass of wine. Random snuggled up next to me, and I enjoyed a long, relaxing inhale.

Life had gotten so stressful lately. Death, demons, deceptions… Thank Brightness for dogs. Instead of turning on the movie, I let my head fall back on a pillow and closed my eyes, stroking Random's warm, furry head.

I should've felt worse than I did. The horror of the wedding, my illness, the confrontation with the genie…

Ah, that had to be it. The healing magic had soothed my spirits as well. Deciding I might as well enjoy it, I savored the comfort of the couch and Random's affectionate cuddling.

At that moment, my phone chirped with the notification unique to Raynor.

"Demon's balls," I mumbled, squeezing my eyes shut. I didn't move. A moment later it chirped again. "They have no idea what I could've wished for. I could've turned the whole stupid organization into a worldwide chain of toddler dance-and-music centers."

After another sigh, I picked up my phone.

Meet me at Armstrong Woods, the text read.

When? I replied, but I could guess.

Now.

I scratched Random behind the ears, got up and gave him my dinner, which he seemed to feel was a fair trade for being pushed off the couch, and then got dressed in black denim, a black hoodie, black gloves, scarf, and my favorite black boots. If Raynor made the hours-long trip north to chat in a redwood forest at night, he wanted our meeting to be secret. The old-growth redwoods at the state park would block all overhearing and observation once we were inside, but I'd want to cross the boundary unseen as well.

The narrow, winding drive through the dark to Guerneville was slow, and I couldn't help but muse how fast apparating would've been. I parked outside and slipped in on foot past the gate, which delayed me even more, and when I finally met him beside a massive redwood over a thousand years old, he'd had time to get cold and irritable.

"Vera's body has been traced to a missing woman in Colorado," he said without a hello, breathing a warming charm into the air around himself but not me.

"What was she like?"

"Who?" he snapped.

"The missing woman," I said. "Demons choose their bodies carefully. Was she a mother? A criminal?"

He enhanced the warming charm, making it glow just

enough to faintly illuminate our faces. "Both, it seems. Her stepson told the police his 'guardian angel' had arrived to take her away. He told them she'd been abusing him and his little brother."

"Ah," I said, my shoulders relaxing. So Vera hadn't been totally amoral then. Most Protectorate witches didn't think it mattered if demons possessed an evil human, but it mattered to me. Relieved she hadn't taken a life indiscriminately, a knot of tension eased inside me.

Could she have been another demon with a heart of gold, like the one I'd met last month? Or had I been blinded by her quirky charms, my father's love, the odd bridal gown?

"Aren't you going to ask me about your father?" he asked.

"I saw your message he was under house arrest," I said.

"Don't you want to know more?"

"I assume he's completely innocent and now you're just trying to save face by keeping him under observation," I said.

Raynor pointed a finger at me. "Don't push me," he said. "You're a valuable agent, but you can't afford to disrespect me, especially now."

"I'm not an agent," I said, angry. It was cold, and my dinner was giving heartburn to my dog instead of to me. "Why did you bring me here?"

He scratched his bald head and turned, looking up the massive trunk of the ancient redwood. "You should leave Silverpool," he said. "Sorry. I know you like it there, but you need to pack up. Probably before dawn."

Chapter Fifteen

I cast my own glow spell and thrust it out on my outstretched palm between us. "No. No way." I tried to catch his eye, but he was looking down at his hands, playing with his array of rings. "Are they going to search for the demon from the hardware store again?"

He looked up and met my gaze. "Kurt Bosko will be coming to Silverpool as the new Protector."

My anger turned into a cold stone in my gut. That murderous, bloodthirsty agent was coming to my little town? Too stunned to speak, and now appreciative of why Raynor had come in secret, I doused my light charm.

"I tried to stop the appointment, but one of the Sapphires in New York overruled," he said. Sapphire-level witches were part of the top management in the Protectorate, overseeing multiple Directors all over the world. "They've given him the resources to have two assistants with him—an apprentice and another subordinate."

"Three witches? Tristan managed the job by himself."

"With so many, Bosko will be able to impose Protectorate rule over every creature in Silverpool, including you."

"Why would he want the job?" I asked, clenching and unclenching my fists, longing to cast a decade-long forget charm on Kurt Bosko. "Why isolate himself in the middle of nowhere? It would be so boring for him." Being the Protector of a wellspring was like being a justice on the Supreme Court —a lifetime appointment. Cushy and well-compensated, usually easy, but forever. Well, until death, which did come for every witch, often by foul play—like what had struck Tristan down over the summer.

"He seems to think the wellspring requires more aggressive protection," Raynor said. "You know, your father thanked him for the Protectorate's action in stopping the wedding. He seemed sincerely anxious about almost marrying a demon. We couldn't find any evidence he'd known what she was."

Malcolm *thanked* him for stabbing Vera? "Nice euphemism. You did more than stop the wedding," I said. "She was a smoky husk the last time I saw her."

"The body was not her own. She killed the poor woman months ago."

The poor child abuser, I thought, but maybe my judgment was flawed. Vera had charmed me as well as my father. "I didn't feel any demon sign on her. Had you? Is that why so many agents were there?"

"No, that was Bosko's doing. He was still angry about the torc. He wanted to find evidence to haul your father in while he was distracted by love." Raynor snorted. "Looks like it could've worked. Whatever love delusion your father was under, it was strong enough to hide the demon's nature from him over all the months they were together. As soon as we cleansed him of all enchantments, he snapped out of it completely. He barely remembered anything about her— where they'd met, how long they'd known each other. She'd convinced him they'd met years ago, which was impossible, of course."

"So it was just the opal ring that tipped him off?" I asked. "Bosko is wearing an amulet that tells him when somebody *might* have demon ancestry in them? What's to stop him from just going around killing everybody he suspects of being guilty of supernatural qualities he despises but doesn't understand?"

"This is why we are standing here right now, my friend," Raynor said. "I've taken the opal away and locked it up again at Diamond Street. But he'd convinced New York to let him have it for your father's wedding, and there's no telling when he'll convince them again. He'll be Protector of a wellspring. He'll have a case for screening unknown visitors to Silverpool for demon print."

"How about existing residents?" I asked. "He'll know about me if he shakes my hand."

"Yes."

Shaking with anger and cold, I closed my eyes and considered my options. If the ring responded to my presence the way it had the last time, he would know there was something inhuman—something demonic—in me. He wouldn't care that it wasn't really *me* who had been touched, but an ancestor, possibly centuries ago. One of my great-great-great-great-grandmothers might have been temporarily possessed, like Samantha had been—and left a mark that carried down the generations. Bosko, indifferent to nuance, could have me immediately detained at the Protectorate, sent off to Death Valley for lifetime detention or—true to his brand—stab me in the chest with a silver stake. Any metal would work on me; I was human. He didn't care. His type never cared about the details.

"How have you hidden your own mark from him?" I

asked. We hadn't discussed our shared trait recently, but as Director he was more vulnerable than I was.

He didn't answer my question. "Will you leave before dawn?" he asked.

"Before dawn? Of course not. My life is here. My house, my magic, my workshop, my friends, even the fae—" My voice cracked. Not wanting him to see me cry, I turned my head into the shadows. I would leave if I had to, but I'd take a few days to prepare. I wouldn't let Bosko drive me out in the middle of the night as if I was a criminal.

Seth… I had to warn him. A tear managed to slip out, and I angrily wiped it away.

Raynor was holding something out to me on his palm. He pointed at it with his other finger, casting a tiny light spell to illuminate a piece of metal. A ring. "I was afraid you wouldn't be logical about leaving immediately," he said.

It was a plain, simple band made out of—I cast out my senses—copper. Tarnished, it didn't sparkle. In fact, it was almost invisible, embracing the darkness around itself. I bent over, found a twig on the ground, and used that to pick up the ring. My affinity for wood gave me enhanced insight to the ring's magic—and would protect me from any curses. Raynor was unlikely to hurt me intentionally, but he wouldn't be a director at the Protectorate if he wasn't ruthless.

The ring held powerful shielding magic. A don't-notice-me kind of charm. The thin band of tarnished copper would never catch another witch's eye.

I looked up at Raynor, who nodded. "Put it on," he said.

"This was why you came in person," I said. There were easier ways to communicate.

He nodded.

After another quick scan, I decided it was safe and slipped it on my pinkie finger. It was too small to fit on any of my others. "I don't feel anything," I said after a moment.

"That's the idea," he said. "Neither will Bosko." He held up his own hand.

It was too dark to see, so I cast a light spell again and peered at his big fingers. Lots of gold, platinum, silver, several stones, a tattoo. But there, mixed in between the others, was a sister ring to the one I wore. I never would've sensed it if I hadn't been looking directly for it.

Excellent magic. I smiled, relieved and grateful. "Thank you. Where did you get them?"

He cleared his throat, gesturing at my glow spell, and I extinguished it. At this point, if anyone was out there looking for us, they could just follow the blinking lights in the forest, but I didn't want to argue with a powerful witch who had just given me a present.

"There was only one originally. I melted it down and cast it into two." He exhaled, crossing his arms over his chest.

I was touched. "Thank you."

"It's purely selfish on my part," he said. "If you're exposed, the trail points directly to me. They'll wonder why I recruited you after your dismissal. What did I know and when did I know it? How about Darius Ironford? Rochelle? Keeping you incognito is necessary for many of my plans, and possibly my job."

"And your life," I said. "You saw how Bosko took out Vera without any silly Protectorate inquiry, self-defense, due process—"

"The demon was about to form a ceremonial bond with a witch," he said. "Bosko had the license to act immediately."

The Circle was an ancient magic, giving all rites a more powerful bond that modern witches didn't understand. The possessing demon might have had reasons we could only imagine for bonding with a witch in a Circle. Could my own ancestor have been a victim of such a rite?

"What's to stop him from doing the same with one of us?" I asked.

"This is why you should leave California immediately," he said.

"First Silverpool, now the entire state?"

"You should avoid New York, too." He ran his hand over his scalp. "Why not find a quiet cottage in the middle of nowhere—"

"I already *have* a quiet cottage in the middle of nowhere," I said.

"*Without* a wellspring. You don't even like springwater. Why stay here?"

"I like it. It feels right." But the truth was harder to explain. I'd come after my disgrace in the Protectorate in part because Tristan Price, the former Protector, had been supportive. Magic infused the land, flora, and fauna, attracting fae. There were also witches here, but it was remote. It was remote, but San Francisco wasn't too far away. And the redwood trees… they'd called to me. I didn't want to live without them.

"It's going to feel wrong very, very soon," Raynor said. "That ring will buy you a little time, but he's persistent. And, as you've noticed, likes to kill things. Swear to me you'll leave within the week."

"But—"

"Swear it, or I take the ring back." He held up his hand, fingers splayed, and I felt a sizzle of power in the copper band around my pinkie.

"Wait, just—" I began. The ring twisted and began sliding up my finger. "Wait!"

"Swear it."

I fisted my hand to slow the ring's departure and buy myself a few seconds to think. Was there a way I could protect myself from Bosko without the ring? If I refused to shake his hand, he and his assistants would turn all his powers of detection on me. Herbs and other hearth magic would probably work with a weaker witch, but he was strong and had methods and tools I could only imagine.

Just because I left within the week didn't mean I couldn't come back. My gut told me Bosko wouldn't stay in Silverpool for years, let alone decades. But was it just wishful thinking? Wishes had gotten me into enough trouble lately.

All I could do was live in the present moment with the circumstances as they were. Meeting Raynor's gaze, I felt a bonding spell flare into life. "I swear it," I said. "I'll leave within a week of Bosko coming to town."

"And you'll stay away," Raynor added.

That vow I would not make. "While he's here, I'll stay away."

His brow furrowed. "The Protectorship is a lifetime appointment."

"In theory," I said. "We can't see the future." Even with magic, it was useless to try.

"Don't count on him leaving anytime soon. He pulled a lot of strings to get this position. I don't know why, but Kurt Bosko really wants to be in Silverpool."

I inhaled a deep breath. "Yeah. Me too."

Chapter Sixteen

It was almost two in the morning when I got back to Silverpool and knocked on Seth's door. I'd thought his fairy senses would've warned him somehow to be waiting for me, but it took him five minutes to hear my knock and finally open up and peer at me outside in the dark. His face was as sleepy and confused as any human's.

"I know you'll ignore me like all the other times," I said, "but a really bad guy is coming to Silverpool as the new Protector, and I thought you should know as soon as possible."

He yawned. "Really bad guy," he said, nodding. "Got it."

"His name's Kurt Bosko," I added.

"Right." He nodded again, leaning against the door with his eyes half-closed.

His lack of reaction annoyed me. "He killed the woman who was marrying my dad because the opal ring told him she was a demon," I said. "Day before yesterday. Maybe you heard about that?"

His eyes snapped open all the way. "Sorry. That must've been stressful."

"It was kinda."

"And now they're sending him here to find more demons, I assume," he said.

"Aren't you worried? Why aren't you worried?"

"None of this is news," he said. "This is what the Protectorate does. There's a wellspring down the street. Tristan has been dead for months. They were bound to send somebody eventually. I'm just surprised they waited this long—but that's probably your doing."

"You're welcome."

"I don't want you to do anything for me, Alma. Please. It's hard enough carrying the burden of one human life." He opened the door, inviting me inside. "You look like you need a drink."

"I can't come in. From now on, I'm going to stay as far away from you as I can. It's the least I can do for you, which is more than you want, but tough. They're probably following me. My father's reckless lifestyle strikes again." I felt warm, tired tears pool in my eyes. "I have to leave Silverpool."

He pulled me inside and closed the door. "I'm sorry," he said. "He's got the opal ring?"

"Not at the moment, but he'll probably get it at some point," I said.

"Then it sounds like you don't have a choice," he said. "You can't risk running into him. When does he get here?"

"I don't know. Any day now." I couldn't muster the panic I should've had. It just didn't feel real.

"What are you doing here? You should be packing up right now."

"That's what Raynor said." I looked down at the ring on my hand. "We worked out something to protect me for a while. I'll be fine. It's you who needs to worry."

He followed my gaze and stared silently for a moment. "There's something there on your finger, isn't there?"

"You can't see it?"

He shook his head. "Barely. It's... brass?"

"Copper."

"Neat," he said. "Raynor has his uses."

I felt a surge of affection for Seth, who was willing to say a kind word about a Protectorate agent whose career had been founded on killing supernatural creatures just like himself. "You could borrow it," I said impulsively. "When you need to leave home—"

He scowled. "Then *you* would be exposed."

"Only temporarily. I can avoid them. If they scan you once and determine you're not a threat—"

"Alma, why? Why do you feel the need to protect me?" he demanded, fully awake now. "You've ruined your career, risked your life, and seem compelled, no matter the cost to yourself, to protect me. Why? You're a witch, not a—" He cut himself off and stared at me.

"It's not what you think," I said quickly. He had a long history of flirting with me and was probably going to suggest I was in love with him. I did have feelings for him, but I didn't think it was romantic. He was only joking, anyway.

"I'm having that urge again," Seth said. "The one where I want to crawl into your lap and purr."

"Now I really know I have to leave," I said, reaching for the door.

He blocked me. "Your ancestry. It's what drives you to sacrifice yourself, for me in particular. Powerful spirit beings have always been fond of the fae. My mother used to tell stories about angels who were as nurturing of us as demons were... hungry."

"Right, I'm an angel," I said with a snort. I didn't pretend to understand all the subtleties of creation, but I was sure of my own imperfections.

"One of your ancestors was possessed by something similar, at least briefly," he said. "That's my theory."

I was just starting to accept I had a demon ancestor. Now an angel? I wanted to believe such Bright creatures existed, and I would love to meet other demons who didn't want to possess innocent people and make kebabs out of every wood sprite they met, but I didn't have enough evidence. One thing I knew, however, was that I was too imperfect—too human—to consider myself one of them.

Seth was just teasing me again.

I nudged past him and opened the door. "Theories are cheap. I'm going home to shore up my wards. You should do the same."

"I'm sorry if I've offended you," he said. "I meant it as a compliment."

"I'm a human being. A witch. Just because I'm a little different from average doesn't mean there's some big weird secret about me." Big weird secrets were dangerous. It meant powerful witches like Kurt Bosko might want to kill you, and others would fire you from your job, and genies would grant wishes and demand unaffordable prices. It meant you were alone in the world, forced from the only real home you'd ever had in your life.

I strode away without another word and quickly strengthened the boundary spells around my house, extending them into the yard—and then, with a little spite, around Seth's property as well. I was more powerful than I'd been a year ago; I could feel it. I used to have to scan my own front door before I entered, once finding my father had broken in, but now I didn't have to. Could it be something about Willy? Or my advancing years? The alternative explanation was less pleasant: the deaths of other witches, fae, and supernatural beings who had crossed me—and died—had deepened my personal well of magic. I hadn't intentionally killed anyone, but there had been deaths. Tattoos had appeared on my arm. And now I was stronger.

Did I really have to leave Silverpool? Maybe I was strong enough to stay. There was the vow to Raynor, but I could negotiate a compromise if I convinced him Bosko wasn't a threat to me. The opal was locked up, he'd be occupied with Protectorate duties, and I had centralized a tremendous amount of power here at my house to protect myself, more every day. And if Bosko did somehow shake my unprotected hand and expose me as having the demon mark, the most likely thing he would do would be to expel me from Silverpool—so why jump the gun and do his work for him?

I went to bed hopeful but woke before dawn in a cold sweat. The dark ceiling seemed low, pressing down on me, and the walls felt too close and creeping closer. I got out of bed and dressed quickly, craving fresh air.

Something was coming. My hair stood on end, and every creak of the floorboards made me touch my focus string. When the sun finally broke over the treetops to the east, I picked up Random's leash and took him out for his morning walk through Silverpool, resisting the idea it might be one of our last.

❧

GIVEN MY NERVES, I was prepared for the Protectorate to visit me, but when Random and I returned from our walk, the witch standing at the end of my driveway was an old friend.

Well, that's what my father had called her right before she'd ensnared him in an arrest spell for Kurt Bosko to take him into custody after the execution of his bride.

I pulled the leash tight so Random couldn't greet Flor with his usual warmth. He was too friendly. She didn't deserve it. "What are you doing here?" I asked coldly.

She was wearing an official black-and-silver Protectorate sweater. Archivists, her former position, only wore civilian clothing. The hair bow in her helmet-shaped bob was still there, though. Today's was red velvet.

She put her hands on her hips and frowned at the overgrown botany of my front yard. "I understand if you're a little annoyed, but you can't be seriously angry. You've got to admit I had no choice. Some of us can't afford to turn down an opportunity when it literally falls at our feet."

"You arrested him while his bride's corpse was still warm."

Flor snorted. "Warm? She was on fire. Because she was a *demon*."

"My father invited you into his home. He was your *host*. Talk about a breach of protocol."

"He's been released," she said. "Let's not overreact."

"I'll act however I want." I scratched Random behind the ears, fondly remembering how, when in dragon form, he'd been able to blast things with his fire breath. It was safer I didn't know how to command him to do that. "So. Bosko took you on as his apprentice. You're on your way to having that life of meaning you've always wanted. Congratulations."

"Thank you. I don't think you're really angry. You always did hide your goodness under sarcasm." Before I could correct her, she continued, "But I'm not quite his apprentice. Not yet. That position is filled at the moment. I'm in line to fill it when Percival moves on."

"You're just a Flint flunky?"

"I don't have a title. You may refer to me as his assistant."

I opened my mouth to tell her I didn't plan on referring to her as anything because I was leaving town, especially now that she was there, but I stopped myself in time. Sleep deprivation, even with herbal remedies, made my tongue too loose. "His app is here in Silverpool too?"

She shook her head. "He's coming later. I came with Protector Bosko at dawn. He said it would make the right impression."

"That he has a sleep disorder?"

"That he means business." She turned to look at my house—into which I was not going to invite her—then back to me. "I'm only here for the wellspring, Alma. With it so close, I can research the fae as I've always dreamed. *Some* of them will let me see them—new, wild ones who have never been studied by researchers before. I can compile the research to write fresh and exciting theories. And with Kurt Bosko's name on my dissertation, some people will actually read it. That will be the start of me making a name for me and my children's children's children."

What a fanatic. She and Bosko were meant for each other. "Don't you think you're getting ahead of yourself?"

She smiled. "Maybe. I don't care. Big goals take planning." She walked past me toward the street, patting my shoulder. "I just wanted to say hi. Clear the air. We'll come by for a real check-in later."

I promptly sent an erasing spell to the patch on my arm she'd touched. "Interrogation, you mean."

"Not at all. There probably won't be much talking required. Just a scan or two." She waved and kept walking down the street.

It was then I realized she'd come on foot. The winery, where the Protector and his staff lived, was just over a mile away on the other side of the Vago River.

It was smart to walk. Easier to sneak up on the unwary. I vowed to keep a sharp eye out for doll-headed pedestrians from now on.

Chapter Seventeen

Deciding Flor and Bosko would be busy at the winery on their first day, I took a nap on my living room couch, holding my magic staff. It was a rough-hewn piece of lumber I'd carved from a broken beam in my attic, holding a fragment of the power I'd infused in my home. A witch's house contained, expanded, nurtured, and amplified her innate power—as long as she was in it. If I held the staff while I was inside the boundaries of my property, it was powerful, enabling me to lift bodies and blast hexes. Away from home, unfortunately, it lost most of its strength, although I was working on expanding its radius. It was now able to light a match a mile from home.

Maybe the comfort of the warm wood, vibrating softly, would help me rest. My sleep hygiene had been poor lately, and I needed to recharge. Random didn't join me, instead choosing the tile of the kitchen floor, which was both pleasingly cool after his long walk and gave him first dibs on any intruders.

We were both on edge. He'd learned to dislike any

stranger I didn't let into the house. If Flor ever came back to see me, he'd bark at her. We had an excellent system.

The next time Flor wanted my attention, however, she simply texted. It was around two in the afternoon.

Come at highest moon, she wrote. *The Protector wants to talk to you.*

I pretended not to see the text right away, but I couldn't ignore the summons.

What about? I texted an hour later. I didn't expect an answer, but the nonanswer might be interesting.

Bring all your unregistered amulets.

I made a face at my phone. Nobody registered their magic anymore. Nobody. *My garage is full of jewelry material,* I wrote. *Can't bring it all.*

Not that! Real magic.

Although I did get tired of the dismissive attitude toward hearth magic, sometimes there were benefits to being under-estimated. Almost everything I had was either uninteresting to Bosko or was under safe, undetectable storage in my living room filing cabinet.

But I did spare a thought for how fun it would be to bring the torc and wave it around like no big deal, just to see his reaction.

BTW high moon is 2059, she wrote. *See you then.*

I didn't reply. Scheduling by moon position was an old-fash-ioned protocol, and nine at night was lucky. Sometimes a mage would demand attendance at highest moon even if it was three in the morning and then wouldn't show up himself until after breakfast, keeping the lesser witch waiting in sleepy misery.

I spent the rest of the day trying to pack, but it didn't feel right. It took two hours for me to fill one suitcase and a single box of kitchen supplies. Even if I was really leaving, how much did I want to bring with me? With nowhere to go, I'd need to travel light. Birdie could have everything I left behind.

When night finally came, I gathered the magic I was willing to show Bosko. I filled a plastic box with a few harmless pieces of my jewelry, a tarnished silver spoon from babyhood, and all the pieces I'd been wearing to the wedding, which he might remember, and then locked up the house. I was nervous and stopped a moment to gaze at the sky and breathe. It was only a few days until the full moon, and the forest was well lit. In rural Silverpool, the moon's phase made a big difference. I made some of my most powerful necklaces, all of which I was wearing now, in the backyard under its bright glow.

I got behind the wheel of my Jeep, my pulse higher than I would've liked, and twisted the copper ring on my finger three times for good luck. Then five. Then seven. I made myself stop before I sawed my finger off.

Suddenly I remembered that unfriendly Protectorate agents had seen me that summer with my staff. Reluctantly I went back inside to get it, grumbling to myself. I'd rather hide it at home, but it wasn't worth the risk of looking like a scofflaw from the start.

The winery was a very short drive down the hill, over the river, and up a nicely landscaped vineyard driveway to the private residence, the winery, and a small structure with a tasting room overlooking the valley. I'd had a complicated relationship with the former Protector, Tristan Price, and had spent a lot of time there. Including after his murder.

Flor met me at the open door and looked past me at the Jeep. "Did you bring everything?"

I held the storage bin with both hands, the staff held under a belt at my waist. "I'm wearing it or it's in the box."

"What's the stick?"

I was happy not to bring it inside. "Should I put it back in the car?"

"Just kidding. Nice staff. Very wizardish." She patted me on the shoulder. "Come on in. The Protector is on the back patio. Want a drink?"

"No, thanks." I didn't want anything to slow me down. When she turned to lead me into the house, I cast a quick spell to wash off her touch again on my shoulder. Remembering how I would be unable to wash away Kurt Bosko's touch, I clenched my teeth.

The ring, I reminded myself. *I'm wearing the ring. It worked for Raynor. Relax.*

The patio had an excellent view of the vineyard. Bosko stood in front of a low stone wall next to a potted lemon tree, gazing at the rolling hills of dormant vines under the moonlight. One pleasant night a long time ago, I'd kissed Tristan in the same spot, warmed as much by his company as the large propane patio heater.

I swatted aside memories of the past. I couldn't afford to get lost in soft feelings at the moment. Setting the box down on a bench, I pulled the staff out of my belt and turned to Bosko.

"I feel a somewhat strong piece of magic in your hand, Alma," he said, scratching the side of his neck with his left hand as he turned. The right held a drink of some kind.

I stepped closer to see if he wore the opal ring, but not so close to antagonize him and risk an aggressive probing. The staff, which I hadn't wanted to bring, suddenly became indispensable. With a stealth I wouldn't have been able to manage without it, I scanned both his hands with a swift, powerful probe of my own.

Ah. He wasn't wearing the ring. I let out the breath I'd been holding. The drink in his hand was laced with springwater.

"Yes, Protector," I said. "Flor said to bring everything."

The corner of his mouth curved in a disdainful smile. "There's no metal inlay or hardware on the wood of that staff, though, is there?"

"No."

"It's barely more than a giant pencil," he said, then snorted and added, "Less. At least the pencil has graphite."

"And aluminum," I said.

His smile softened as if he felt sorry for me. "Indeed." He sipped his drink and held out his right hand for a handshake —the inevitable display of witch dominance. "Set the stick down first," he said.

He'd spoken contemptuously about my staff, but I noticed he was afraid of my using it to block his magic. "Sure." I set it on a bench and took his hand with a careful blend of innocent wariness and indifference.

His grip was painful, like other bullying men I'd known, crushing my finger bones together like too many books on a shelf. His skin was cold, and the magic he swept over me had a stinging, prickly character that went uncomfortably deep into my spirit. Given his new job in town, I could only grit my teeth and wait it out. His probe was similar to what the Protectorate mages would do with young Flints who joined the organization to measure their innate abilities.

Finger by finger, he released my hand and then took another drink, watching me carefully. "You're stronger than I expected."

I made no comment. I knew why he'd expected me to be weak. He was a man who measured strength by its ability to hurt, overpower, and destroy.

He went over to my storage box and opened it. Not putting down his drink, he reached inside and rifled dismissively through my things as he cast a probing scan. Unimpressed, he put the lid back on carelessly and turned to me again.

"My assistant said you were at the top of your class," he said. "Just beneath her."

I glanced at Flor, who lifted a hand to adjust her red hair bow. She probably had been at the top of our class, but I had no memory of my own ranking. I'd been to so many schools and seldom paid attention to grades or competitions. "That was a long time ago," I said.

He lifted his glass to his lips. "Spoken like a child. You're both too young to take seriously." The rings on his hand caught the light as he drank. Because I had the staff, I could tell he wasn't wearing the opal. He had so many other rings, though, and I wondered what they did, if they told him other things I'd rather hide.

What an unpleasant witch. Why did he have to come to Silverpool? I wish—

No. I picked up my staff and drew a bubble of magical nullity around me. No more wishes. Cypress Hardware was less than a mile away.

"Assistant, I need a refill," he said to Flor. She nodded, took his glass, and went back into the house.

Bosko gestured for me to sit with him on unpadded teak chairs facing one another. "I brought you up here to give you the opportunity I'm sure you wanted," he said, crossing his legs, "but didn't know how to go about getting."

Opportunity? He couldn't be talking about giving me the chance to push him headfirst off the patio into the rows of golden-brown grapevines, but that was the first thought that came to mind. "Excuse me?"

"Your father thanked me immediately," he continued. "The first moment he was able. The Protectorate truth spell had just been cast, so it was especially heartfelt."

I stared at him, realizing he was talking about the

wedding. "He thanked you for killing V— The demon, is that what you mean?"

"Of course. Even with his crimes, Malcolm is a human being—a witch and a Bellrose—and didn't deserve to be bonded with a demon." He reached over and patted my knee. "They took you home before you too could thank me personally, but you must be unspeakably horrified at the thought a monster from Shadow almost became your mother."

"*Step*mother," I muttered. Oh Brightness, I had to say more than that, but my lips wouldn't move. The touch of his hand on my knee made me want to vomit.

I was glad it was dark enough to hide my features from close scrutiny. Pretending to like somebody had never been one of my strengths. It was taking all my energy to hide how much I loathed him.

The staff. It had come through once for me tonight; I'd try it again. Balancing it over my knees with both hands, I tapped into its strength and poured the magic into a smooth, convincing lie. It was worth the risk of using a spell he might detect; even a powerful witch was disarmed by hearing what he wanted to hear.

"I was unspeakably horrified at the idea, Protector Bosko. Thank you from the bottom of my heart." The staff was warm under my fingers, giving me more power to build on my deceit and hopefully shield its use from him. "You were a hero. And at such risk to yourself, jumping into the Circle when the rites were just about to begin. Thank you. Thank you so much."

Bile rose into my throat, but I clenched my teeth together and swallowed it back down while holding a smile on my face.

He nodded, smugly satisfied. "You're welcome. Now, on to business. I'm sure Tristan had his own methods"—his smug expression twisted—"but I'll expect all witches in Silverpool to report to me every week for scanning. In addition, I will be notified of all supernatural activity, minor and major, within an hour of its occurrence. This includes so-called benevolent creatures."

"So-called… Do you mean the fae?" I asked slowly.

"Of course the fae. But I was speaking in particular of the tiniest of them that are generally forgotten—wisps and other insect-sized fairies, for instance. With special amulets, we can see the microscopic ones. If they let themselves be seen, they need to be dealt with, no matter how quote unquote cute they seem to the ignorant." Flor returned and handed him his drink, which he took with a grunt. "My assistants will be compiling an inventory. We can't let these things run loose anymore. Your friend here has a pretty good track record with wild fairies. She worked in Sweden, Ireland…"

When he trailed off, Flor said, "And Costa Rica," and Bosko gave her a mock salute.

He was nuts. I assumed Flor was just humoring him to get ahead. What did he suggest doing to the tiny creatures—blasting them with fire and burning down the forest?

Maybe he did.

"Alma?" he asked sharply.

I'd been gaping at him. He would be scanning witches weekly, expected frequent updates, and wanted to create an inventory of even the tiniest of fairies, who he believed to be dangerous. The larger beings could cause trouble, of course, and had rebelled just that summer, but the vast majority were as harmless as dragonflies.

Given their mythical name, he probably wanted to kill the dragonflies too.

Raynor's insistence that I leave town was making more sense. I got to my feet. "Forgive me, Protector. It's getting late. Do you mind if I go home and we can continue this conversation when I return for my first weekly, uh, scan?" I'd make sure to be gone by then. He was going to be worse than I'd imagined, which made my departure easier to accept. He would make life intolerable for me and every other witch within twenty miles of the wellspring. I didn't believe he'd be able to control the fae—they'd hide or leave, as they had left other places humans made inhospitable—but I'd be miserable. I just had to face reality. I'd gotten too attached to my life there. I should've remembered how much it hurt when I was a kid to be uprooted. It was better to never put down roots at all. Better not to get attached to anything or anyone.

"You may leave after my apprentice arrives. I want him to meet all witches here in person." Bosko had his phone in his hand and was tapping the screen impatiently. "He left San Francisco an hour ago. He never mastered the art of casting spells on the road. I should've sent the new girl. She at least doesn't drive like an old woman."

I looked over to see if Flor was irritated with the way he'd addressed her. Protocol called for addresses like "Protector" or "Apprentice" or, at the very least, "Witch"—and although most trainee agents were called by their first names, that was an improvement over "the new girl." I wondered if he knew her name. I wondered if he'd ever bother to learn it.

The nasty thought cheered me enough to ask Flor for a cup of herbal tea, and I sipped it as I endured twenty minutes of Bosko's complaints about California freeways before his apprentice arrived from San Francisco.

When Percy, the apprentice, finally arrived and came out onto the patio, Bosko's temper had deteriorated.

"Sorry to keep you waiting, Protector," Percy said. "I came as soon as—"

"This is Alma Bellrose. Malcolm's daughter," Bosko snapped, pushing his empty glass at him. "She lives here."

Percy was a thin, dark-haired man about my age or a

little older who might've been tall if he stood up straight. He had onyx plugs in his ears, a heavy gold necklace, eyebrow and nose studs, and numerous rings of metal and stone. He took the glass from the mage he served with a polite bow of his head.

"Hi," he said quietly to me. "I'm Percival Tuff. Everyone calls me Percy."

Bosko pointed at the sky, where the moon was sinking. "It's late."

Percy's head sank farther. "I'm so sorry, Protector Bosko." He took out a small black leather pouch from the front pocket of his jeans. "I had to wait for Mage Dupo."

I sucked in my breath and held it. When I'd first seen the opal ring at a house party, it had pained me to get near it. Would it give me away now? The Circle at the wedding seemed to have shielded me. I hoped the copper ring was doing the same.

Bosko strode over and took the package from him. "Don't blame Dupo. It was your nervous driving that made you late." He weighed the pouch in his palm, magic probes flying, then smiled in satisfaction. "This is it. I thought they might try to send me a fake, but I'm attuned to it now. This is the opal."

"Why didn't they want you to have it, Protector?" Flor asked. "You'd think they'd want the best demon detection available near a wellspring."

"You'd think," Bosko said with a snort. "But that's politics for you. Powerful people are afraid of losing their privileges, no matter how just that might be. Because this little stone, witches, has the power to uncover demons—yes—but also demon *stain*." He closed his fist around the pouch and thrust his arm into the air.

Percy began cleaning up the crumpled napkins and

empty glasses from around the deck. "You really think there are powerful mages who have demon stain?"

"I'm sure of it," Bosko said. "It's past time for the Protectorate to go after the Shadow in its own ranks. The ring will help me weed out not only the demons from Silverpool, but any witch with demonic ancestry who comes near it. Such witches are tainted, impure, and dangerous. Amulets like this ring have been locked in storage for too long. They need to be *used*. This is no time to be cowardly."

Then he lowered his hand, tucked the ring into a chest pocket, and pointed at Percy. "I missed my dinner. The kitchen here is empty. Go out and find me steak. I'm in the mood for iron."

"Certainly, Protector," Percy said, bowing his head over the dirty glasses.

Bosko stared at him, scowled at the glasses, and then shook his head. "Never mind, you're busy." He turned to Flor. "You. I'm not particular, just make it beef. Percy will stock up the kitchen tomorrow."

Flor's mouth opened to protest—she'd been in town for only a day, but it was long enough to notice there probably wasn't a twenty-four-hour drive-through—but then she smiled tightly. "Of course, Protector. Thank you. It's my pleasure to serve you." She mumbled a quick goodbye to Percy and me, then marched into the house, her bow bouncing.

Just a hint of magic tingled the back of my neck, and I looked around, feeling for its source, unable to find it.

Percy stood unmoving, facing the vineyard. The moonlight sent deep shadows across his eye sockets, casting his skin in an ashy glow.

"Well, go on," Bosko said to him. "Finish cleaning up. Party's over."

Percy jerked into life and scurried into the house without a goodbye. The hint of magic lingered. One of them had cast a spell over the other, but I couldn't tell who had done what to whom.

Sitting down, Bosko crossed his legs and frowned at me. "Well? What are you still doing here? Go on. I'll be seeing you soon enough. You'll be coming here every Wednesday at highest moon from now on. Don't watch the clock—I go by the old ways."

I gripped my staff and nodded, relieved he wasn't going to test me with the opal ring tonight. The copper Raynor had given me would probably work as a shield, but it was always safer to completely avoid the conflict altogether.

"See you," I said, careful not to promise Wednesday since I fully planned on being gone by then.

Of course I didn't want to leave Silverpool, but it was irrational to argue with reality. Bosko was an Emerald, armed with both position and power. I was outmatched.

But I hoped a fame-hungry witch like him would get tired of being in Silverpool. When he did, I could come back. It didn't have to be forever.

Who knew what the future would bring?

Chapter Eighteen

Early the next morning, before the sun had risen high enough to cut through the shadows of the redwood forest, I knelt down in a pile of dried leaves near some vicious blackberry brambles and held out the torc.

There wasn't any spark, snap, or stink—a person walking by wouldn't have noticed a thing—but I felt a tug in my cheeks as if I were hanging upside down, and then back up again, sideways, up, down, around, and back up. I'd tried resting the torc on my lap instead of holding it in the air, hoping its immobility would make the spell less nauseating for me, but it had made no difference. When my vision cleared, I saw a pool of water form beneath the leaves in the dry earth in front of me: the wellspring that gave Silverpool its name.

I filled up the bottles I'd brought with me, appreciating the magic that kept any of the leaves from sticking to the water, and carried them to my Jeep parked nearby. Storing large quantities of springwater was dangerous, which was why it was hard to come by. It attracted demons and fae, potentially putting you in the middle of the brutal conflict between them. I'd have to be careful and spread out my stash as soon as I could.

We hadn't had a big storm yet, and the news mentioned it might be a drought year again. If it did finally rain, water would drain into the valleys, fill the Vago River, and rush the remaining miles down to the Pacific while the wellspring would rise up to the surface in the patch of ground where I'd filled the bottles. Until then, only the torc could get large amounts of water from the dry earth. Only the person holding it. Me.

I returned to the wellspring, which had already drained mostly away, leaving only a shallow patch of water amid the mud and leaves. The fairies didn't want to be seen, but I saw them gathered around the puddle: wood sprites and flower fae, the bridge troll, a thin goblin in a brick-red dress. As at an oasis in the desert, ancient enemies kept an uneasy truce, watching each other out of the corners of their eyes as they crept up to the remnants of the precious springwater.

I lifted the torc with both hands, enduring the vertigo again, and more water bubbled to the surface. The fae didn't thank me—the green-faced bridge fairy gave me a sour, bitter look—but I enjoyed watching their pleasure secondhand. My favorite were the tiny flower creatures who flashed gold sparks and fluttered down to the drink with delightful enthusiasm. The wood sprites, some as big as human toddlers and who could be dangerous and nasty when stressed, were now cheerful as they took out wood bowls and discarded human bottles to collect the liquid for later. Until the wellspring rose naturally to the surface after the winter rains, only these local fae would enjoy my generosity. Late December, countless other spirit creatures from far away would arrive in town to celebrate. It was that crowd that Flor probably intended to study.

If they let her. I wondered what magic she had to compel them to show themselves to her. There were amulets witches used, or perhaps her years of fae research had taught her methods I'd never had to learn because of my innate, secret talent of seeing them naturally. Tristan, the former Protector, had used a combination of metal magic and old herb lore. Many of the plants in my front yard had ended up in Tristan's potions and potpourri gift bags.

Lots of unwanted memories of Tristan were coming to me since I'd been to the winery last night. He hadn't been perfect, but he'd been a good witch, and the town had prospered under his Protectorship. Back in my car, I sat with my grief for several minutes until I felt strong enough to drive home and pack up the car.

It didn't have to be this way, my mind argued. *It's not fair!* my heart cried. But I started the engine and pulled out onto the road, watching the drunk fae in my rearview mirror, accepting it might be the last time for a while. How old was Bosko? A lifetime appointment could mean decades. Or maybe…

As I drove home, I consoled myself with dark thoughts about him adopting a ten-pack-a-day smoking habit or passion for solo free climbing in the Himalayas. When I turned the corner to drive up the hill to my house, I was feeling a little better.

But then Flor jumped out from behind a bush and ran in front of my car. She was waving her arms and screaming. For a split second I thought she might be part of my guilty daydream, but I snapped out of it when she slapped the hood of my car with both hands, then stumbled out of sight.

Adrenaline surging, I slammed on the brakes and killed the engine. When I jumped out, Flor was already there, seizing me by the shoulders, her eyes wild.

"He's dead!" she shouted. "He wasn't asleep, he was dead!"

"Who?" I demanded.

"Bosko! The stupid bastard died! Our first day! What in Shadow am I supposed to do now? He was my ticket! I planned so long for this! It's not fair!"

Chapter Nineteen

Flor shook me by the shoulders, repeating the same words over and over—*it's not fair, he's dead, what in Shadow do I do now? Why me?*

I twisted her fingers loose and squeezed them. "Tell me what happened." By instinct I cast a calming spell over her. I could feel her racing pulse through her hands.

"I don't know," she gasped, falling quiet. Then, under the effects of my spell, she began to speak more slowly. "He fell or something. He… he's in his room. Just lying there. He doesn't use a bed, so I thought he was sleeping, but his mat is in the corner and he's in the middle, sprawled out in a weird way. Like he fell. He looks like he fell."

I squeezed her hands harder. "Who's there now with the body? Percy?"

"No, I couldn't find him. We were supposed to meet first thing this morning, that's why I went looking for Bosko when he didn't show up."

Now I was the one to start shouting. "So Bosko's body is alone up there?"

"Of course not. The cleaner is there. She's not a witch,

but she used to work for Tristan and knows about us. We locked the door. She's standing guard."

"What did Raynor say?"

"I'm hardly important enough to have his direct number," she snapped. "That's why I came to get you."

"You could've called somebody else at Diamond Street," I said. "You worked there."

"He's dead, Alma. He would've promoted me. Percy was always getting on his nerves. I would've been an app before the equinox if I'd had the chance to prove myself, but he's dead… I worked so hard, so hard, you have no idea… and now he's dead…" Her voice rose to a wail.

I sent a stronger sedating spell into her nostrils. After her third breath, she slumped forward, put her arms around me, and began to weep softly.

"I'll go with you," I said in a soothing voice, patting her back as I indulged in an eye roll. She should've called Diamond Street, not come to me. "Don't worry. Get in my car. Let's go." She was easy to guide over to the passenger side and seemed relieved about my driving her back to the winery.

For Brightness' sake. The last thing I wanted was to get swept into another crime scene. Or was I too hasty to assume it was a crime?

"You said he might've fallen from something?" I asked. "How?"

Silence. I looked over.

She was asleep. Her head was slumped forward, and drool was hanging down her lip onto the seat belt, leaving a shiny trail on the black strap.

Great. I'd have to wake her up to deal with the Protectorate, because I sure wasn't going to be the one. And where was Percy? If Bosko had been killed, which was likely, the apprentice might have been hurt too. Of course, if he'd been the murderer, he could be fleeing the country. Had he finally snapped? Or had Bosko used the opal ring on him, discovered he was a demon, tried to stab him but this time the app was prepared and—

It was fruitless for me to speculate on so little information. And it wasn't my job to figure it out.

I parked in front of the tasting room and went around to the passenger seat to wake her up. Only more magic could overcome the spell I'd knocked her out with, so I had to draw upon my beads again and send stimulating energy into her nostrils this time.

The moment her eyes opened, she began muttering, "He's dead, he's dead," but she wasn't shouting, so I left her alone until she calmed herself down. A minute later, she shuddered and got out of the car. "What in Shadow did you do to me?"

"You were hysterical," I said.

She rubbed her temples. "Where did you learn that kind of spell?" She gave her head a shake, sighing. "I feel like I've been partying for a week."

"Sorry."

"No, seriously," she said. "I didn't have a chance to fight it off. Did you do something to my nose?"

"You inhaled a little calming energy, that's all."

"I didn't know that would work." She frowned at me. "I guess they teach agents the good stuff."

I hadn't learned it at the Protectorate—I hadn't learned it anywhere; it just seemed natural—but it was easier if she believed that. "I guess." She seemed awake enough now, so I waved my phone in front of her face. "I'm going to dial Raynor. You're going to tell him what happened."

"You aren't going to introduce me?"

"He knows who you are. Just give your name and tell

him what you told me. Without the shouting." I hit Raynor's number and handed her the phone.

She touched her hair, adjusting a bright yellow bow—as if he'd care how she looked—and then lifted the phone to her ear. "No, Director. This is Florence Werner. Alma gave me her phone." She paused. "Do you want to talk to her?" She gave me an *I-told-you-so* look and thrust the phone back at me.

"Hi, Raynor," I said quickly. "Flor's going to tell y—"

His voice was an uncompromising growl. "I want to hear it from you. What happened?"

I sighed. "Bosko is dead. She found him in his room this morning."

"Who else knows?"

"The housekeeper. The door is locked. She's standing guard outside."

"The nonmagical woman who worked for Tristan Price?" he asked.

"Yes. Her name is Donna. She knows about us." I clenched my jaw, braced for his disapproval.

He immediately began ranting that it was completely inappropriate for a nonmagical cleaner to be left in charge of a potential demon-attack scene.

"Not my idea," I cut in.

"Where's the app? Percy."

"Missing," I said.

"Demon's balls."

"Anyway, just thought you should know," I said. "I'm going home now."

"Absolutely not. You're going to secure the scene and alert me of any developments," he said. "Florence doesn't have the experience for this. At least she had the sense to get you involved instead of calling just anybody at Diamond Street, or Brightness forbid, the police."

"I don't work for—"

"This is really bad for you, Alma. Really bad for your father. You should do exactly what I say."

"Bad for me? Why?" Now I wouldn't have to leave town. I was feeling secretly upbeat.

"Another Protector is dead within a year, and the man who killed your father's bride is now dead, and I bet neither of you has an alibi."

"I barely knew her!"

"He got the opal ring last night," Raynor said quietly. "Do what I say."

"If I'm—" I turned away from Flor, who was watching carefully. Nobody else needed to know I had a motive to fear a man wearing the opal ring. "Why me?"

"Keep Flor and the housekeeper with you at all times," he said. "Until I get there."

"Hex me," I muttered. My car was filled with jugs and bottles of illicit springwater I'd gotten with the stolen torc. If anyone scanned it, they'd sense the powerful water and, given the drought, realize it was me who had the stolen object. And then quickly see through the masking spell that hid it under the front seat. I didn't know if I could wiggle out of that one, even with Raynor's help.

"Raynor, I just can't," I said, thinking desperately for an excuse. "It's too… traumatic. You know how much I've been through."

"You might face worse if you don't listen to me," he said.

I wanted to bargain—what about Seth?—but Flor was standing there, obviously hanging on every word.

"Fine," I mumbled.

"I'm on my way," he said. "You know what to do." He clicked off.

I swallowed another curse and walked to the front door.

"We're going in together," I said, gesturing for Flor to follow. "Do what I say. I'm in charge now."

She walked slowly, frowning at me. "In charge? But they fired you."

"You're the one who came and got me," I snapped. "Open the door, please. I don't have a key."

Pursing her lips, Flor took out a key, cast a spell that she actually tried to hide from me, and went in first. "His bedroom is past the living room, at the end of the hallway on the right."

I knew where it was. There was only one master bedroom, and I'd slept with Tristan in it. Better times, though I hadn't thought so at the time. Another reminder to be grateful for what you had—although I supposed that went for every moment, including this one. Bosko was dead without a single free climb or unfiltered cigarette, making the world a better place.

As we walked through the airy, expensively decorated rooms of the single-story house, I sent out probing spells for evil or danger but detected nothing I could isolate as foreign to the current residents. Even as we got closer to Bosko's bedroom, I detected nothing at all unusual.

The housekeeper, Donna, was sitting where Flor had left her, in the hallway beside the closed door of the master bedroom. The last time we'd seen each other was right after Tristan's death.

"Hi, Donna," I said. "It's me, Alma. We met—"

Her eyes lit up, and she scrambled to her feet. "Thank God, somebody I know." The winery had changed hands twice since the summer, and she was probably disoriented by the changes. "Tell them I'm not— I'm not one of you. I can't do anything about whatever is going on here. In fact, I told Flora here—"

"Florence," Flor said.

Donna waved impatiently. "Told this one I'm not going to work here anymore. The money's good but not that good. Tristan was bad enough, but now—"

"I understand. Stick around for a few more hours and they'll make it worth your while, I promise. Get yourself a drink from—"

While I spoke, Donna suddenly looked at the ceiling, made an "ooh" sound, and swayed into Flor, who grabbed her under the arms and guided her to the floor. The remains of a knockout spell wafted up from Donna's mouth.

"You didn't have to do that." Kneeling down, I took off my sweater, bunched it up, and set it under Donna's head. Her pulse was slow but steady, and her color was good. "She would've stayed for a few hundred bucks. Now we've got to erase her memory."

"Her memory will have to be erased anyway. Besides, if you didn't want me to do that spell, you shouldn't have taught it to me." She flashed a wry smile. "What do we do next, boss?"

Chapter Twenty

When Raynor arrived, Flor and I were sitting with Donna's unconscious body in the hallway, staring at our phones. Even witches wasted time online. Flor had already set up a boundary spell at the threshold and outside windows, and there was nothing else I could do.

"Where in Shadow is Percival Tuff?" Raynor's booming voice came from inside the house. Then he turned the corner and saw us just as we were hurrying to put away our phones. "Reassure me you haven't taken any photographs."

He was alone in the hallway, but I was sure he had agents on hand waiting for orders to approach.

"We haven't opened the door," I said.

Raynor pointed at Flor. "But *she* did this morning," he said. "Open it now. Your aura is already on the doorknob. It needs to be you."

"Now?" Flor asked. "Don't you want witnesses?"

"There are almost three of us here," he said, glancing at Donna's unconscious body with disapproval. "How many do you think we need?"

Flor flushed. "Sorry. I don't know. Never been to a demon hit scene before."

"Why do you believe there was a demon here?" Raynor asked.

Looking even more embarrassed, Flor said, "Isn't it? I mean— it's Silverpool. Isn't that why the Protector is here in the first place? I was told there had been a demon attack recently."

Raynor nodded, absorbing her response but not agreeing or disagreeing with it. "Before you open the door, tell me exactly where you stepped this morning."

"I didn't go inside. I just looked through the door," she said. "He told us to never step on his floor."

"So you've *never* crossed the threshold?" Raynor asked sharply.

"Never," Flor said. "I just pushed the door open but stayed out here."

"I'm surprised you opened it at all," Raynor said. "Weren't you afraid of making him angry? His temper is legendary, and it's only your second day, isn't that right? Everyone knows you want to make apprentice. You're just waiting for him to chuck Percy overboard and take you on."

Flor shot me a panicked look, asking silently for help I didn't offer. She adjusted her yellow bow and said, "I... I called out and there was no answer. I... I probably shouldn't have done it, but I had a sixth sense that something was wrong."

Raynor's voice dropped. "What did you do?"

"Just tried the handle! It was unlocked, so... I opened the door." She looked as if she wanted to apparate to Alaska. "It's just he told us emphatically to be on time this morning. Maybe his spirit gave me a shock or something, letting me know there was danger, because I got so worried all of a sudden and *had* to see inside. And sure enough, he was lying there. Not moving. And I sent out a probe, just a little one, and I knew he was dead."

Raynor glanced at me. He would ask me later if I believed her. I thought he should rely on magic and agent legwork to determine the truth instead of my intuition.

"Do exactly what you did this morning," Raynor said.

Flor clasped the knob, pushed the door open, and peered inside, her toes never crossing the contrasting wood inlay of the threshold. "Like this," she said.

I stared past her at the body of Kurt Bosko, demon killer. He was flung out on his back, his head facing the door, twisted at the shoulders with his neck and limbs in an unnatural position. There was no blood. His hands were bare of all rings but one, a simple platinum band. He wore black knit pants and a T-shirt, probably what he wore to bed.

The only furnishings in the room was a narrow futon along one wall, a leather trunk near the door, and a meditation cushion and yoga mat under the windows that were both surrounded with bottles and drinking glasses of a liquid I sensed was springwater.

"He does look like he fell," I said.

"But from what?" Flor asked.

The three of us looked up at the vaulted ceiling, higher than the rest of the house, about twenty feet at its peak. "Maybe it was an accident," I said. "He was doing some spells—using wellspring water—and landed on his head. Maybe he was doing some crazy yoga pose."

"All right, stand back," Raynor said. He took out a black bag and began setting pale round pebbles in a spiral pattern on the floor in front of the door. When he had a pattern about as large as a human head, he set a ruby in the center, an emerald at the tail, and then dusted it with a fine sand.

The spell was supposed to illuminate the magical imprint of any spells done recently—the time frame and accuracy depended on the skill of the witch, the stones, and the crushed minerals that were used. I watched the air above the spiral and in the room for any sign of activity. Like hitting the rewind button on a video, it took a few long moments before we reached far enough back into the past to see any sign of life.

But it was only Bosko's magic that had left its ghost in the room. A mist near his hands appeared, then grew thick and cloudy as if remembering his life force. The same cloud moved around the room, tracing Bosko's steps to the trunk, the cushion, the drinking glasses, the bathroom, and then to the door where we stood.

"So maybe it was an accident?" Flor asked, watching the smoke. "I'm not an expert on memory mist charms, but isn't that what it's showing? That he was alone when his spirit went out?"

"It only shows the magical residue of the witch casting spells. If a person was in the room but wasn't casting any magic, we wouldn't see them." Raynor let out a slow breath. "Flor, go get my agents. You two need to be probed officially. And the housekeeper needs to be wiped and sent home with a gift bag or something."

"I can wake her," Flor said.

"Might as well let her sleep," he said. "Is his jewelry in the trunk?"

I looked over at the area below the light switch at the entrance of the room. Tristan had kept his own magic trunk in a similar position—as far from the sleeping Protector as possible while still being inside the warded room.

Witches took off most of their powerful amulets before bed because its magic couldn't be fully controlled by a sleeping human brain. I left my beads on because I'd made them myself, but if a witch had a large collection of silver, gold, and platinum jewelry well-adorned with diamonds and other gems, they would store them overnight in a safe place. I kept most of my uncontrollable magic in my steel filing cabinet.

"Yes, everything went into that trunk," Flor said. "Except the platinum band he's wearing now."

Raynor glanced at me, no doubt thinking about the opal ring. To Flor, he said, "Get Agent Ironford. I'll take it from here."

When Flor was gone, Raynor turned to me and spoke with a very quiet voice.

"He had the ring when you saw him?"

"Percy brought it," I said.

"Did you shake his hand?"

"Before he got it."

"Good. Safer that way," he said. "See him shake anyone else's?"

"No," I said. "He didn't take it out of the package."

He tapped his lips and turned back to the room. "We'll look for it."

"Percy would know if he stored it in the chest or was wearing it," I said.

"Or the new assistant. Your friend, Florence." He pointed at the bottles discarded around the room. "Long day, but he still found time to have a solo cocktail party before kicking off."

"Maybe that's why he wanted the job in Silverpool. He's a springwater addict."

"Maybe he was," Raynor said.

"Was," I echoed. Past tense.

"I came up here today with five agents, but there will be more." He gave me a worried look. "This is bad for you, Alma."

I gazed into the room, watching the remainder of Bosko's faint, ghostly mist moving around. "If it had been a demon, there should be some sign of it entering," I said. "The magic would've left a trace."

"Should be," Raynor said.

"Is there magic that can evade your spiral's detection?"

He gave me a look. "The daughter of Malcolm Bellrose is asking me that?"

I flinched and turned away. My father was a whiz at escaping detection. It had been his key to evading imprisonment. There was never enough evidence to convict him.

"Go get yourself scanned and go home," he said. "Enjoy your life while you can. Things might get uncomfortable for you. And for everyone in town."

"Everyone? Why?"

He slid a hand over his bare scalp. "New York is tired of hearing about this little backwater. There's no telling what they might do now."

◈

THE PROTECTORATE AGENTS let me go home less than an hour later, which made me suspicious. In case they had me under surveillance, I didn't go to Seth's to tell him about the short-lived Protector. As a fairy at heart, he had his own ways of finding things out, and the death of the powerful witch would send shock waves through the supernatural community for miles. I told myself I'd already given the changeling every warning I could give.

Because of my stash of wellspring water, I parked the Jeep inside my detached garage—after spending an hour moving aside my worktables, storage boxes, bulk toilet paper, an old bicycle, spare lumber, dirty garden tools—I used the rust for spells—and a rechargeable lawn mower without a working battery.

I'd only lived there a couple of years. How had I already

collected so much junk? If anyone looked inside my garage, they'd see immediately what a powerful motive I had to kill Bosko: moving it all would've been a nightmare.

With the Jeep safely hidden inside the garage, I walked over to the redwood tree and squatted down near Willy's door with a bottle I'd filled just for him. He didn't come out to see me, however, even after I waited awhile and called his name, so I left it propped against the shaggy, massive trunk and went inside the house. When I let Random out a minute later, the bottle was gone.

He'd gone underground. That itself made me more nervous than anything else I'd experienced in the past week.

I wanted to talk to Birdie, but as with Seth, I didn't want to draw a target on her back. They almost certainly had me under watch. Anything I did inside my house was private, but the moment I interacted outside of it, they'd know.

And so I stayed inside, fretting and casting misleading, ineffective spells in an effort to see into the future. They never worked, but it was impossible not to try sometimes. It was past midnight while I was watching a distorted maybe-future unfold in the steam rising from a whistling teakettle filled with wellspring water when Darius dropped by.

Random loved Darius, and told me my former partner was outside by suddenly rising from his cozy bed near the heater and whining to be let out. I picked up my staff, grateful Bosko hadn't confiscated it the night before, and opened the door.

He was standing in the driveway ten feet away. "Quite some wards you've put up," he said. "Will you let me into the house, or do we need to talk out here?"

Thumping my staff, I dismissed the spells that kept people from touching my land. "Hi Darius. Come on in." I was glad to see him. Although he wasn't always on my side, I trusted him. "Do you have news for me, or should I find a dog sitter for Random because you're dragging me into custody?"

He came inside, flinching from the screening spell at the threshold and then frowning at the teakettle. The prophecy I'd called forth in the mist had dissipated, but he'd be able to feel the residue of magic. "So you look into the future now?"

I shrugged, pretending not to be embarrassed. It was an inaccurate, exploitative magic, as scorned among witches as it was among nonmagical humanity. "I got bored."

"What did you see?"

I pulled out a chair at the kitchen table and got him a bottle of mineral water—he preferred Calistoga to Silverpool. "The usual crazy stuff," I said, thinking about the contrary futures the teakettle had displayed over the past few hours. "In the last one, Seth seemed to become Protector of Silverpool."

"Very realistic," he said. "And?"

"Unfortunately, Silverpool was swept away by the Vago River like a sandcastle at high tide."

"Sounds like what happened over the summer when the fae revolted," he said.

I nodded. "It's probably picking up the memory of that." I sat across from him. "I know it's ridiculous. I couldn't resist. Is there any news?"

He uncapped his water bottle. "I'm sorry, Alma."

"You didn't come all this way to tell me you can't tell me anything," I said.

"No." He met my gaze. "They've arrested Malcolm again."

"Seriously?"

"I thought you should know." He started to stand up.

"Wait! You have to tell me more than that."

"I don't know any more. They took him into custody because he has motive and opportunity. I wasn't there, but

Bosko didn't have to take down the demon like that, on display in the Circle where everyone could see and nobody would forget…" Darius took a long swallow and wiped his lips. "Maybe your dad didn't appreciate being humiliated like that."

I stood up. "My father wouldn't murder somebody for embarrassing him. He'd be a serial killer if that was the case. He's shameless! That's his superpower."

"There's some jewelry missing," Darius said, raising both eyebrows.

My stomach tightened. I was afraid to know more. "How would the Protectorate know what was missing?"

"That opal ring from Mendocino was released to him yesterday. Now it's gone."

Oh Shadows inside Shadows, I thought. "The room was warded. He was alone."

"Your father can apparate. Hardly anyone can do that."

"There wasn't any trace," I said. "Raynor cast the spiral himself."

"Malcolm is famous for getting around magic like that," he said, then added when I began to argue, "Don't blame me. I don't think he did it. I'm just explaining how they see it. Did you ever get that New York advocate like I told you to?"

"He didn't need my help after all," I said. And I'd been unconscious for a full day after the wedding.

"He might need it now, but who knows?" Darius said. "He's a lot better at taking care of himself than you are."

Chapter Twenty-One

I had trouble sleeping again.

Was Darius right? Did I need to get my father an advocate? I'd avoided interfering—helping—in Malcolm's life for a reason, but my rational mind couldn't get my heart to stop worrying.

Malcolm had already spent time in Protectorate custody, as well as house arrest, and they might see that as an excuse to prevent him from seeking counsel from his current defenders. They'd been known to accuse the witch lawyers of being accomplices, and therefore deserving imprisonment themselves. Who else was able to help him? His cronies wouldn't stick their necks out. His bride, a demon, was dead.

Surely my own situation was more secure now that Bosko was dead. The Protectorate would come in and make a fuss, but I wasn't in personal danger. I had time to help my father. It was for my own peace of mind, not his.

Luckily nobody had explicitly commanded me to stay in Silverpool, so after we'd both had a good breakfast, I loaded Random in the car and hit the road for San Francisco. It was almost noon when we reached Diamond Street in Noe Valley.

But I wasn't going to the Protectorate office. Just next door, in an unmodernized Victorian, lived Helen Mendoza, an irritable, cynical but brilliant witch who would help me if it somehow helped her. She'd become a mentor of mine over the years, first when I was a lowly trainee agent next door and then more recently as I struck out on my own. I believed she secretly liked me as a person, not just a source of payment, but I had brought several vials of torc-drawn wellspring water to make it easier for her to be nice to me.

I wasn't technically hiding from the Protectorate agents, but I parked several blocks away and then got my cardio workout in for the week by trekking back over the hills to knock on Helen's door. The bribes I hoped to tempt her with were tucked away in the pockets of my leather jacket.

She opened the door on the fifth round of my knocking. "How'd you get out of Silverpool?" Helen demanded. She wore jeans and a royal-blue sweatshirt that flattered the silver of her short, spiky white hair.

"Nobody told me I couldn't leave," I said. She always seemed to know everything, which was why I'd come to her. "May I enter, Dr. Mendoza?" I really didn't want agents from next door to see me on her front step, and I couldn't get past her wards until she invited me.

She waved Random in first, rewarding him with a piece of cheese. Although she pretended she didn't like dogs, she always had a snack ready for Random when I visited. All I got was a shrug and a head shake, but it was enough to let me step past her boundary spells.

"Are you telling me they didn't set up a blockade to keep witches from coming in and out of town after the Protector—another one!—was killed violently and mysteriously, possibly due to a demon possession or revenge for same?" Helen locked the door behind me and recast the spell.

"Well…," I said. "They weren't really serious about it. Nobody stopped me." There had been a PG&E truck at the road out of town, with a few cones and a sawhorse, but I'd been able to drive around it.

"What did you use?"

I rubbed the back of my neck, feeling the truth charm she was using on me. "You don't have to do that. I'll tell you the truth without it."

"Well?"

"I bungeed my staff to the roll bar. It was just a small bit of extra magic to help me over the hump, so to speak." It had gotten me past the PG&E truck, and then when I'd parked in San Francisco, I'd left it there to guard my Jeep from all trouble, magic or nonmagical, while it was parked on the street. Car break-ins were common, tickets were expensive, and it was likely an agent or two would be out combing the city for it within the next hour. I'd evaded the first agent tailing me in Occidental and the second in Robin Williams Tunnel in Marin, but there would be more.

"Great, so now you're an outlaw too. How exactly is this going to help your father?" Helen ushered me through the old house stuffed with dusty antiques to the kitchen in the back. Like me, she was a hearth witch, and had a rooftop garden to grow and harvest her herbs, roots, and other magical tools from living things.

"I'm not an outlaw." I helped myself to a glass of tap water. I didn't trust anything she poured for me. "If they're going to blame Malcolm for the murder, then they've got a weak excuse for grounding me in Silverpool. I'm his daughter. Naturally I want to be by his side."

Helen snorted. "Why are you really here?"

"Seriously. I want to help him."

"Why?"

I patted my jacket pocket. "I brought you springwater I got with the torc."

"You're going to pay me, all right, but not with wellspring water. I've got plenty of that now, thanks to you," she said. "What I want is knowledge. The real stuff. The truth."

"I want to help my father," I repeated. "Scan me. Probe me. You'll see I'm telling the truth."

"I get that—but why? Why now?"

I sipped the tap water, my pulse rising. Did she know something I didn't? As far as I knew, I wanted to help my dad so he wouldn't be tortured, brain-scrubbed, or sent to retire permanently in Death Valley.

But was that really it?

I closed my eyes and turned my own truth spell inward. I let go of what I thought I knew and focused on my breath. It came in, went out, in again, out again.

And then I saw something I didn't expect. Although it was *mostly* true I didn't want him being locked up... I *would* appreciate the peace and quiet. But beneath that... deeper than that... *truer* than that...

"I want to find out about my mother," I whispered, each word hurting as I spoke it.

"Ah," she said, long and slow.

The truth spell continued to work. "If they do something to Malcolm, I might never find out the truth about my mother. He might not even know it himself, not consciously. And whatever he does know... I don't want them to wipe his memory. And they might find..."

"The Protectorate might find out something about your mother you don't want them to know."

"If they find out I'm part demon, or my grandmother or great-grandmother was, then I'll be the one sent to the Mojave or stabbed in the heart."

"And even if they don't do anything with the information, they might not share it with you," Helen said. "You want the truth more than you fear them knowing it. You're a witch, Alma. You need to know. Of course you do. That's a motive I can believe in. So. What can I do?"

⬥

HELEN LET me stay at her house while I found an advocate to defend my father. She even let Random run loose in the wild garden beneath her deck and greenhouses. When I'd been a trainee agent, I'd paid her a nightly fee to sleep in her basement, a better location than the under-the-desk arrangement most young witches put up with during their early years at Diamond Street. San Francisco rent was too expensive for underpaid witches who weren't allowed to hex or steal from their landlords. Now, however, Helen let me stay in one of the many small bedrooms on the second floor—and I even got a bed.

It took four hours Monday afternoon to track down an advocate who could come right away. Although Darius had pushed New York, I was a California girl. There was a glut of witch lawyers in LA, no time zone to worry about, and short, hourly flights. The woman flew into Oakland just after sunset and banged on Helen's door at eleven. She was shouting on the phone at a Protectorate official in the bedroom next to mine as I fell asleep that night. The sound of her strident, angry voice through the wall soothed me to sleep, confident I'd chosen well.

And I was right. On Wednesday morning, without an apology or explanation, the Protectorate released Malcolm on the sidewalk between our two houses and told him to call himself a ride or walk. His advocate was prepared to sue for the insult, but Malcolm talked her down. By noon, I was driving him, with Random in the back seat, across town to his house in Pacific Heights, and the advocate was flying back to LA.

"She wasn't cheap," Malcolm said as we walked up the stairs to his house. It looked smaller than it had on his wedding night, making me realize he'd enchanted the property to look more luxurious than it was. An empty parking space out front, which had only appeared as he approached, had to have been part of the spell as well. "I had to vow to give her one of the gold necklaces I put in my will for you."

"As if you'll ever die, Father," I said, bringing Random inside the house on his leash and closing the door. Malcolm always liked to talk about his will, manipulating me with its contents, but I no longer believed he'd ever written one.

In the foyer near the front door was a pile of suitcases and a few boxes. I recognized an antique tapestry bag from my childhood. He'd already packed up his life's belongings. He'd always traveled light.

The house was empty—chilly, dark, and cold. The chandelier was gone, the carpets were gone, the wall decorations and furniture and potted plants—gone. I touched my focus string and pushed my senses into the floor at my feet, searching for a hint of what had happened. Had the Protectorate taken everything as evidence? Should I call the lawyer back from the airport?

I unleashed Random, who trotted off to explore the empty mansion. As I followed him, walking deeper into the house, I realized nothing had been taken. It had all been an illusion.

I let out a low whistle. "You're kind of amazing, Dad," I said, impressed.

"You think I'd actually pay for all that? Or this?" He smirked. "I'm a little disappointed you didn't see through it right away. It's a rental, of course. I'm paid through tomorrow. It was worth paying the advocate her outrageous fee to get my luggage before the landlord threw it out on the street."

"How did you hold the spell while so many witches were here, poking and probing it? And it even held after Bosko—" I cut myself off when I saw the sad look on his face.

"Even after Bosko killed her," he said with a sigh. He walked over and sat at the bottom of the stairs, propping his chin in his hands. "I should've seen it coming. He'd had it in for me for years."

I went over and sat next to him, feeling oddly protective of him. "How could you see it coming? You didn't know what she was." I looked at him more closely. "Right?"

He shrugged. "Doesn't matter. He would've found some other excuse to stop the wedding. I'm sure he came here ready to get *me* somehow. Stabbing somebody was just a bonus."

I noticed his uncritical reference to his dead bride. "I know she was a demon, but I kind of liked her."

He turned his head and regarded me the same way he looked at a locked museum. "Did you kill Bosko? They've already scanned me. It's safe to unburden yourself if you—"

"No, of course not! I have an Incurable Inability, haven't you heard?"

He continued to study me, weighing my tone, my expression, and my magic aura, then finally nodded, satisfied. "Good. Now I can enjoy his death without worrying about you being sent to the Mojave for it. I'll never forgive him for what he did to poor Vera."

Poor Vera? It was my turn to study him. "*Did* you know what she was?"

"Of course I didn't know," he said. "She had me enchanted. Oh Brightness, did she ever. It was great. I wish she'd come back and do it to me again."

I flinched at the word *wish*. "Don't say that, Dad. She'd possessed a human being. I'm not glad she was stabbed at the wedding, but you couldn't marry her. The Circle would've bonded you for eternity, which for her true spirit is a really long time."

"Maybe it would've been worth it." He smiled at the empty space in front of us. "She was so pretty. I liked her skin, too. It was really soft."

"It was a stolen body. Don't forget."

"I loved listening to her sing in the shower," he said. "Such a beautiful voice."

"You're still enchanted," I said. "We can find a witch who specializes in breaking love spells…"

"Why would I want that? It feels nice. I haven't felt this good since I was with your—" He got to his feet. "Never mind. Well, I might as well unpack a few things. That advocate told me I'd better stay here a week or two so the Protectorate doesn't have an excuse to abduct me again. I suppose I could hex someone at the property management company to cover the rent—"

I jumped up. "No, I'm not going to let you change the subject. Not this time."

"Will you be staying here tonight? There's only one real mattress in the place, and I'll be using it." He cocked his head, listening to Random's toenails echoing on the hardwood floors in another room. Just a few months ago, the dog had been his indentured accomplice in burglaries. "He can relieve himself on the patio, but make sure you pick up anything solid he leaves behind. I want to get my security deposit back. Those flower petals were expensive."

He started to walk over to the suitcases, but I blocked him.

"Dad," I said, hoping the familiar name would kindle some empathy in him. "You've got to tell me about my mother. You've got to. You can't leave me hanging like this for the rest of my life." I put my hand on his—without magic, just skin against skin. "Please. Whatever it is, I can take it."

He stilled, pursing his lips. Random trotted back into the room and sat at my feet. Finally he said, "You'll judge me." He glanced at me out of the corner of his eye. "You always judge me."

I fought off a pang of guilt. He was manipulating me again. "When has that ever stopped you from doing what you want to do?" I patted his hand. "Tell me what she looked like."

"I don't remember."

"Dad—"

"See? I knew you'd judge."

"Seriously? You don't remember?" I asked.

He shook his head. "I remember how I felt. I was in love. We had a good time. And then she got pregnant and disappeared." Dropping his head, he clasped his hands together and stroked his bare fingers. The Protectorate must've confiscated his rings. "A nonmagical woman, a nurse or social worker I think, called me from a hospital in Berkeley, said your mother had died in childbirth. She'd named me as the father."

I stood flooded with a mix of emotions until I could bring myself to speak. "I researched. There was no Bellrose born in Berkeley."

He gave me a disappointed look. "You know, for a witch, especially a Bellrose, you're awfully gullible."

"You changed the records," I said.

"I deleted the records and helped myself to a giant balloon, a floral bouquet, and a year's supply of formula."

"Dad," I said, thinking, *Berkeley. I was born in Berkeley.* Something tight inside me eased and let go. I wiped the tears off my cheeks. "You should've told me."

"I would have, sweetheart. I would have. But I forgot."

"Right," I said, fed up with his evasions. But then I caught myself. His expression was so serious. "You really did?"

"I've never been good with emotions. I don't know if you knew that."

To my credit, I managed to keep a straight face. More than anyone, I knew he wasn't good with feelings.

"So when I knew she was gone and never coming back," he continued, "I— Well, I didn't think there was any reason for us to suffer, dwelling over the past. So I... *forgot*."

Something about his tone told me he meant more than what he was saying. A chill ran through me. Casting destructive spells on your own brain was dangerous. "You hexed yourself?"

"That doesn't work. I had to pay some guy to do it. Naturally I don't remember anything about him."

"But you remember my mother now," I said. "How?"

"Something about being with Vera brought it back. The love triggered more love or... I don't know. Maybe I'm just getting old. I wanted to remember. I wanted to feel more than I could from stealing a piece of gold."

Could I believe him, or was this another one of his cons? "The Protectorate was convinced you were glad they killed Vera. Maybe you're lying to me."

"Maybe I'm lying to everyone, even myself. Maybe I've been at this so long I don't know what's true anymore." He bent down and scratched his old dog's head. "Does he still like pad Thai?"

Chapter Twenty-Two

Before we could order the Thai food, I got a call from Birdie. "Alma? Where are you?"

I had to walk out to the front landing to get better reception. "San Francisco. How are you? What's going on there?"

"Are you with your father?" she asked.

I closed the door behind me so Random couldn't escape and my father couldn't hear. "How did you guess? I was about to come home."

"I know your father lives in San Francisco," she said. "I'm here in Silverpool."

"I figured," I said.

"There are a lot of cars in front of your house. Motorcycles, too. I was going to visit, but I couldn't get through."

My gut clenched. "Motorcycles?" Protectorate agents with the authority to investigate, interrogate, arrest, and kill rode motorcycles. "What are the riders wearing?"

"Wearing?"

I studied a bearded man walking down the street with a little dog. He didn't look at me, but I eyed him suspiciously.

"Agents usually wear leather jackets heavily adorned with silver," I said. "Remember?"

"Right," she said. "Right, of course. They were agents. That's why I'm telling you."

The man disappeared around the corner, but another rode up on a pink scooter, pulled over across the street, and took something out of his pocket. I touched my beads, bracing myself, but then I saw it was just his phone. I let out my breath and stepped back into the house, where Random, frantic to be reunited, danced around my legs.

"I better come home," I said. The Protectorate was jumpy, I could feel it. And when agents got nervous, spells got thrown around like pixie dust on the winter solstice. "Did you see Seth? Were they at his house?"

The line went quiet for a moment, and I asked again, thinking we'd lost the connection.

"I don't know. I'm sorry," Birdie said. "When are you coming home?"

"Now. I'll come right now." I bent over and stroked Random's neck, thinking he'd be glad to go home too. Helen had fed him treats—and in typical dog fashion, he'd forgiven Malcolm for all crimes—but he liked his familiar bed. "Go home and stay there as much as you can. The Protectorate is freaking out about Bosko's death."

"Will you come see me when you get back?" she asked.

"I'm not sure that's a good idea. I don't want to draw attention to you."

"Everyone already knows we're close," she said. "You're my best friend."

Already emotional about my mother, her sweet words brought tears to my eyes again. "I promise to check in as soon as I get back to Silverpool," I said, then repeated my advice to stay home before hanging up.

Malcolm seemed relieved when I told him I was leaving,

although he held Random's collar for a few seconds at the door as if reluctant to let him go with me. Noticing the suspicious guy on the scooter brought him back to the present, and he wished me well and slammed the door between us.

It was a slow drive north to Sonoma County. The sun had already gone down when I reached Riovaca, the largest town before Silverpool on the Vago Highway west of Santa Rosa. My remaining miles through the forest hills to Silverpool, a rolling, twisty drive that was treacherous even during the day, impelled me to set my staff across my lap to drive the fairies away from the Jeep. They liked to lure travelers over the bluffs into the ravines with their enchanting songs. The vertical drops weren't usually enough to kill, but sometimes... The skeletons of wrecked cars, overgrown with sword fern and oxalis, told the tale.

I held the wheel and cast spells around my car to keep me safe. More than other witches, I was vulnerable at night because I could see the tempting fairy lights, sparkling and elusive, as they celebrated another turning of the earth. The closer we got to the winter solstice, the more dangerous it became.

Because my attention was fixated on the forest, I failed to notice the Protectorate blockade until the agents on duty—in disguise as utility workers, firefighters, and police—had already seen me. If they hadn't, I would've parked the car a half mile back and sneaked by on foot, well hidden by my spells.

But they had seen me.

When I'd left, there'd been a nondescript utility truck at the end of the winery driveway, but now there was a full-blown landslide marked by sputtering flares and orange traffic cones. A crew of Protectorate agents in disguise as police, firefighters, and utility workers stood around their officially marked trucks and cars, turning everyone who wanted to enter Silverpool away.

I slapped the wheel. Why did they always have to use brute force? Hex first, ask questions later. They thought they were being strong, but it was fear that drove them, exposing their cowardice.

Chewing my lip, I weighed my options. I considered walking up to one of the fake cops and identifying myself as a close personal friend of Darius Ironford, but it was possible Darius had orders from Raynor to turn me away. I'd managed to escape on Monday, and maybe the director thought it was better for me to stay that way.

But I wanted to go home. Bosko was gone; I was still here. It would take more than a few Flints in high-vis jackets to block me.

With a tight inhale, I touched my beads and gathered a cloud of power around the Jeep. Then I pulled into the left lane and floored it, using a spell to erase a path through the imaginary rubble. When the "utility" woman shouted at me to stop, I used the staff to knock her safely out of the way. Then I barreled over the bridge, sped around the corner, and drove up the hill. The rearview mirror showed a pair of agents following me on motorcycles, which was inevitable. Once I was on my property, I'd have the power and position to keep them away.

Using the staff, I concealed the turn for my narrow lane, buying me enough time to get down the street to my house. I screeched into my driveway, jumped out with Random, and ran to my back door. In my hurry, I dropped the staff in the grass, Random picked it up, I had to tug it away from him, he thought it was a game, I yelled at him, he barked…

By the time I'd slammed the kitchen door behind me and set up a fresh boundary spell, I was breathing hard and swearing at the universe.

"Alma Bellrose, what in Shadow are you doing?" boomed a voice from the other side of my back door. It sounded like Darius, but I couldn't be sure it wasn't enchanted.

I looked over at Random, who was drinking from his water bowl without a care in the world. Sometimes dogs were more trustworthy than magic. If he thought it was safe, it probably was.

I opened the door. "Hi, Darius. What's up?" I leaned casually against the doorframe, tightening my abdomen so he wouldn't see the heaving of my lungs from the chase.

"You knocked over a Flint," he said. "It was her first day."

That explained why she'd been so easy to hex, but I didn't say so in case it pushed his temper past its breaking point. He already looked irritated. "I was in a hurry," I said. "I heard the Protectorate was looking for me, and I didn't want to keep you waiting."

Approaching from the driveway, Raynor himself appeared in the beam of my porch light, holding his helmet against his hip. He looked huge and was thrumming with magical power.

I froze, my throat going dry. Had I finally pushed him too far? It took me a second to get air into my lungs. "Good evening, Director. Would you two like to come inside for a cup of coffee or a beer or—?"

"Who do you think you are?" Raynor demanded.

"Look, I'm sorry but—"

He pointed a finger at me. The tip was glowing faintly. "I've gone out on a limb for you, and this is how you repay me?"

I stepped back into my house and closed the door. Putting my palm on the wood, I silently rescinded my invitation for the two angry witches to cross the threshold. Maybe after they'd calmed down, I'd offer the drinks again.

While I waited, I peeked through the curtains, still

holding the staff. It was much more powerful at home, especially with its tip pressed against the kitchen floor that was old enough to have a layer of asbestos underneath. The natural mineral could cause lung disease, but it also amplified my power.

To my alarm, Raynor was attempting to blast his way through my door. The glow at the end of his finger had grown into a transparent golden rectangle as big as he was, and he was pounding it like a pile driver against my invisible wards.

Until that moment, I'd felt a little guilty about knocking over the Flint, and maybe even for leading them on a chase. But now—

OK. Now I was mad. This was my home, and what had I ever done to deserve the kind of harassment, insults, and extortion I'd experienced at Protectorate hands? *Male* Protectorate hands. They jumped into brute force when a peaceful conversation might resolve the dispute. Their egos caused so much damage.

I banged my staff against the tile, using my magic as a conduit for my anger. A single wave of defensive power rolled out from the walls of my house and knocked Raynor back a step. Without putting the helmet down, he pointed again.

"You've gone too far, Alma," he called out. "You have to listen to me and do what I say."

His words only made me angrier. Why? Why did I always have to do what somebody else wanted? When I'd been nine years old, my father had made me steal a pack of cigarettes from a gas station in Virginia for another witch, a blond guy with grabby hands, to stop him from identifying us after a heist.

Us. That's how he'd put it, like we were equals, in it together, both with the same motives, values, needs, and desires. If I hadn't stolen the smokes, it would've been *my* fault my father went to jail. That was how he'd pressured me.

I was so sick of being pressured. I banged the staff harder this time, and then again. My mood had flared into a white-hot rage.

Raynor lost his feet in the blast of my power and fell forward as if he'd suddenly decided to drop to the ground and do a few push-ups.

Brightness forgive me, but I grinned. He thought he could just—

Whoops.

One push-up was all Raynor had needed to regain his feet, and now he was blasting me with both hands. Darius stood behind him, amplifying his strength.

Random began whining. I looked down at the big, worried eyes gazing up at me.

What was I doing? I'd just attacked *Raynor*. He'd been pretty nice to me, but he was a director of the Protectorate. He was a powerful demon-killing agent with, like me, secret gifts bestowed by an unknown supernatural ancestor. Bosko had just been killed, and my father had been a suspect. Why would I risk antagonizing him now?

It must've been the conversation with my father. The story about my mother. There were too many old memories, scars, and bruises rattling around in my soul. I'd lost control of myself.

One more minute and Raynor was going to blast a hole in not just my boundary spells, but the wood frame and siding of my house. Talk about losing your security deposit.

I set down the staff and went over to open the door, silently preparing my humiliating apology. He'd want me to say I'd had no right to defend my own home, which rankled, but I'd have to say it. I'd have to *mean* it. I turned the knob and began to pull it open.

There was a loud crash, then a blinding flash of green light that lit up the patio, yard, garage, driveway, trees. Raynor and Darius sailed into the air and…

I couldn't see for a few seconds because of the shock to my eyes. I listened for a thud, shout, blasts, sirens, explosions, thunder, lightning…

With angry witches, anything could happen.

Slowly my vision returned. The yard was dark except for the area lit by the porch light and the rising moon. And over by the redwood, the tiny red glow of a lit pipe.

"Willy?" I asked. It had to be the gnome. "What did you do?"

An ancient, unforgiving voice shot through the dark. "Your visitors had poor manners."

I pressed my hand to my mouth, flattered by his caring but terrified he'd killed them. I cleared my throat and managed to ask, "Where are they?"

"On their round wheel machines on the shared human property you allow others to use when traveling to you," he said.

"You mean the road?" I pushed Random back into the house and ran outside and down the driveway.

Thank Brightness, they looked OK. Both men were wearing their helmets, sitting on their motorcycles—which were running—facing the opposite direction.

Instead of running inside, I forced myself to stay and wait as they turned around, parked, and dismounted again. This was really going to infuriate them. I held my hands up in a show of surrender, resigned to my fate. It would be foolish to expect forgiveness after such an insult to their bodily autonomy. And men hated it when you messed with their wheels.

But Raynor and Darius stood next to their bikes, helmets on, facing me. Afraid they were shoring up their power to hex me, I lifted my hands higher, spreading the fingers wider, and waited with my heart pounding in my throat.

Very slowly, Raynor lifted a hand to his helmet and popped the visor open. "Our apologies, Witch Bellrose," he said. That method of address was an old-fashioned, formal term of respect, more typically directed at elderly witches from respectable families. "Lower your hands and we can express our regret over that drink you mentioned."

Darius stood still next to Raynor. Was he shaking slightly?

Very belatedly realizing they were afraid of me, I lowered my hands. They'd thought I was threatening them, not surrendering. For Brightness' sake. How was I going to get out of this?

"Of course. Please enter my home," I said quickly. Maybe I could defuse the situation by pretending I'd thought they were imposters. "This is all just a terrible misunderstanding. Raynor, is that really you? And, don't tell me, could that possibly be Darius Ironford, my former partner and current and future friend?"

They looked at each other, then Darius took off the helmet. "Witch Bellrose, forgive me for disrespecting you. I vow I shall never do it again."

I risked a glance over my shoulder at the redwood tree. Was it me they feared or my gnome neighbor? The tiny glow was gone. Job done, Willy had gone back to bed.

I put my hands behind my back and turned to the men. "Look, guys, I'm really sorry," I said. "I've had a stressful week. Will you come in?"

They looked at each other again. Raynor gave a small nod, and a few minutes later they were walking into my kitchen without a single golden sledgehammer or patronizing demand.

I'd have to give Willy a wine barrel filled with wellspring water.

"I didn't believe it was you," I said, not too contrite to lie.

"You knocked over a young woman wearing the uniform of a nonmagical utility worker," Darius said.

"That was really bad, you're right," I said, "but I thought the Protectorate agents were here, wanting to talk to me, and would be angry if I didn't show up as soon as possible."

"How did you know agents had been here at your house?" Raynor frowned in Seth's direction. "Is that wise, being in contact with the changeling, especially now?"

"Birdie called me on my cell and told me she'd seen them," I said. "I'm allowed to talk to my best friend, aren't I?" Smiling to break the tension, I went to the fridge and got everyone a beer.

Raynor sat at my kitchen table, drank most of it down in one go, then wiped his lips. To my surprise, the look he gave me wasn't angry, but sympathetic.

"They're burying Silverpool," he said.

Chapter Twenty-Three

F eeling weak, I sank into a chair with my untouched beer. "Burying? What do you mean?"

"Before the solstice," Raynor said. "All witches are to leave as soon as possible and not come back. Nonmag people will get the impulse to move away. We've already arranged for a fleet of one-way rental trucks and trailers to be available at Cypress Hardware."

"The solstice is in less than three weeks," I said, gripping the table.

"There's going to be a massive landslide before then," Raynor said.

"All this because of Bosko?" I asked.

Raynor peeled the label off his bottle. "The town will become more inhospitable than usual."

I shook my head. "What about the investigation into Bosko's death? That'll destroy evidence."

"They've concluded the demon he killed at your father's wedding returned and took revenge," Raynor said. "They can't punish an evil spirit, but they can eliminate the draw to future demons by burying the wellspring."

I didn't believe Vera had killed Bosko. "That's insane," I said. "The wellspring provides the only springwater for hundreds of miles, and its location here, with the old-growth redwoods and the Pacific nearby, makes the water especially powerful. More fae gather here than in any other—"

"New York doesn't care about the redwoods, the fae, or the springwater," Raynor said. "They have their own wellsprings they protect and draw from. By their thinking, California might as well be on Pluto."

I couldn't believe what I was hearing. Nobody could've loved Kurt Bosko enough to destroy a town because of his death. Could somebody be trying to cover up a crime? Was there someone else in Silverpool they were trying to destroy? "But—"

"You'll need a new house, and for that you'll probably need a job, given the astronomical rental market these days," Raynor said. "I'm pleased to report that the Protectorate no longer considers your Incurable Inability bad enough to preclude your employment."

It just kept getting worse. My head spun. "Even after I attacked you?"

Raynor brushed that aside with a large hand. "That was the gnome. You're hardly in control of him. Nobody can control a gnome." He put the hand on Darius's shoulder. "Darius has decided he'd be honored to have you as his partner again. If you're willing."

Maybe they *were* imposters. This was crazy talk.

Darius took a long drink from his beer and shrugged. "Yeah. It's true."

"I don't believe it," I said.

"He thought you were the worst partner a witch could have," Raynor said. "Then he discovered you had hidden qualities. Isn't that right, Darius?"

"Let's just say I've had a run of bad luck," he said. "And

working with you in Mendocino… Well, it showed me you've learned a lot since the old days."

Raynor hadn't changed. He still insisted on trying to get me back into the Protectorate. "I don't want to work for—"

I stopped myself. As if by a green flash of blinding gnome magic, I saw a way out. I didn't believe Kurt Bosko had been killed by a demon—the murder scene just didn't feel like demons had been involved, and not Vera in particular.

"What if I found out who *did* do it and could prove it wasn't a demon?" I began. "Would that stop New York from destroying Silverpool?"

Raynor peeled the rest of his label off the bottle, frowning, and then looked at Darius. "Did you hear that?"

"I did, Director," Darius said.

"Looks like you two have a job to do together." Raynor got up and dropped his bottle in my recycling bin near the door. "Better hurry. This is all unofficial, of course. I'll deny everything. But it sure will be nice to ensure our local source of wellspring water. New York might not care, but we do, don't we?"

I closed my eyes. I'd been had.

Darius slapped the table. "Well, guess I'll see you first thing in the morning," he said. "Maybe tell your gnome friend I'll be coming by. Cool? Cool."

"Hey!" I got up and went over to the door, blocking their escape. I expected Raynor to be ruthless; he'd become Director in San Francisco. But I wasn't ever going back as an agent. I would work odd jobs when it suited me, but those amoral mages weren't ever going to own me. "That's what this was all about? Trying to blast your way into my home, just to trick me into investigating another case for you?"

Raynor looked at Darius. "She's not much of a morning person," he said. "I wouldn't come by until at least eight."

"I'll work with Darius to help Silverpool, but it's *temporary*," I said. "Unofficial. I'm not going to be an agent again."

Raynor shrugged, his lips curving in a mild smile that suggested he really didn't care what I called it. "I look forward to hearing your first report," he said.

"I refuse to fill out any repo—" I began.

"I'll do them," Darius said. "You always get the dates wrong anyway."

"We are not partners," I said tightly.

Raynor gestured at the door behind me. "It's late. I accept this is a temporary agreement. But you…" He trailed off, his dark eyes meeting mine and holding them, inscrutable and probing.

I frowned until my curiosity—always a problem—got the better of me. "Yeah? What about me?"

"You've shown to me, Darius, and, I hope, yourself, just how powerful you are. You carried me and a fully trained Protectorate agent through the air for at least—what was it, Agent Ironford, thirty meters?—against our will." His eyebrows reached toward his smooth scalp. "You don't know how strong you are. And neither do I. Wouldn't you like to find out?"

Reaching behind me, I turned the doorknob and pulled the door open. "My powers are my own business. Time for you to go." I would love to think I'd lifted the two witches on my own, but Willy had played a strong supporting role in my show of strength.

"I'm not going to let you waste your talents." Raynor stepped past me, his massive shoulder brushing my ear, and went outside.

"Get out of here before I use them to hurl you through the air again," I said.

"Don't let him tease you. We're going," Darius said,

waving as he stepped out to follow Raynor. "See you tomorrow."

Hot with anger, I slammed the door and cast a spell at the kitchen towel hanging on the oven door. It burst into flames, which I had to run over and extinguish with another spell, which helped me get a grip on my temper.

I set the singed towel in the sink and braced my hands on the edge as I counted to ten. What was the matter with me? I'd always had a temper, but I was out of control. And the magic I was using was beyond anything I'd used before, especially against other powerful witches.

I'd felt Willy's fingerprints in the magic that had expelled them down the driveway. Was he interacting with me still? Had I absorbed his power inside me, or was it consciously given to me only as I'd needed it to defend our shared property?

My questions needed to be answered—but not because Raynor said so. Without the answers, I might hurt myself or somebody else. Or at least burn the house down. But I'd do them at my own pace, on my own terms, and keep my secrets to myself.

Wrapping my hand in an empty velvet pouch, I took Raynor's bottle out of the bin, tied it closed with a silver-threaded cord, and locked it in my filing cabinet. There were things I could do with his spit—some illegal, some dangerous, some terrible. And all required at least a week to marinate. But some of the spells were fairly mild and could provide an escape hatch for me if he came at me in earnest.

It was time to act more like Helen. She'd survived, even thrived, without the Protectorate. I could too.

JUST AS I put my head on my pillow, a tap on my bedroom window sent Random flying off the bed in a fit of barking. He jumped onto the chair to attack the intruder, but suddenly stopped and began wagging his tail.

I put my hand on my beads, sent out a probe, and felt Seth's presence. Turning on a light, I got out of bed and walked over to push Random aside and lift the window. Cold air wafted in as I frowned at Seth's handsome face.

"Why not knock on the door?" I asked.

"I saw what you did to your last visitors."

The memory still made me smile. "Willy helped me out."

"Sorry for the late chat, but the fae are freaking out. What's up?"

We were still speaking through the open window, both of us hunched over. "You better come in," I said.

"Can't. Your spells are worse than ever. Even being this close to your house is giving me a rash."

I never knew when he was kidding. The situation was too serious to joke around. "The Protectorate is about to drive everyone out of town and bury the wellspring."

"Ah," he said.

"Ah? That's it?"

He shrugged. "Thanks for the information. I'll let the fae know. They won't understand, but it'll make me feel better."

"They're going to find you, Seth," I said in a rush. "You can't stay here. You've got to figure out how to survive away from Sil—"

"I've tried everything."

"Try again!" My back was aching, so I held up a finger to tell him to wait where he was and then ran through the house to go outside to talk to him. When I reached him, he looked taller—and I realized he was floating several inches above the ground. "I didn't know you could do that."

He patted his chest. "I'm amazing, aren't I? A miracle of

supernature. Except for the little side effect of me dying whenever I travel a few miles, it's great."

"You've got to find a way to survive. You could try digging up the earth and bringing it with you, like in a bag or a huge bag, a *truck*—"

"Tried it. All kinds of containers."

"You could try new metal alloys, or springwaters from other wellsprings, maybe gems and stones, herbs…"

The light streaming out from my bedroom illuminated his sad smile. "It's all right, Alma. I've accepted my fate. It was sealed the moment my mother put me in a human baby's body."

"Is that it? You still think you *deserve* this? Maybe your mother does—I don't know—but you didn't ask to possess a human. And now the original guy is gone. He's not coming back. There's no moral benefit to you… passing on…"

"Dying," he said. "I think I'll just be dead. My spirit is melded with this mortal form now."

"Nobody knows what happens to us, not even fairies like you," I said. "Stop being so fatalistic and self-hating and fight for yourself."

"I have fought, Alma. I've done everything I can think of. When the Protectorate comes for me, I'll fight some more. And then I'll be at peace." He reached out and cupped my cheek, a rare moment of physical contact between us. "Don't feel bad. Promise me."

Tears came to my eyes. I scowled at him. "I won't promise anything. You're just depressed. You're afraid to hope, but I'm not."

He stroked my cheek, smiling. "You really are an angel."

I pushed his hand away. "Stop staying that. I'm no better than you are, you… you—" My words failed me. I could hardly motivate him by calling him names.

"It was nice knowing you. Really. A bright spot in a Bright world." With a bow, he vanished.

"No! You—" I buried my face in my hands, feeling the essence of his sweet-smelling spirit on my skin. Even knowing his origins, I'd always thought of him as a man. But he wasn't. He was unique. Irreplaceable.

And the Protectorate was going to kill him. Even if I caught Bosko's killer and they allowed the wellspring to exist, his replacement would be even more brutal. The years of casual management of Silverpool were over.

Tired and demoralized, I stood in the cold dark and cried.

Chapter Twenty-Four

W iping my cheeks, I grabbed my shoes and jacket from inside and set off walking down the street. Given the Protectorate presence, I couldn't risk driving the Jeep. If somebody tried to stop me, I'd put myself into a convincing trance and claim it was sleepwalking.

I also cast a subtle hiding spell over myself, not too strong to be noticed. I didn't see anyone, only the lights of agents at the blockade, and walked across the parking lot of Cypress Hardware without being stopped.

I stood in front of the front doors and looked through the glass at the rows of stored shopping carts, waiting for the genie to come to me. In case such creatures slept, and she needed a motive to rise, I lifted my hand and tapped my beaded bracelet against the glass.

"Hello," I said softly. "Anybody home?"

Before I could tap the glass a second time, the doors slid open. I didn't see Jen, but I walked inside, my arms hanging by my side, a show of defenselessness. The doors closed behind me.

It was dark except for the glow of security lights at the

exits. I didn't want to be seen from the street, so I walked deeper into the store, moving slowly through the shadowy aisles.

Then I saw a light flicker near the back where the clearance patio furniture had been the other day. Swallowing my nerves, I walked toward it.

Jen Bardak had improved the patio furniture; now, instead of weather-resistant brown plastic, her seat was a wingback chair made of walnut with gold leaf accents in the carvings and down stuffed into the silk upholstery. She gestured to a similar chair next to her.

"Welcome," she said. Her clothing was a mixture of goth and gardening. Blood-red corset, black leather skirt, a choker in red velvet, and the hummingbird-patterned plastic clogs. "You witches are strangely nocturnal, aren't you? Like bats."

"The Protectorate is here and—"

She snapped her fingers. "Before you state your wish, let's confirm the price." Her gaze flicked to the bracelet I'd tapped against the glass. "No more beads. You know what I want."

I took a deep breath and nodded. "You want my silence."

"Guaranteed," she said. There was a pause, and then she asked, "What is your wish?"

"What I'd like, only hypothetically, because first we have to agree on the limits of the arrangement, is to prevent..." I hesitated, trying to think of the best way to phrase my wish that wouldn't cause unpredictable damage. "To stop the Protectorate from—"

Jen flung up a hand. "I can't interfere in their business right now. It's too risky."

I stared at her in dismay. I'd expected haggling, but not an outright refusal. "You said my silence was important to you."

"I'm afraid that my interference in the machinations of

dozens of powerful Protectorate witches would cost more than your silence," she said.

"But if you won't help me save the town, you lose all this."

"I love this town, and I love my store." She cast a slow gaze around the shadows of her remote big-box store as if it were paradise, then sighed. "But I can't intervene for love. I can only intervene if the payment is satisfactory."

I was afraid. Giving her a vow of silence was more than I'd wanted to pay, but it was still less than she'd accept. In the back of my mind, I'd been counting on getting her help. "Please?"

She stroked the velvet choker around her neck. "Surely there's another, smaller wish we can agree on," she said. "Every once in a while, a human figures out I'm here, we make a deal that benefits both of us, and life continues."

"Won't you do *anything* to save the town from being destroyed? What about the wellspring? Won't you miss the springwater?"

"You tell me the town will be destroyed, but the future is unknowable, even for a genie." She extended her hands, palms out, and smiled warmly. "Come on, Alma. You can trust me. Birdie can tell you I was a good boss. I look out for my people—just as I did for their parents and grandparents. What can I do for you? There must be something more… *personal*. I find that the best wishes are limited in scope. Fewer unintended consequences. Like asking for world peace and ending up with a planet of only koalas. I can't tell you how often I have to explain…"

While she spoke, I turned my attention inward and asked my instincts to guide me. My mind's eye saw a sad, playful face, and I knew. There had never really been any question.

"I want to help Seth Dumont," I said, feeling the rightness of it loosen a knot in my gut. "Since the death of the fairy Launt, formerly the human who owned his body, he can't leave Silverpool without starting to die."

Her eyes widened. "You would waste your gift on the changeling?" she asked. "What about that house you rent, perhaps? In the blink of an eye, the deed could be yours. Of course, real estate here might be worthless in a few days. How about a house in Riovaca, Santa Rosa... Tiburon is lovely—"

"The housing market is bad, but I'm not going to let a friend die to save on rent money," I said.

She shrugged. "I don't judge."

I took a deep breath and continued, letting my heart guide me. "I wish Seth Dumont was able to travel freely the way he used to. I will give you my silence in exchange for a safe, reasonable cure for Seth's condition. No tricks or hidden costs—you have to infer what I mean and not punish him with some kind of sneaky side effects."

Jen's face spread into a wide, beautiful smile. Her hair shimmered, her eyes sparkled, the velvet ribbon around her throat was as red as blood. "I'm not vindictive. I understand what you want. My motto has always been to make the customer happy." She got to her feet, adjusting her corset with a wiggle. "OK, it's done."

The next time I drew breath, I was standing in my bathroom, a toothbrush in my hand, the sun streaming through the window.

My phone—my phone was on the shelf above the sink—chirped. Massaging my forehead to shake off my disorientation, I picked it up.

I'm outside, a text from Darius said. *Let's get to work.*

Chapter Twenty-Five

I'd done what I could for Seth. Now I'd have to try to save everything else.

Come on in, I texted. *I need a minute.*

Darius quickly replied, *No thanks. I'll wait here.*

I smiled at the screen. In spite of my lack of sleep, I felt refreshed as I got ready. My jacket was already stocked with extra beads and a pouch or two of useful herbs. Darius could be the one to carry a notebook and write things down. My style was more impulsive.

After taking care of Random, who I had to restrain from running out to say hi to his pal Darius, I walked out alone and got inside the black SUV parked way down the street in front of the Souters' house. I did glance at Seth's house, but the quiet bungalow gave nothing away. Did he feel anything yet?

"I see you're not taking any chances," I told Darius, who was alone in the big vehicle.

"I've never felt anything like whatever that gnome did to us," he said. "I respect it. Not going to lie."

"He's a mystery to me too," I said, buckling the seat belt.

"Want to grab breakfast before we get to work?" He started the engine. "Coffee?"

Now that I was outside the boundaries of my home, I felt my optimism waver. Even if Darius and I found out how Bosko died, the Protectorate might not change its mind, and everything I was looking at, the redwoods and sorrel, old bungalows and colorful storefronts, could be magically erased, blocked from human access, forgotten.

I put my hand on my beads and gave myself a shot of energy, a magical pep talk. "I don't drink coffee anymore. Besides, no time. Let's go right to the winery. I didn't get a chance to scan it properly when I was there Sunday."

"It's been four days, and countless agents and nonmagical people have been trampling in and out."

"You never know," I said.

As he turned at the end of the street, Darius handed me his notebook, open to the last page. "Here's a sketch of the scene."

"I remember it pretty well already," I mumbled, reflecting on my nights with Tristan. Most women in town had gotten to know it too.

"I've drawn where Percival and Florence were sleeping, as well as the location of the proposed office space," he said. "They hadn't had a chance to set up yet, but the boxes and standard amulets were there." Standard amulets would include silver jackets for each witch, a few gold chains for dangerous work (which would have to be returned), a vial of springwater, a box of gemstones (also for borrowing only), and an array of silver knives. The junior agent would be in charge of keeping them free of tarnish.

While I was imagining Flor cleaning the silver knife that had killed Vera, Darius parked in front of the winery tasting room. Did she feel the same care for the fae as I did, or was her interest entirely self-serving? I didn't expect anyone to worry about demon rights the way I did, but the fae were widely viewed as innocent. The destruction of Silverpool would be one more blow to fae habitat, already shrinking worldwide.

"I suppose Percy has an alibi, or you would've arrested him instead of my father," I said, remembering the missing apprentice on the morning of the murder. I handed his notebook back to him.

"He was with friends on the coast near Jenner," he said, naming a town less than an hour to the west. "Moon party on the beach. We scanned them. Seemed legit."

"You don't sound convinced."

Shrugging, Darius took off his seat belt but didn't get out of the car. "Percy is known for his mind magic. That's why Bosko kept him around—he has a knack for persuasion. If a witch wasn't careful, he or she would confess their crimes to Bosko without intending to."

"You think he might have tricked his friends into claiming he was with them when he wasn't," I said.

"Maybe. No proof of that, of course. Just wanted you to keep your senses alert when you meet the guy."

"I did meet him on Saturday night," I said. "Very briefly. Bosko wanted to introduce us. He seemed kind of wishy-washy, like Bosko had him well trained."

"Well trained for sure. He idolized Bosko," Darius said. "When he came back to the winery and found out his master was dead, five agents as well as Raynor were on the scene, able to scan his reaction for falsehood in real time."

"And?" I asked.

"Totally broke him up. Fell apart crying. He needed a calming spell before he could speak sense."

I wondered if he'd also been distraught for the man who'd died or if he was actually grieving his career. The death of a master was considered bad luck for the apprentice, both in magical terms and practical ones. An apprentice who hadn't protected the mage he served wasn't worth very much on the job market. Flor would face the same prejudice, although at a lesser scale, given how brief and junior her position had been.

We went inside, where Flor and Percy were working with other agents to comb the property repeatedly for any demon sign, which made me think the Protectorate was determined to find it. Flor was crawling on the floor of the hallway with a silver orb in a glass box, watching it carefully as she inched it across the tile. Percy was in the doorway, swabbing the frame with cotton balls, which he dropped into another glass box, this one filled with a cloudy liquid. I had no idea what it was, but it smelled nasty and throbbed slightly, like a lung.

Flor's hair bow today was black, which I thought was a little overdone. We weren't Victorians. She lit up at the sight of Darius and got to her feet. "Oh thank Brightness," she said. "Please tell me you need to ask me more questions. My neck is killing me."

Darius turned to me with a raised eyebrow. "Which one first?"

Percy frowned, watching the exchange. "Why are you asking her?"

"Witch Bellrose has a special gift I will be utilizing in my investigations," Darius said smoothly. "Naturally, I can't tell you what that gift is."

An awkward silence fell as both Flor and Percy stared at me. They probably thought the gift was a physical magic, like an amulet, and they wondered why the Protectorate hadn't simply confiscated it from me to use as they pleased. Snapping out of her curiosity, Flor put aside the box and came with us outside to the patio where we'd gathered on Saturday night. When we reached the steps that led down the slope to the vineyard, Darius hung back.

"I'll catch up," he said, waving us ahead. "I forgot something in the car."

Flor gave me another curious look, then shrugged and walked down the stairs. At the bottom, I walked ahead to a path that Tristan had used to peruse the grapevines. I knew nothing about winemaking, but Tristan had loved it almost as much as he'd loved women. And his black-market magic collection—a secret I'd discovered after his death. The assortment of potions, herbs, amulets, and other magic had been stored in a custom-built cabinet that was now long gone, taken by the Protectorate over the summer.

"I hear Percy was at some beach party Saturday night," I began, giving her an opener to complain, which she took eagerly.

"So annoying," she said. "So, so, so annoying, but I guess it doesn't matter now since his career is over. Like mine." Her voice cracked, and I realized she was crying.

"I'm sorry," I said.

She flung up her hands. "How could I have such bad luck? Why does this always happen to me?"

I thought about the dead body sprawled on the floor. "I'd say it happened to Kurt Bosko."

Hanging her head, she wiped her cheeks. "You're right of course," she said. "I've been holding it together as much as I can, but sometimes it just hits me. I thought I was finally on the right path. I should've listened to Percy, but I thought he was jealous."

My interest sparked. "What did he say?"

"Oh, just that Bosko would make me miserable and to stay far, far away from him. He told me more than once. Back in San Francisco—twice—and then again on our first night here."

The night Bosko was killed, I thought. Had Percy known something was going to happen, or had he just been trying to protect his own job? "Was Percy miserable? Darius said he'd idolized Bosko."

"I think both things were true. He was like an abused dog, loyal to the end." Flor suddenly stopped walking, shook her head, then continued, adjusting her hair bow. "*He* would've found the steak dinner Bosko wanted, never mind it was past midnight in the middle of nowhere with more fairies than humans. But me? No luck. I tried to find anything that was open, maybe carne asada at the taqueria, but everything had been closed for hours. What did he expect? He'd lived in New York too long."

As I walked beside her, I was momentarily distracted by a tiny structure at the end of one of the vineyard rows ahead of us. About the size of a volleyball, it was large for a fairy house. To most humans, it would look like a misplaced hunk of concrete, perhaps the remains of an old retaining wall. But I had the fairy sight and could see not only the shell of concrete but the tiny windows with their candy-wrapper curtains, the path of plastic bottle caps, and the fairies themselves, three gray-skinned figures in green dresses, watching me from the front door. I wondered if they'd stay if the wellspring was buried, if they felt danger coming.

To hide my reaction to something invisible to her, I coughed and bent over to tie my shoe.

"You saw him tell me, so I assume he'll believe it's true, since you two are obviously working together in some weird, secret capacity that I hope you can explain to me someday." She sighed. "That's hubris for you. I thought your career was over and mine was taking off. Sure got that wrong. Why do these things always happen to me? What did I do to deserve it?"

If I encouraged her pity party, maybe she'd tell me details she hadn't shared with Darius. "What happened when you had to break it to him that gourmet meals aren't available in small towns in the middle of the night?" I asked. "Did he actually blame you for that?"

"That's what made it worse. He'd gone to bed when I got back to the house. Wouldn't even see me." She picked up a stone and threw it into the vineyards. "It was two a.m. before I could go to bed, not that he cared."

I glanced back at the fairies, who were watching us walk away. Their house was beneath a massive rosebush, still heavy with yellow flowers even though it was the first week of December. I wondered if Tristan's old magic kept it blooming. Although their choice of home would put them in the path of frequent human contact, it must've been worth it to them to be near such beautiful roses.

"Well, he's dead now," I said.

She sighed. "I know. I shouldn't talk about him that way, but I figured you're a friend. You'll understand."

"I've never wanted to be an app," I said, "because I knew I'd never be able to suck up as much as you're supposed to. I'm not always good with authority."

With what I thought was an inappropriate level of amusement, Flor laughed. "No, really?" she asked, rolling her eyes.

"And you are?" I asked, my ego stinging a little.

"Better than you are," she said. "I can fake it. At least I am faking it—Percy, on the other hand, is the real deal. Naturally submissive. I don't think he ever would've left Bosko on his own."

"Had Bosko told him his days were numbered?"

She shot me a look. "You don't think Percy could've done it, do you?"

"Do you?" I asked.

Shrugging, she picked up another rock and rolled it between her fingers. "I don't know. Maybe. But only in a heartbroken, nobody-can-have-you-but-me kind of way. He treated Bosko like a god." She hurled the rock into another row of dormant grapevines. "But didn't he have an alibi?"

"That's what Darius said. I haven't talked to him myself."

She gave me a sly look. "Do you have special scanning powers? Is that the 'gift' Darius was talking about?"

"I wouldn't be asking you so many questions if I could read minds," I said.

"I suppose." She looked up at the sky, mostly gray and hinting at rain. "The Protectorate can get the truth out of him if he's lying. He's good at mind spells, but I don't think he could overcome a team of Emerald mages. But who knows? He did all kinds of sneaky stuff for Bosko, I hear. I was hoping he'd teach me some of it so I could take over someday."

"Why would he teach you something that would make him replaceable?"

"You never know," she said. "I just met him last week, but he seems like he's the type of person to be nice even if it's bad for him. Couldn't help himself."

Percy sounded like a witch with a lot of contradictions. I was eager to scan him. Maybe the ring had exposed his demon print to his master and he'd had to lash out to save himself.

But from the way he'd been handling the package on Saturday night, it hadn't seemed to bother him as much as it did me. If Percy shared my demon mark, he should've felt a pain in San Francisco when he'd collected the opal ring. He could've fled with the ring instead of bringing it to a man known for killing so impulsively and cheerfully.

But he could have a shielding amulet like I did. There was something about Percy that didn't feel right.

We'd walked around a loop path and were now walking uphill, returning to the house. "I'll let you get back to work," I said. "Thanks for the unofficial chat."

"Sure. We won't be seeing much of each other after this," she said. "Where are you going to go?"

Up on the deck above us, Percy was talking to Darius. The apprentice seemed a decade older, as hunched over and miserable as a bridge troll. "Go?" I asked, not sure she knew about the Protectorate plan.

"It begins at noon," she said. "They cast an exodus spell."

My stomach lurched. "Already?" Raynor had said it would happen before the solstice, but that was weeks away. He'd enlisted me to investigate Bosko's death, which would take time. "No. Today? Are you sure?"

"The nonmagical inhabitants will feel the urge to go first," she said. "I *overheard* the agents talking about it." She used finger quotes to indicate her eavesdropping had involved magic.

I swore. The confidence I'd felt earlier vanished. They'd already started to bury the town. When the exodus spell turned on the resident witches, too, I'd be driven out as well.

"When do they hex the witches who live here?" I asked.

"Sorry, I don't know," she said. "Do you feel anything yet?"

A quick scan told me no. "I need to interview Percy," I said, hurrying ahead.

Flor grabbed my elbow and leaned close to speak into my ear. "Watch out for him. His mind skills are stronger than you'd expect."

I wrenched my arm free, automatically swept the remains of her touch away, and turned my attention to the miserable man up at the house. "Thanks for the warning."

Chapter Twenty-Six

D arius stood on the deck next to Percy as if he'd been keeping him from leaving, but from the look in Percy's dejected face, he didn't have the energy to walk ten feet. Heeding Flor's warning, however, I used my beads as I approached to draw power around myself, focusing on buttressing my brain from outside influence. Even a pleasant smell could work to trick a person.

I stopped a few feet away without offering my hand. "I'm sorry about Protector Bosko's death," I said to Percy.

The overcast sky made his complexion appear colorless against his dark hair. He looked more dead than his boss had the last time I'd seen him. "You want to talk to me?" he asked.

I had no idea what Darius had told him. "Nothing official," I said. "Just helping out, given the crisis, as much as I can."

He shrugged without interest. "Do you mind if we go into the house? I have to finish screening the bedrooms."

Darius nodded, and I followed Percy inside and down a hallway to a familiar guest room. A few months ago, after

Tristan's death, I'd found a magical storage cabinet inside it, well protected by enchantments. I'd needed to use odd metal objects from home to break through and examine the contents.

Percy lifted an iron bar out of his pocket and held it in the doorway, frowning at it. Iron was a hearth witch's metal, common and domestic, often used to create or detect herbal magic. "There's something here," he said. "It's hidden, but I'm picking up a lot of residue. Can we talk while I work? They've already begun to secure the region. I owe it to the Protector to find out what happened to him."

I wrapped my fingers around my beads and cast out my own senses. They'd removed the cabinet, but there had been other spells. One of them... I squinted... was still there.

And he was about to throw something.

"Duck," I said.

A flash of light flew past Percy's head. He cried out and dropped the iron bar to clutch his right ear. "What was that?"

"The last Protector put an enchanted jade gargoyle in here to guard some property of his," I said. The small creature was now perched on top of a large computer monitor on a desk near the door, grimacing and pointing at us. "Let's talk somewhere else before he strikes again."

Another flash of green light shot out of the room. Jade was a lovely stone that was also excellent for guarding property. The gargoyle might not have been as effective if made out of granite. This time Percy pivoted with surprising speed, dashing into the hall and avoiding the blast. "Demon's balls," he said, breathing hard. "Didn't the Protectorate clean the place out?"

"I guess they missed him." I leaned against the wall next to him, safely out of reach. "Tristan set a lot of traps to protect his stuff. You'll need to—well, you would've needed to do another sweep."

Percy leaned his head back and closed his eyes with a long exhale. What energy he'd displayed to jump out of the gargoyle's attack was now gone. "Just scan me. That's what you're here for, right? I did the same thing for Mage Bosko. I'm too tired to put up a block or a dispersion. Do your worst." He opened his eyes and gave me a sad smile. "Or your best, I suppose. Are you a mind mage like me?"

I shook my head. "I make wood jewelry. Darius was my ex-partner. I got fired for—"

"Spare me the official story," Percy said. "I don't want to know your secret. Just do whatever you're going to do so I can get back to work."

The hallway was as good a place as any, and his guard was down. Casting a scanning spell, I asked, "Where were you Saturday night and Sunday morning?"

"Friends of mine invited me to a moon party on the beach in Jenner," he said, staring straight ahead. It was obvious he'd told the story several times already. "I left at midnight and got back Sunday morning at nine thirty."

"Why were you late? You were supposed to be working with Flor and Bosko earlier."

"I lost track of time." He tilted his head and looked me in the eye. "I drank some springwater spiked with borage leaf and dried quail eggs. One of the locals sold a bottle to a friend of mine. I don't have any tolerance for potions, never have. I woke up on the beach with my face in some kelp and came as fast as I could."

His story was comically common. Metal witches scorned the organic magics professionally but then would go to a party and play around with ingredients they didn't understand and get into trouble.

I couldn't detect any deception, but he did have a lot of

experience tricking people. "Did you ever get tired of working for him? Wasn't he awfully demanding and critical?"

He held my gaze. "He was brilliant. A genius. Nobody could see Shadow the way he could." His aura was steady and unwavering, and I believed he was telling the truth as he saw it. "Yes, he was uncompromising. He saw the world in Bright and Shadow. But that was his job, wasn't it?"

Rather than answer his question, I asked, "Why did you tell Flor to find another position?"

"She already disliked him," he said. "She thought she could fake it, but I knew he'd see through her within weeks. She would've been much worse off than if she'd never worked for him. A down vote from Mage Bosko would end your career."

"Why have you stayed so long? You could've moved on to something more advanced by now. Something more independent."

He leaned back and smiled at the ceiling. "Everyone asks me that. My mother asks me that. I guess I'm just not the ambitious type who's always looking for the next step on the ladder." His voice roughened. "All I wanted was to work with him."

Again, my scan could find nothing false in his words. I asked him a few more questions, all confirming what I'd already heard about him, and thanked him for his time. But just as I was leaving to look for Darius, Percy stopped me.

"Pardon me for mentioning it, but it's such a rare magic, and you haven't bothered to hide it," he said, looking down at my arm. "Do you mind if I take a closer look? It's quite interesting."

I followed his gaze to my left wrist, where the inked rings were visible under one of my beaded bracelets. The skin was still red around the tattoo but wasn't painful anymore.

I gave him a sharp look and lifted my arm. "You've seen this kind of magic before?"

Eyes widening in alarm, he took a step back. "Sorry, I didn't mean to intrude. It's none of my business. Forgive me. I'll get back to w—"

"No, please, you're not intruding." I looked around to make sure we were alone and lowered my voice. "The truth is, Percy, I don't know what it is. It just showed up."

He took another step back, swallowing nervously, looking as if I was trying to get him in trouble. "How strange," he said. "I wonder what it is? It just caught my eye. I've always been too observant for my own good. I'll keep my mouth shut. Don't worry."

"No, I'm serious," I said. My stomach clenched at the thought it might be some kind of mind magic he knew about, and I'd just left it burning there in my skin without trying to get rid of it. "Please. I'd really appreciate anything you can tell me about it. You said it was a rare magic. What did you mean?"

He chewed his lips, glancing between my face and my wrist. "You really don't know?"

I shook my head. "Not exactly. There was another witch who had it. He's dead now."

"Did you kill him?" he asked. "But no—you can't kill, can you? That's what I heard. Incurable Inability."

"I was there when he died," I said. "Let's just say that."

Percy nodded, seeming to relax, and leaned down to look more closely at the dark circles around my arm. "The spell has changed since its first casting," he said after a moment. "It's got your fingerprint now."

My patience was thinning. "But what is it? Is it dangerous?"

"Oh no," he said. "Although you might want to cover it

up if you don't want to talk about it. People will wonder why your life is so dangerous."

"Dangerous?" I was afraid it was something worse, that it indicated I'd been responsible for death. "Can you be more specific?"

"May I send out a little probe?" he asked.

I nodded.

He tapped my arm with a forefinger, and a sizzle of energy leapt into his hand. "Ah," he said, studying me. "It's a near-death mark."

"Near death?" I asked. "You mean me? It's not... indicating the death of people who get too close to me?"

He frowned. "I can see how they might be related, among our kind. Witches can be bloodthirsty monsters." He cast a dark look toward the room where his master had met a violent death. "I don't know what the original spell was, but on you, it's a survival mark. Centuries ago, parents would cast them on babies after they'd passed their first birthday. A new one would appear every year after that."

"That's what it was like on the other witch," I said.

"But he didn't survive," Percy said, "and you did. So now you've got it."

"But I've gotten three rings in less than three months," I said.

Percy's eyes widened. "Three?" He began to look nervous again. "Sounds like you've been busy," he said, stepping away. "It really isn't any of my business. Please don't tell them in San Francisco I offended you by asking. I'm going to need all the help I can get, finding another job after what's happened here."

"I won't tell anyone. I'm not like that," I said, annoyed to be lumped in with the witches at the Protectorate, although it was understandable he would. "I'm really grateful you told me what you did. Thanks."

He forced a smile and got back to work. I was relieved to know I wasn't carrying a killer's checklist on my arm. My life *had* been crazy lately. Now I knew the demon attack at the hardware store had been more dangerous for me than I'd realized. Another brush with death.

I thanked him again and went looking for Darius. He was in Bosko's room, scowling at his notebook. I wrapped another focus string and my watch from my right wrist over to my left to cover the tattoo before I went in.

"It has to be a demon. Nobody else could've gotten in here," he said.

"Could a witch have apparated in here somehow?" When he gave me a raised eyebrow, I made a face and said, "Other than my father."

"We're pretty sure nobody here can apparate," he said. "We did the probes."

"Percy's talent is manipulating minds," I said quietly. "And he does seem the type to be underestimated."

Darius crossed his arms over his chest. "I tested him myself. I'd bet my great-grandmother's diamond tiara on it."

From what I knew of the Ironford family, they'd kill him to hear he'd bet such a treasure on a hunch. "OK, not Percy then. Flor?"

"No way," he said. "If that witch could apparate, she would've put that on her Protectorate application in giant letters. She's been bugging every mage for an apprenticeship for years."

He was right. I looked around the room. "Can I have a few minutes to scan it myself?"

"It's been wiped pretty thoroughly," he said.

I took a moment to gather my focus, then turned it to the floor, walls, windows, furniture, open space. The only magic I felt was the residue of other scans. "And? Is there demon sign?"

He licked his lips and glanced at the hallway, where two agents were cleaning up the scanning supplies and talking about how the Warriors were playing that year. He turned back to me and shook his head. "We're still looking."

Yet they'd already officially labeled it a demon attack.

"Who else benefited from Bosko's death?" I asked, leaning back to probe the vaulted ceiling. "Is there anyone visiting from New York who might have it in for him?"

Darius quickly went over and slammed the door. "What are you up to?"

I looked at him, my ceiling probe only half-finished. "What do you mean? Nothing. I'm just asking questions."

"You shouldn't ask those kinds of questions unless you have something to go on," he said. "If there are any Free-witches around you want to investigate, that's fine, but leave the Protectorate out of it."

Freewitches were a revolutionary fringe group of witches who opposed Protectorate authority around the world but mostly in the US. They were an easy scapegoat for all kinds of problems.

"Freewitches don't have the motive or the ability to do what happened here," I said, gesturing around the room. "No sign of witch activity. A Protector with a broken neck. It doesn't add up. There's no evidence."

"Agreed. And there's no evidence of some evil New Yorker popping in and dropping him on his head either," he said.

I looked back up at the ceiling. If somebody had dropped him, it would've been from up there. Stun him, lift him by his feet, let go. Easy. If I were in my house with my staff, I could've done it. I'd trained Birdie by holding her on the ceiling. My father liked to steal things by floating above the ground, leaving less of a trace. All kinds of creatures—fae, witch, and demon—could use magic to defy gravity and move objects for brief periods.

"What about the trunk?" I asked. Maybe Bosko had owned a levitation amulet or some other tool that had been used against him.

"We've already removed it," Darius said. "Diamond Street went through it first. Now it's in New York. So far, the Emeralds haven't been able to find anything inside with residue of his murder."

I rubbed the back of my neck, massaging away tension. "Did they find any residue on the outside?" The old leather would hold human prints for longer than metal or plastic. "Had he tried to get into it, maybe in a panic, or somebody else as they came in?"

Darius paged through his notebook. "A preliminary scan showed it was touched by Percy, Florence, the housekeeper, a vineyard worker, and, at least recently, two Uber drivers, one in New York and one in San Francisco."

I gaped at him. Bosko must not have feared anyone or anything, to let his precious trunk be handled by so many people. But the apex predator hadn't been invincible after all. Even with his most recently acquired tool.

I lowered my voice. "Was the opal ring inside?"

Darius wouldn't look me in the eye. "Not supposed to talk about that." He gestured at the room. "You done here?"

"Just give me a yes or a no," I said.

"Can't."

With Darius, I didn't know if that meant magic had sealed his lips or if it was just his ethical code. There wasn't much difference with him.

This was why that ring didn't belong on *any* witch's finger. Bosko hadn't held it for a full day, and now he was dead. I didn't know what was worse—the murderer having it or the Protectorate bosses in New York. Either way, witches like me were in danger of being exposed, our careers ended, our lives threatened.

I closed my eyes and cast my senses up again for long enough to make myself dizzy, but I couldn't feel any magic I was familiar with.

The room wasn't giving anything away. I needed more to go on. "I'm going to follow Flor and Percy's trails into town on the night of the murder," I said. "Maybe one of them is lying."

"We're calling it a death, not a murder," Darius said.

I snorted.

"OK, the Protectorate is," he said. "Let's go in an hour. I need to talk to the guys in the hall when they finish."

"No, stay here," I said. "I need to do this by myself. I'm a local. People will talk to me."

"People might be too confused, reacting to the exodus spell, to have anything useful to tell you."

"Another reason for me to go by myself," I said, walking to the door. "And now."

"Don't try to do everything on your own. Keep me in the loop."

Opening the door, I waved my phone at him and stepped out into the hallway.

Chapter Twenty-Seven

The agents cleaning up watched silently as I walked around the containers of cotton balls, bubbling liquids, and iron bars, and in a few minutes I was back out in the driveway, alone except for one young agent standing guard.

I put my hand on my beads and imagined Flor. Because we'd known each other as children, I had an existing connection to her and found her trail after a minute of concentrating. She'd walked in and out of the house many times, some quite recently, and I could feel her aura on the concrete and flagstone. The black Audi sedan near the tasting room, where the trails ran to, must've been hers.

Percy's was less obvious. I was only sure it was his because of the concentrated sense of him around an old Honda hatchback. I went over to the driver's side door, wiped the handle with a sycamore leaf I kept in my pocket, then wrapped it inside a swatch of velvet. It might help me follow his trail.

It was just past ten on a Thursday morning, so I drove to the taqueria on Main Street and parked. The town did seem busy for a weekday, with people driving and walking faster than usual. The spell was unfolding, compelling the nonmagical to pack up and leave, and even giving me a stressful, anxious sensation. A voice in the back of my mind promised how much better I would feel in another town, another county, another state. Wasn't I tired of the flooding? The fog, the potholes, the underfunded infrastructure, the wildfires? The cost of living was so much lower in New Mexico. Arkansas. Minnesota.

Seth was from Minnesota, I reflected, staring off into space. He'd been born fae, then placed into the body of a human baby and raised as a nice Minnesota boy.

My thoughts continued to drift pleasantly. There were lots of lakes there. Lakes were nice. And loons—Silverpool didn't have any loons, and they made such lovely sounds, haunting and hypnotic...

I put both hands at my throat and gripped my beaded necklace as if it were a handle on sanity. The exodus spell was very strong. No wonder people were leaving.

I found a hint of Flor's trail on the sidewalk and followed it to the door of the restaurant, where it stopped, backing up her claim that she'd been there when looking for a late-night beef dinner for Bosko. The trail then led to the road, then the faded crosswalk; holding my beads, I held her image in my mind and followed the sense of her to the other side. I lost her for a few minutes and had to walk up a few blocks and then back again before I regained it outside the gas station. I walked over to the pumps and found a trace of her there, on the handle and the keypad. Closing my eyes, I felt a larger sense of her near the trash container beneath the windshield fluid and squeegee. Reluctantly I put my hand inside, following my instincts, and felt a jolt of power when I touched a crumpled tissue. I pulled it out.

It seemed like a used tissue, nothing more. It was now

stained with coffee and ketchup from other items inside, but it was her… fluids… that had drawn me. It was definitely Flor's snot. And tears. As a witch, they held some of her power, concentrated in the paper fibers as the water had evaporated. I took out another velvet bag and stuck it inside, grimacing as the ketchup wiped across my knuckles.

Holding the bag, I asked it where else Flor had been. I felt a tug behind me and tried to hold the feeling lightly as I walked slowly toward the sensation. The fog hadn't burned off, even though it was midday, and heavier clouds had rolled in, dulling the old storefronts of downtown Silverpool into shades of gray. The trail went dim, so I closed my eyes and waited for the sensation to strike again. It took me to a Thai restaurant a block to the west, one that had closed last year. Flor seemed to have lingered at the door, touching the glass, and I could feel more frustration. Then I followed the trail to the deli, which always closed before four p.m. I could feel the panic in her throat and almost felt sorry for her. Silverpool simply didn't have the population to support many businesses. Cypress Hardware had been an exception, and now I knew it was because an ancient genie had made it possible.

Speaking of Cypress, she even tried there. I followed her scent back to the hardware store, around to the side entrance, where a hot dog truck was parked next to the garden center gate. It would've been closed at midnight, of course, but she'd stood and begged for it to open, pleaded with the universe to give her just this one break. Although now it was almost lunchtime, the counter window was shut, and a guy was walking around the back, wrapping the power cord into a loop. They weren't local and would be feeling the unavoidable urge to go park their truck somewhere else.

I lost her trail for a few minutes, so I walked back to the Thai restaurant, wondering if she'd found the pizza place up the hill. Then I looked across the street where Birdie's building stood. She'd moved into the apartment above the store, but downstairs was the same as when she'd bought it, dirty and cluttered with an expired travel agency. A bookstore would've been a tough sell even without an exodus spell or burying of the wellspring. A surge of compassion rushed through me. I'd been neglecting her. I'd been rude about Thanksgiving and hadn't yet seen her since she called me in San Francisco. I should've already told her about what the Protectorate was doing.

I walked across the street and rang the bell for the unit upstairs, then stood waiting, noting the absence of Flor's trail. There weren't any restaurants near that part of the street. I concluded Flor had done exactly what she'd said she'd done: looked for her master's dinner and failed.

Birdie flung open the door and threw her arms around me. "Alma!" She held me close, wiggling from side to side. "I've been so worried!"

I hugged her in return for a few long seconds before drawing back and looking into her face, which was unusually strained. "Are you OK?" I asked.

"Of course," she said. "You're my best friend. How could I not be OK?"

Guilt struck me again. "Don't say that. I bailed on you again." On the street, cars were going too fast, honking at the stoplight, screeching their tires. Silverpool wasn't supposed to be like this. As we continued to stand on the landing, I could feel the boundary spells she'd erected. Combined with the exodus spell, it pushed me in different directions, making me queasy. "Can we go inside?"

She reached up her hand and touched my face. "You're worried about something. Was it the Protectorate? Your father? I've"—she squeezed her eyes shut, pinching her face together—"got a bit of a headache. I was trying to ignore it, but it just won't go away."

"Let's go upstairs and you can—"

"No, I'm working downstairs. Let's talk there." She gestured to the glass door that led to the former travel agency, still filled with laminate desks and twentieth-century cabinets and shelving, furniture to assist the needs of a different age. We walked through the dusty remains and sat down in a corner decorated with posters advertising Paris, Mexico, Hawaii. "How about some coffee? I set up the machine. I don't think it's old enough to kill. See?" She lifted a foam cup from an end table and gulped it down.

"Oh, Birdie, no. Don't drink that." I reached over and took the cup out of her hands. "You really drank something that was left here from the old travel agency?"

"It doesn't seem to be hurting me, but I've only had two pots so far." She grinned. "You're so nice to care. I won't drink it if you don't want me to."

"It's not that it'll hurt you," I said. "It's just... ancient. Doesn't it taste bad?"

"I don't mind. Maybe it'll help the headache." She rubbed her temples.

"I think that headache is you fighting the exodus spell," I said. "That's why I'm here. The Protectorate is driving everyone out of town. Or trying to. You need to stay in your apartment—you've got the boundary spells up, which is great —and just ignore it as long as you can."

"Exodus?"

I set the cup down on a wrinkled 1998 issue of *People* and told her everything. When I was done, she got to her feet.

"We should go," she said seriously. "Now. While there's still time."

Disappointed, I looked up at her from my chair. Didn't she want to fight for her dream? "Please don't panic yet. I'm going to fix things. Just stay put. You can start planning your bookstore layout. Were you still thinking about having a café—?"

"Alma, it's not safe. Please, let's go. You and me." She bent over and caught my hands, squeezing my fingers in hers. "I'm tired of dealing with the Protectorate, aren't you? Let's get away. We don't need them."

I eyed her critically. The exodus spell could be clouding her judgment. Holding her hands in mine, I spun a cleansing, fresh-air spell around us to temporarily break the influence of the Protectorate magic.

Seeing the confusion in her eyes as the magic went to war on her senses, I said quickly, "Think about your bookstore. How much you want it. You just bought this building. You have the money to make it work. Remember?"

She closed her eyes, obviously in pain, and shook her head. "It's not safe," she said. "I don't want you to get hurt."

I held her more tightly. "I won't. Nobody is going to get hurt," I said. "The Protectorate witches are casting spells that make us feel like we need to leave, but—for right now anyway—we don't have to."

"There's wildfires, there's floods, there's murder—"

I held her shoulders. "Birdie. Listen to me. Go up into your apartment and stay there. Your boundary spells should help you feel better. You can clean up and plan the store down here later." I turned her and guided her to the door. From the way she was talking, the best place for her now was safely tucked away in her apartment. Or maybe…

I stopped in the doorway. "Would you like to come over to my house? You can sleep over. Random would love it. My spells are stronger than yours. You won't feel nearly as much—"

"No!" She pulled away from me, then shook herself and laughed. "Sorry. I love your house, of course, and you're so nice to invite me like you have done in the past. But I need to be independent. You don't need to take care of me. In fact, I think I'm the one who needs to take care of you. Why are you out here trying to save other people when they don't even appreciate what you do?"

I could only stare at her. Of course I had to fight for Silverpool. Didn't she want to? Were we really that different?

As she continued to stare back at me, not backing down, I realized Birdie had never confronted me about my actions before. In fact, I couldn't think of a time she'd confronted me about anything.

Although my first impulse was to get defensive, I stopped myself. It was good for her to push back, to challenge, to question. To stand up for herself. We were friends, right? I'd taught her some magic, but that didn't make her my apprentice. I didn't want to be a bully like Bosko had been.

"Thanks for your concern," I said. "Really. I'm not just trying to help other people. I'm trying to help myself. I love this town. It's worth fighting for."

"Other Silverpool people can fight for it."

Sadly, the declaration was ridiculous. I was the most powerful witch left living in town and the only one to be trained at the Protectorate. The others I knew were retired, indifferent, untrained, or self-centered. "Like who?"

"I'm sure there's somebody," she said. "We can leave tonight. I have a lot of money. I'll buy us new stuff. Stuff is never as important as life. Life is everything."

The glass door to the outdoors was the only thing blocking us from the Protectorate exodus spell, and from Birdie's odd behavior, I realized it must be a lot stronger than I could sense myself. "You need to go upstairs," I said firmly, turning her toward her apartment entrance. "Drink the wellspring water I gave you. Don't be stingy. Drink it all. Then we can text each other about what to do next."

She tried to argue, but I opened the door and pushed her

through it. Her boundary spells sizzled on my knuckles, making me gasp. She struggled, but I wasn't going to let her sacrifice herself for me. I cast a secondary boundary spell between us, blocking her, then pivoted on my heel and hurried out the door and down to the sidewalk. I flung up one last spell to stop her from following and hoped she'd forgive my pushiness once she was out of range of the Protectorate enchantment.

Chapter Twenty-Eight

In just the time it took me to walk to my Jeep a block away, three trailers and pickups loaded with belongings sped past me, heading east on the road to Riovaca. I hadn't realized there were so many nonmagical people living in Silverpool. The enchantments to protect the wellspring had always made everyday life so difficult. How had they survived with so little reliable contact with the outside world? UPS trucks got lost, friends and family forgot the turnoff, landslides cut off the road…

But for so many people, especially in the north coast of California, getting lost was a feature, not a bug. Returning to the normal world would be a shock for them, and if the exodus spell held, they'd never be able to find their way back again.

The thought made me sad and angry. It wasn't just the witches like me or magical creatures like Seth or even Jen who deserved to stay—it was the nonmag weirdos too.

As I stepped off the curb to get into my car, I noticed a couple sitting close together, kissing, in a familiar car a few spots down. When I belatedly recognized Percy's old hatchback, I was embarrassed my tracking abilities had completely missed him. I'd managed to trace Flor's steps from days ago, but Percy had been sitting right in front of me, and I hadn't felt a hint of him.

I got into my Jeep and used my nonmag senses to watch him now. They weren't kissing anymore. His companion, a dark-haired woman in large, stylish glasses, was upset with him—that was clear from her expression and his. I wondered if she was emotional, like Birdie, because of the exodus spell, which was a grating, irritating feeling that never went away. She pulled away from him and got out of the car, slammed the door behind her, and strode down the sidewalk in front of me.

"Yuki!" Percy shouted out his window but didn't get out of the car.

Yuki waved, annoyed, and went into the taqueria. Pulling the shade down and using a subtle spell to hide my face, I waited to see if Percy followed. No. After a minute, he backed out into the street and drove away, back toward the winery.

I waited until he was out of sight before going after her. Percy had a girlfriend. Had she been at the moon party? He was an expert at mind spells, but maybe she wasn't. If he'd lied, I might be able to unravel it from her brain instead of his.

The spell I'd just used on Birdie had drained my power, and I needed a moment to recover. I reached under my seat and found a pouch I'd put there with several other items a month ago—my emergency stash. The bag held dried needles from a bristlecone pine tree in the Inyo National Forest—at least that's what Helen had assured me when I'd paid her for them. I put my nose in the bag and inhaled slowly and deeply. Its tingly, citrusy scent filled my head with energy, and the strength of its ancient lifespan fed my cells.

When I jumped out of the car and strode into the taqueria after Percy's companion, I was completely refreshed —at least for a few minutes.

"Yuki!" I exclaimed. "Is that you? I can't believe it! What are you doing way up here?"

The woman turned to me, confused, and I struck her with a borderline Shadow spell often used by con artists, one that said I was safe and familiar, like family. It was usually too weak to be used on trained witches, but she'd just been in an argument with her boyfriend and was still visibly upset, crying and blinking away tears. Staying an unthreatening distance away, I used another spell to make myself look shorter, my voice higher and softer. "Are you OK? I saw Percy. Were you fighting?"

Looking at me with hope, convincing herself she knew me, she nodded. "He— Bosko— Are you here because of what happened to him?"

I couldn't lie—that would break my innocence spell—so I approached and whispered, as if sharing a secret, "New York thinks a demon did it." My hope was that she was in the Protectorate, like Percy, and would assume I was a colleague. We were standing in the middle of the restaurant, which had a few agents in a corner having a lunch break but was otherwise empty. The fortysomething woman behind the counter was staring at us, waiting for us to approach and order. She had to be a witch herself to be resisting the exodus spell, but I'd never talked to her. Many Silverpool residents, for all kinds of reasons, kept to themselves.

"I'm not hungry," Yuki said absently, looking at the menu board above the counter. "I just wanted to get away from him."

"You could sit down? I'll get us some horchata?" I made everything a question. Optional. "Maybe it has wellspring water in it?" I pulled a chair out and smiled in the most nurturing way I could manage. "I heard it gets into every-thing here?"

She sat down, and in a few minutes I'd bought us each a glass of the sweet drink. Before handing her the glass, I dipped my pinkie into hers and cast another spell to enhance my harmless vibe. Unsanitary, but she'd just been sharing spit with Percy, so I didn't feel too bad.

After one sip, she let out a huge sigh and began to cry. "I told him not to come," she said. "I'd heard about Silverpool. The last Protector died, and it was never cleared up."

I bit my lip, tempted to tell her what I knew. "You thought something bad would happen to Bosko, too?"

"No, I guess not," she said, taking another sip. "I thought he'd get stuck here forever. I thought Bosko was too mean to die." Her nose wrinkled.

"I thought he was kind of mean to Percy," I said casually.

She put the glass down. "Percy adored him. He admired him more than anything. Everyone knew that. Percy gave up promotions of all kinds because he loved, just loved, Kurt Bosko." Nodding, she looked at the menu above my head behind me. "Maybe I will get something. Do they have fish tacos here?"

In spite of my spells, she was lying to me. I could feel it. "I think so?" I said tentatively, trying to regain my unthreatening status. "Probably?"

So, what part of her statement had been a lie?

Yuki got up and ordered something, then stood there waiting for it instead of rejoining me at the table. When she finally had her plastic basket of fish tacos with a pile of tortilla chips, which she began to eat first, she'd put up a figurative wall between us. Why would she lie about Percy hating Bosko? Most apprentices felt hostility toward their masters. Or had she been lying about Percy passing on promotions?

I waited for her to finish one of her tacos before trying another question. "When did you get here?" I asked. "It looks like they've got a blockade up now."

"Percy came and got me this morning," she said, pushing the basket away and wiping her hands. "I came up with Sarah Rock, don't know if you know her, she's a Flint now. We had to sleep in her Pilot on the side of the road. I knew it would be remote, but I didn't expect so many fairies. They kept waking us up, turning the windshield wipers on, the headlights, the hazards—really annoying."

"Did you see any of them?" I asked. Even regular witches without unusual sight like me could see fae who wanted to be seen.

"Just the lights," she said, yawning. "If only Percy had listened to me. I've been telling him for months to get a new job, but he was afraid of looking su—" She cut herself off. Eyes opening wide, she turned her attention to the basket, pushing a soiled napkin into the uneaten taco.

"Suspicious?" I asked.

Face flushing, she stood. "I've got to get back. Nice seeing you…" She stared at me and began to frown.

My spell wasn't strong enough to stand up to a direct challenge from a trained witch, and before I'd drawn my next breath, she'd pulled a boundary spell around herself and hurried out of the restaurant.

❦

I GOT up to follow her, but Darius walked in the door, pointing at me.

"You were supposed to keep in touch," he said.

"I was just about to call." Standing up, I looked at Yuki's basket and considered bagging it and scanning it at home, but then I'd have to explain what I was doing to Darius, which made me decide there wasn't a sensible reason to do it. Whatever she was hiding, the secrets wouldn't be unraveled with her saliva. Percy was the one who needed investigating. "I just met Percy's girlfriend."

"Yuki Kimura," he said. "She's his alibi. They were at the moon party together. All night."

"Are you sure?"

He looked around the restaurant—where everyone, I realized, was staring at us. Without a word, we turned away and went outside together. The exodus had quieted down for now. The rest of the people were probably like Birdie, holed up at home with headaches.

"We didn't find a reason not to believe either of them," he said. "Percy wasn't supposed to leave his master's side on their first night in town. Keeping that from us would've helped him save his career. Now he'll never live it down. His master killed while he danced under the moonlight with his girlfriend and a bunch of counterculture witch hippies."

"I'm not convinced Percy loved Bosko as much as people thought he did," I said. "Yuki was lying to me, but I'm not sure exactly about what."

"All right. So, you think he killed his master?" Darius asked absently, flipping through his notebook.

"If you're not going to take my ideas seriously, maybe I should just go home."

"I think you *should* go home," he said. "Isn't the exodus spell wearing you out? I've got a silver bracelet the Protectorate gave me, but your boundary spells must be exhausting to maintain."

I stifled a yawn, realizing how tired I was. Without being consciously aware of it, fighting the Protectorate hex had strained me. "Look into Percy's story. This might help you break through any spells he put down to cover himself, if he did." I took out the scrap of velvet holding the sycamore leaf

I'd rubbed on Percy's hatchback. "Maybe he can apparate. He's got skills with mind magic, maybe he's got other talents."

Darius looked inside the bag, frowning. "A leaf?"

"It has Percy's aura."

With a sigh, he took out a second velvet bag of his from his chest pocket and pushed mine inside. "Maybe he's secretly the most powerful mage of our time. That's why he worked for Kurt Bosko, who emotionally abused him and paid him Flint wages."

I flung open my car door, afraid I might lose my temper. Darius didn't mean to be patronizing. He was just careful. "Maybe Percy was only sticking around until he had the chance to kill him," I said. "Will you investigate him more thoroughly? For me? Please?"

Darius stayed on the sidewalk but nodded and slipped the wrapped leaf inside his jacket. "Sorry. You've really got a feeling about him?"

"Yes." Mollified by his belated helpfulness, I asked, "Did you need a ride back to the winery?"

"It's not far. Why don't you walk more? It's good for you."

"I will if the town survives," I said. "Promise."

❧

MY HEAD CLEARED AS SOON as I went into my house, and I felt a surge of energy. Fighting the exodus spell was going to drain me if I wasn't careful. I made myself some toast with almond butter and sat down for a minute to recharge. It was dinnertime. When had I last had a proper meal? I made myself a second slice of toast, added an apple, and ate.

What if Percy had actually hated Bosko and had used the idea of demons in Silverpool as a cover for murder? He'd have to have a way of getting into the room without leaving a trace. Lifting and dropping Bosko, a powerful witch, without him fighting or saving himself would take an amulet or an unusual skill. Perhaps both. But did he have a motive?

I picked up my phone and called Helen.

"Are you calling me for a place to stay?" she asked.

"No. I need information."

"Good," she said. "I was afraid you were fighting your destiny again. You can't run away now. Too many questions. A witch answers questions. And finds new ones. It's our true nature."

I licked almond butter off my thumb, skeptical. Was she really in a mood to cooperate? "You know what's happening in Silverpool?"

"They're trying to drive out the people before they bury it."

Helen was still better informed than any other non-Protectorate witch I'd ever met. "Percival Tuff. Goes by Percy. He was—"

"Bosko's apprentice. Think *he* dropped Bosko on his head?"

"I don't know. People say he idolized Bosko. Can you find out if he might have it in for him for some reason?"

"I have an idea," Helen said. "Maybe, like your father, he was in love with that demon. She enchanted your father, why not a Protectorate witch?"

"That makes no sense," I said. "First of all, he's much younger—"

"You think a young man wouldn't be interested in an older woman? She was barely fifty, if that," she said.

Helen's ego was as fragile as a fairy's wing. "All right, maybe he was. Will you find out and tell me?" I poured some milk into my cup and put it in the microwave. The nights had been dropping into the thirties, and my house was drafty. "Go way back, too, if you can. Where'd he grow up? Go to school? Did he always want to be an app? What's his family—?"

"Hello, I'm not your Flint," she said. "I might ask around because it pleases me, but that's all. If you want to know how he felt about his mommy, you'll have to find her yourself and ask her."

"I have wellspring water I could pay you with."

Silence. I'd spoken her language.

"It has to be solstice drawn," she said. "I already have the off-season. And you have to use the torc to get it so I can compare."

"The wellspring might be buried by then. I need your help before then. Like now."

"Do you really think they'd bury it? The income potential alone—"

"Yes," I said. "I think they might. It seems like somebody powerful wants all the questions here to go away as soon as possible. Forever."

"If the wellspring is buried, even if I help you, what do I get?" she asked.

I looked around my kitchen and saw a nicely carved piece of wood leaning against the wall behind the door. Bosko had said it was barely more than a giant pencil, but he'd soon realized that was wrong. The staff would be weaker away from my house, but with time and skill, which Helen had, she could take control of it for herself and tap into its powers in her own home.

"My staff," I said. "If I can't get the solstice-drawn well-spring water, I'll give it to you."

I could hear her smile over the phone. "Deal," she said.

Chapter Twenty-Nine

In the dark, before the moon rose above the tree line, I took Random for a quick walk down our street. The poor dog hadn't had a good run off leash in days. There was still no sign of life at Seth's house, and I wondered if he'd left without saying goodbye. I told myself—unconvincingly —that was for the best. The Souters' house was also quiet, which was unusual for the seventy-something nonmagical homebodies.

As I walked by, I studied the Souters' property more closely. All the lights were off, even the electric lanterns Chuck had wired along the ground to light the path up to the front door so Marge, with poor night vision, wouldn't fall. Then I realized the lighting was gone entirely, torn from the ground. The living room shades were still up, too, which meant they'd left before it got dark. Even the chicken coop was empty.

I shouldn't have been surprised. They were a nonmagical couple, and the exodus spell would've hit them first, but their departure made me sad. They were good neighbors and good people, and at their age, even if the exodus spell was halted and Silverpool survived, they might not come back. It was hard enough to find the town once. Returning to it later might be harder, even after living here for years. They could be on their way to Arizona by now.

Looking at their dark house reminded me of how little time I had, and I pulled a reluctant Random away from the Souters' bushes to return to my house.

My heart jumped into my throat. Seth was right behind me, floating above the road.

"What did you do?" he demanded.

Only the fae could creep up on me like that. Taking a breath to calm myself, I looked up at his face, which looked healthy and strong, though angry.

"I paid a fair price," I said. I couldn't talk about the genie and had no idea if he knew what she was. She'd been the original owner of his house but smart enough to use intermediaries. He'd sensed her on me as one of the three spirits who had messed with me, but he'd been unable to specify her identity.

"You had no right to take that burden." He crossed his arms over his chest. He wore a yellow hoodie over dark sweats, giving me the impression of a skinny, furious bee. "I can't repay you."

It was pointless to argue. "I know," I said. "I did it anyway."

"Why?"

I opened my mouth to explain the limits of my wish, how the genie hadn't really given me a choice, but my jaw locked. Right. It was hard to remember my vow. Silently agreeing to avoid the topic, I said instead, "You need to leave town. The Protectorate is going to bury the wellspring."

He scoffed, tossing his head in disgust. "You have put me eternally—and the fae don't say that lightly—in your debt," he said. "I'm not a child. I've never been a child. I'm a monster, the kind you were trained to kill. And now you've given me a life I didn't ask for."

"None of us asked for life," I said. "We got it anyway. Congratulations."

He levitated another foot into the air, looming above me. His face glowed from within, showing me a pair of dark eyes that were still angry and might be angry for more years than I could fathom. "I'm back to myself again. It's as if Launt never existed. I'm human with fae powers."

"Great," I said. "Now you can leave."

He slowly lowered himself to the ground in front of me. "I'm not going anywhere unless you do," he said.

"You can't let the Protectorate destroy you," I said.

His hand came up and cupped my cheek in the same place it had last night. Warmth flooded into me, eliminating every ache, every pain, knots in my muscles, fog in my brain. The glow in his face enveloped both of us, creating a circle of blinding, yellow light in the middle of the road, a small sun below the moon on a cold, dark November night. "I'll do whatever I want," he whispered. Then he snapped his fingers and disappeared.

Swaying on my feet, dizzy from the loss of warmth and comfort, it took me a moment to open my eyes and look around. Random was sitting calmly at my feet. A light flicked on in Seth's house, and then loud music, '90s grunge, began to play.

He wasn't going to leave.

Fine. He could leave if and when he needed to. I had no regrets. Someday I might miss the sweet, vulnerable Seth I'd come to know as my neighbor, but I'd done the right thing.

Shivering, I clutched my beads to erase the residue of his touch.

❧

EVEN WITH MY BEADS, I felt a growing pressure in my skull as I walked home. Seth's warm touch was being overwhelmed by the Protectorate hex to evacuate. I had to get inside my house before the spell broke through my defenses.

There was a slight improvement in my discomfort when I walked onto my driveway; my magic was getting stronger as I approached the center of my power. Before I went inside, I had to warn Willy. I dropped Random's leash and walked over to the redwood tree.

He appeared instantly at the base of the trunk, hands on his little hips, bare-headed and chewing his pipe. "What is this very horrible magic you are doing, human friend? It is most terrible and I think I will feel worse soon."

"The Protectorate is driving all the humans out of town," I said. "They're threatening to bury the wellspring."

He stared at me. "But they were trying that long times ago. I thought they learned their lessons."

"When was that?"

He took his pipe out of his mouth and shook it on the ground. "Your time and mine don't speak the same language," he said. "It was before the old humans were baby humans. Witches like you were here, afraid of the demons and all the other ones they don't understand. But it was silly to try. The water always flows. Water is always the strongest magic. It can bend to anything, crush the largest stone, dissolve the strongest metal. Without it, we die. With it, we die. Even my kind."

"They're going to try again," I said. "Unless I can stop them."

"Protectorate is not being as strong as water," he said, giving me an approving nod. "You will be winning this conflict, I am thinking. Best wishes to your quest in this matter. Please before then, please I hope you stop the horrible spell coming out of your people. It is disgusting."

His tone was unusually passionate. "What does it feel to you?" To a witch like myself, it was just magic, one spell like any other, just stronger and meaner.

"A crime, that is what I would be saying, something very wrong. The balance of life here does not deserve this insult." He pointed at me. "You will be turning it off for us, thank you for that. Now I will be going into my home, where the stink from human magic is not quite so nasty." He turned toward the little red door that had appeared.

"Would you consider leaving?" I called after him. "If I fail, this forest might end up…" I trailed off, afraid to admit what the Protectorate might do.

"Ending up is meaning what?" he asked.

"Under a pile of mud," I said. "Or boulders. Whatever they can get in here to bury the place. They've done it before."

"As I was saying to you, they have tried."

"But sometimes they succeed," I said. "There are well-springs in Los Angeles and Modesto, for instance, human cities not too far from here, that no longer have ground access to the wellsprings. They're buried under sewers and concrete and made so disgusting even the trolls won't go there anymore." That had been the idea. Without fae, the demons wouldn't come either.

"Your story is very sad. I will think about it in my home while you make the work happen to stop the sadness here." He touched his forehead and disappeared.

He had too much faith in me. I turned and went inside. The moment I closed the door, the pressure on my mind ceased completely. It was only nine, but I decided it would be good to get as much sleep as I could before the sun rose. They had gone after the nonmagical people first, but witches would be next. The compulsion to leave would become irresistible.

I texted Darius. *What have you learned about Percy?*

He didn't reply until after I'd changed into a pair of sweats and brushed my teeth. *It's barely been four hours*, he wrote.

I climbed into my bed and patted the mattress for Random to join me as I texted him back: *Time's running out what are you doing hurry please*

He called me. "I've got some calls in," he said. "I don't think it's the app though. He's here at the winery with me. He's not faking it. He's wrecked."

"That's his talent," I said. "Fooling people. Maybe he's drinking springwater cocktails in his room and plotting his next kill."

"Have you met this guy? A silver jacket wouldn't give him a spine."

"But maybe that's—"

"His talent," he said. "Yeah, I hear you. Just not buying it."

"How about fae or demon activity? Any hint at all it wasn't a witch?"

"Well, here's the thing," he said. "We didn't sense that gargoyle either until it started chucking things at us. With years of Tristan living there, and all the fae in this town and the demons coming in and out, hunting them, and the well-spring, I'm starting to consider we've been overconfident in our screening."

"Great," I said. "So it could be anything or anyone."

His voice lowered. "I might have found something. Promise me you won't overreact."

"Found it where?"

"Promise to stay chill?"

"I'm in bed in my pajamas with my dog," I said. "What are you afraid I might do?"

"I never know what you might do," Darius said.

The line was silent. "OK," I said finally. "I promise I won't overreact."

He made a skeptical *humph* sound and then said, "I found a hint of Percy's footsteps in the room. I know what you're going to say—"

"He wasn't supposed to cross the threshold," I said, perhaps a little too loudly.

Darius didn't answer right away. "I knew you'd overreact," he said finally.

"It was the leaf, wasn't it? It helped you see the evidence."

"I felt like a complete idiot waving a leaf around a crime scene, but yes, it showed me he'd been in there, but—"

"I knew it!" I pounded the bed, disturbing Random, who got up and jumped to the floor.

"You promised."

"I'm not overreacting," I said. "I am reacting appropriately. What's his excuse? I assume you confronted him about it?"

"He said he didn't think it counted since it was what they always did—reaching into the room but not entering. He said he'd tried not to touch the floor, but he must've slipped when he was helping Bosko take off his jewelry for the night, as usual." I began to interrupt, but Darius raised his voice and spoke more quickly. "The trace of him didn't go more than one or two paces into the room. Even with the leaf."

"You're sure? Maybe I should come—" My feet were already on the cold floorboards.

"Absolutely not. The exodus spell is about to ramp up. You might find yourself in North Dakota."

"You'd like that," I said.

"Not quite yet. Raynor would blame me. Stay where you are, and I'll keep an eye on the clumsy app." He sighed. "Seriously, Bellrose. Of all the people to suspect of murder. If you ask me, he's got more of an Incurable Inability than you do. Just today I watched him rescue a fly from a spiderweb."

"I suspect everybody," I said. "So should you."

"You realize, of course, that includes the daughter of Malcolm Bellrose."

"Yeah, yeah. I'm a serial killer," I said. "Let me know if anything turns up. Don't be afraid to wave that leaf all over the place. If any of the other agents give you a hard time, tell them to talk to me."

"Good job not overreacting." He hung up.

Chapter Thirty

I woke up before dawn in a sweat, my heart pounding. I'd been having a bad dream about Birdie, a toxic mixture of reality and anxiety.

Wiping the sweat off my forehead, I rolled over and picked up my phone. It was too early for a polite call, but letting my friend suffer wasn't polite, either. The exodus spell was now strong enough to reach me through the wards of my house. Even Random, curled up next to me with his head burrowed under my hip, seemed to be trying to get away from it.

She picked up so quickly, I decided she'd already been awake.

"Sorry to call so early," I said.

"Are you all right?" she asked.

"I'm fine. I'm worried about you," I said. "How's your headache?"

"Don't worry about me. I'm snug as a bug at my place. You taught me such good boundary spells, didn't you? I can barely feel a thing."

I was relieved she was so calm. "So your head doesn't hurt anymore?"

"Do you call all your friends before dawn to ask them about a little headache?" she asked. "I'm not a child. You don't have to take care of me."

Her words echoed Seth's, and I was momentarily embarrassed. "Sorry, but you're new to magic, relatively speaking."

"I've decided you're the one who needs looking after. You neglect yourself," she said. "Tell you what. Let's have a pact. I'll load up my car and you'll load up yours. Then if we have to leave, we can make sure we leave together."

"Load it up and come over here," I said. "It's safer."

"I told you. I'm safe here."

Maybe I could appeal to her intrinsic helper nature. "Random would be much happier if you were here with him. He misses you." I scratched his ears, sending out a spell to soothe him. He took this to mean he was getting an early breakfast and jumped up and ran to the kitchen. He couldn't be suffering from the spell too badly.

Birdie fell silent on the other end of the line. Finally she said, "He has you. What else could he need?"

Her compliment struck me dumb for a moment. "I-I— I'm worried about you. I'd feel better if you were here."

"I'm just down the road, ready to go when you do, anywhere you want," she said. "But I'm not leaving until you are."

It was typical of Birdie to be so loyal, but I didn't want the burden of her well-being on my conscience. An unwanted image of Seth flashed in my head. We did what we had to do for the people we cared about. Or changelings. Whatever kind of creature.

"All right. You promise you'll load up your car and be ready to go?" I asked. "You'll need to be ready to leave. There might not be much warning."

"Same goes for you. You're strong, but you're still human. Just because you're a witch doesn't mean you can't get hurt."

"All right, all right," I said. "I'll finish packing." I'd already started.

"Load up the car. Get all ready. Swear it."

"I've told you, Birdie, it's too dangerous for a witch to make vows."

"It's too dangerous not to, right? That's why you're calling me before dawn?"

I sighed and closed my eyes. She was the first real friend I'd had in a long, long time. The realization made me feel better than any spell. "I promise. I'll do it right now," I said.

"Me too," she said warmly. "I'll be here. I'll be right here, waiting to go with you."

The sky was lightening with the rising sun when I put down the phone. True to my promise, I hurried to gather my essentials and load them in the Jeep. Heartbreakingly, most of my jewelry supplies would have to be left behind—blocks of wood; pine cones; bags of dried evergreen needles, sorted by species; stacks of lumber; dusty strips of bark; boxes and boxes of stones I'd collected from beaches, hiking trails, and ravines—it was far too much to bring with me.

The thought of never seeing it all again made me kick a bag of compost, but I had to be realistic. The metal and finished beads, smaller and more valuable, were in separate boxes, in preparation for a day like this one, and I stacked them in the back seat with a frustrated sigh. At least, no matter what happened to Silverpool, I'd have the seeds to begin working again.

Daily items like clothing, kitchen tools, home furnishings —all could be replaced. With money I didn't have, but that was a separate problem. It was real enough, however, to make me even angrier.

At last I sorted my filing cabinet. It was a massive, old-fashioned hunk of steel that would take a crew of muscled bodies to get it out of my house. Given its contents, magic wouldn't budge it an inch; it was brilliantly, permanently warded (by myself), and even I couldn't cast a spell to lift it now. Instead, I moved my treasures into plastic tubs and stacked them up by the door. I wouldn't risk putting them outside the walls of my house until I had to.

Because I was leaving most of my belongings behind, I was done loading the Jeep in less than an hour. Sweaty and short-tempered, I paced around my kitchen and shoveled trail mix into my mouth as I tried to make my brain unravel the mystery of Bosko's death.

The genie. Percy. The ring. Flor. Raynor. Darius. The Protectorate. Seth. Birdie. Helen.

Helen. What had she found out for me? If I was going to give her my staff, she was going to have to work for it. I picked up the phone and hit her number.

"Do you realize what time it is?" she snapped.

"You picked up right away," I said.

"This is my thinking time," she said. "I don't like to be disturbed."

"I was thinking too. I thought of you. What have you learned for me?"

"I hear the town you live in is about to become even less hospitable than it has been to date," she said. "What kind of precautions have you taken for your payment to me?"

"Gee, Helen, I didn't know you cared so much about me. I'm fine, thanks. I've got the Jeep loaded up, ready to go."

"I of course encourage you to continue the hunt for knowledge, but maybe you could move the staff to a safer spot. There's a shipping store in Riovaca that takes odd-sized items."

I stopped pacing around my kitchen, struck by her callousness. Of course she was mercenary and drove hard bargains, but I'd thought we had something stronger between us. A mutual respect, a camaraderie, a warm alliance. More than my own absent, anonymous mother, she'd been there for me during my lonely young adulthood. I'd had to pay her, but wasn't that better than nothing?

"You could just hide it a few miles up the road in the forest and wrap a protective enchantment around it for a few days," Helen continued. "Just tell me where. My phone has this thing on it that can read location links. Cast a spell above it with one of those bags of herbs I've given you, maybe that cast-iron frying pan, and I'll be able to see through the enchantment. Even if you don't make it, I should be able to find it."

I sank into a chair at my kitchen table. She didn't really care about me. I'd been too eager for scraps, being grateful for whatever minimal assistance she'd given me, thinking it actually meant she cared.

What a dope.

"What have you learned about Percy?" I asked coldly. "The more useful your information, the more likely I'll survive and you'll get the staff."

"Can't you just hide it—?" she began.

"No. Tell me what you've learned now."

She huffed lightly into the phone. I heard birds chirping in the background, and I could picture her outside on her deck, looking up at Diamond Heights and Sutro Tower. She'd built quite a cozy fortress of solitude in her old Victorian, trading in knowledge, hearth magic, and influence to pay for it all, and there was a time when I'd thought that was what I'd wanted too. Just my own space. My work. My art. A source of income to pay for things that didn't cost me too much emotional or physical toil.

But hearing the callousness in Helen's voice, I saw my dream differently. How lonely it was. How pathetic and sad to only interact with other people in a commercial, selfish, unemotional way.

I didn't want to be Helen when I grew up. She was no better than Jen Bardak, an inhuman spirit forever bound by buying and selling. Humanity was better than that. All of us, witches or no, were forged in that magic.

Remembering Birdie's caring voice, the love she'd always been quick to share, a warm flush came over me, bringing tears to my eyes.

And how about Seth? He was angry with me, but he was alive, he was safe. I'd done that for him just because it had been too painful not to. Brightness was powerful in a way Shadow could never overcome.

I was running out of time. "Well?" I asked.

My tone must've broken through to her, because she replied in a more humble, agreeable voice. "Percival Tuff was a student of the Steelgrass School when he was a teenager," she said. "Up in Oregon—I don't think you ever spent any time there. It was never much and it's closed now. Your father wouldn't have wanted to be associated with it. I have a friend whose wife used to work as an herbalist there. She remembers Percival."

"And?" I asked.

"Kurt Bosko killed a teacher there who'd been a favorite of the students. Unfortunately for the school, when Bosko put a silver stake in his heart, his entire class saw him turn into a charcoal briquette."

"Unfortunately for more than the school," I said. "The kids witnessed a brutal killing."

"It was a history class," Helen said. "They'd thought the teacher was nonmagical. Just one of those guys who learns about witches and sticks around. He'd taught human history with an emphasis on the magical. Kids loved him."

"Including Percy?"

"Especially him. Word was Percival was a big fan of the demon teacher. The other teachers liked him too, which should've tipped them off right away—regular teachers usually hate the popular ones. They get all the love."

"If I were a parent of one of those kids, I'd pull them out the next day," I said. "Is that why the school closed?"

"Bosko convinced most of them it was the best lesson they'd ever have for their entire educational career," she said. "No, the school closed in spite of the killing, not because of it. Witch parents draw the line at schools being stupid enough to put a demon on faculty."

So, Percy had a reason to carry a grudge. But had he had the guts to actually kill him? And why now, after all these years?

While I was still talking to Helen, Raynor broke in somehow and kicked her off the line. One moment I heard Helen's voice suggesting I wouldn't want a demon teaching any theoretical child of mine if I were a parent, and the next moment I heard Raynor apologizing to Helen for cutting in but suggesting she get her nose out of Protectorate business if she didn't want to spend her sunset years in the Mojave.

"Hey," I said. "I was talking—"

"I'm taking you off the case," Raynor said.

"What? After one day? Right. Listen, I've learned Percy had reason to kill Bosko," I said. "I think his timing was because of the ring. He couldn't bear to watch him kill again, and he knew the ring and the job in Silverpool would lead to more killing. So he used some magic we didn't know he had, killed Bosko, and took the ring. He took the ring because he knew some other agent would just take his place and use it to k—"

"Stop. Forget what I told you. Leave it to us."

"But I'm so close—"

"I'm only going to say this once, and I'm wrapping it with a spell to hide the fact we ever spoke. Got it?"

A chill ran across my shoulders. Was I finally on the right track? Raynor knew more than he'd been able to tell me. Something involving powerful players in the Protectorate. Did Percy have connections? Somebody from his old school? "Got it," I said.

"As soon as I hang up, you're going to say goodbye to your gnome friend, get in your car, and start driving," he said. There was a long pause. "Agreed?"

He didn't specify *where* I would drive. Right now I felt an urgent need to go to the winery and confront Percy. "Agreed."

He sighed long and loud into the phone. "I was forced to tell the Protectorate that the opal ring, which was entrusted to Protector Bosko on the day before his death, was missing from the trunk in his room when we discovered the body."

"Percy took it," I declared, seeing my theory unfold.

"No," Raynor said. "I did."

I fell silent, reeling with disappointment. I'd been so sure. "When?"

"When nobody was looking," he said. "I think it's for the best if it goes missing permanently, don't you think?"

I leaned against the kitchen counter. I'd been sure it was Percy. But if Raynor had the ring, and Percy hadn't killed him for it, then… my theory fell apart. "Maybe Percy just couldn't take it anymore, and he snapped. Silverpool seemed remote, as good a place as any to do away with his hateful master."

"Forget it. Nobody cares who killed Bosko. If it was his app, if it was a demon, if it was you. They don't care. He'd been a loose cannon for years, making a lot of powerful witches uncomfortable. They made him Protector to get him out of the way. Now that he's dead, even better."

"Could one of those guys have killed him? Is this a cover-up?"

"Stop searching for conspiracies and see the obvious: Bosko made lots of enemies, and one of them caught up to him." Raynor let out a frustrated grunt. "Now New York wants to look as if they've done something without actually working at it. Burying a distant wellspring is easier than tracking down the dozens, possibly hundreds of enemies Bosko made over the years."

"But just yesterday, you wanted me to do it."

Raynor sighed again, loud and long. "I'd thought you'd have more time. Silverpool is my jurisdiction," he said. "They really hated Bosko. I didn't realize how many witches had a well-known motive for killing him. Some of those mages are powerful and would like to be off the hook as soon as possible."

"So if they're innocent, let me prove it," I said. "Give me a few days at least."

"Sorry, Alma. I tried. It's too late. They want to blame it on a demon and close the case. Destroying the town is an easy way to end the investigation." I heard him sniff the herbs he liked up into his nose. "They're moving in today. In fact, it may have already started."

Chapter Thirty-One

I grabbed my staff and ran outside. The morning sky was the wrong color. Instead of a pale blue or yellowish gray, it was orange. And I smelled smoke.

Jogging to the driveway, I searched the sky to see if I was overreacting. Maybe a neighbor was barbecuing their breakfast. But no—a plume of liver-brown smoke rose up from behind the trees to the north.

They were going to *burn* us out? *Today?*

I ran in and called Birdie. In spite of her promises, I had to leave a message. "Leave now! The hills are on fire!"

Random had been restless ever since I started packing up the car, and now he was pacing and whining near the door. Concerned he might bolt in fear, I put a leash on him and locked him in the car before I ran out with the plastic storage cases of my strongest magic.

How could they burn the forest? The buildings? All the animals, humans, and fae were going to be driven away, not just demons and witches.

With the Jeep packed, I returned with my lungs burning to the backyard to say goodbye to Willy. But the area about the redwood tree was empty, and he didn't appear when I called for him.

The thought of leaving him behind without a word made me pound my staff into the ground near the tree. Those arrogant, shortsighted witches. So much loss and destruction for something so stupid as an institution's reputation. The Protectorate had lost its way, assuming anything it did was for the benefit of humankind just because it benefited itself.

"Willy!" I shouted again. "I'm sorry!"

If he heard me, he didn't want me to hear him. Shaking with anger, I sprinted to the Jeep, dropped my staff in the passenger seat, and patted Random to soothe him. He'd licked and fogged the windows trying to get out.

This was wrong. Scaring my dog was wrong. Scaring my gnome was wrong. Scaring me was easy, but it was also wrong.

Somebody had to stop this. The smoke was over the ridge, showing the fire hadn't yet struck town. There was still time. But I couldn't leave Random alone. Was Seth— No, I'd have to ask Birdie.

Just as I put the Jeep in reverse to drive to her house, I saw her pull up behind me in the road, honking and waving as if we were going to the beach.

The beach would be perfect. Random loved the beach.

"Good news, buddy," I said to him, scratching his cheeks. "Birdie's here." I grabbed his leash and pulled him with me out to Birdie's SUV.

She waved again, smiling, and rolled down the window. "Time to go, right? I thought so. It's terrible, but at least it looks like you're packed." She frowned at Random. "This smoke can't be good for him. Where are you—?"

I opened her back seat, half-filled with her belongings, and pushed Random inside. He was worried, dancing on the seat and trying to follow me, so I latched the leash to the seat and slammed the door.

"Take him to the beach," I called to Birdie. "Drive west!"

Birdie shook her head, her smile vanishing. "But— You—"

"I'll follow in a few minutes!" I waved at her, avoiding eye contact, and ran back to my car. As I backed up, I glimpsed her face, still protesting. "Please? The beach! Thank you!"

Just in case she tried to follow, which would only put her in more danger, I cast an enchantment over her Toyota that should make her think driving to the coast was her idea, just like it usually was. Random's presence at her side would enhance the illusion.

It was a very short drive to Cypress Hardware.

Chapter Thirty-Two

Would the genie stop the fire to save her store? I didn't think so, not with the Protectorate having lit the match, given her fear of exposure. But for a *price*—a higher price than my silence—maybe she would interfere. I'd have to convince her. I couldn't bear to watch Silverpool burn.

I pulled into a parking spot and cast a spell around the Jeep to hide it. Birdie was about to drive by, and I didn't want to risk distracting her from her desire to go to the beach, but I also needed to protect the contents. A tilted sign nailed to a lamppost in front of my bumper warned about leaving valuables unattended in your car, and all of mine would be inside the Jeep.

All but one. I reached behind the passenger seat and snapped open the top box. The torc rested inside its velvet bag on top of my baby blanket, a jewelry box, bottles of well-spring water, and a chunk of my house's window trim.

Please, I asked all things Bright in the universe. Please help me fix this.

I got out and locked the car, setting up several wards

around it, wards that wouldn't be enough to stop wildfire, and jogged over to the sliding glass doors of the main entrance. The smoke filled my lungs; unaccustomed to running, I coughed. Darius was right; I needed to walk more.

There should've been a crowd of people coming in and out of the big hardware store with supplies, residents and emergency responders shouting at each other to hurry, asking for help, but it was dark and quiet. Only the smooth-moving traffic on the road behind me suggested anyone had noticed the fire.

Covering my mouth with the collar of my shirt, I peered through the glass into the darkness. Was that a glow in the back near the clearance patio supplies?

"Hello, Jen," I said softly but urgently. "I've got a deal for you."

I was about to break the most important rule of negotiating with a genie: not acting in a moment of crisis. It would be so easy for her to take advantage and walk away.

Was I willing to risk my life to save a tiny town filled with misfit humans and supernatural oddballs in the forgettable edge of nowhere?

Of course I was.

Leaving the torc in its velvet bag—it was dangerous to remove it too soon, because she might confiscate it and make her own terms—I tapped it against the glass.

I waited, breathing through my shirt to filter the smoke, but nothing happened. Behind me, the flow of traffic moved east, toward the winery, toward the freeway to San Francisco, to civilization, where people had been making terrible decisions since the beginning of time.

When I moved the torc to strike the glass a second time, it swung through open air. The doors had vanished. I glanced behind me at the orange sky for courage, then stepped into the store. Given the daylight and row of windows, it was impossibly dark, and I had to wait for my eyes to adjust. The glow led me to the place she'd been before, but now the patio throne room was a rainbow-colored hammock supported by a freestanding gold frame. The genie held a bottle of Russian River beer in one hand and a vape pen in the other as she reclined in the hammock, wearing denim shorts and a tie-dyed sweatshirt. One shapely leg, barefoot, dangled over the side.

Although my limbs were shaking with the urge to flee—I felt as if the blaze was going to sweep down the hills and ignite the first houses on the ridge any minute now—I forced myself to sit on a tilting recliner with padded arms and two extra-large cupholders. I couldn't rush. She could probably feel my accelerated pulse, knowing I was an easy mark, but I had to control myself.

I leaned back in the recliner, holding the torc in my lap. "There seems to be a bit of a fire up in the hills," I said casually.

She lifted the pen to her lips, nodding. "Seems like it."

As my eyes adjusted to the gloom, I realized that in spite of her recreational posture, her facial expression was miserable behind the billowing white vaping smoke.

I played with the velvet cord holding the bag closed. If she'd sensed what was inside, she hadn't let on. "Can you do anything to stop it?"

She lifted her beer and sipped it, then shook her head. "Can't pay my own price. Paradox in the space-time continuum."

"That's from *Star Trek*."

She shrugged. "Art reflects life."

Her attitude was probably just a negotiating trick. She could snap her fingers and put out the fire any second; she just wanted all the humans to come in and offer her their treasures first. Win-win.

"I'd really tried to make a go of it this time," she said. "I thought I'd found a system that would work long-term for me and for my customers. Nobody would feel tricked by the evil jinn—we'd all walk away happy."

"You really can't help yourself?"

She lifted her legs up and curled into a ball. "That's my curse."

Watching her sink deeper into her hammock, the white smoke forming an opaque cloud around her entire body, I started to believe her. Maybe she really couldn't help herself.

I took the torc out of the bag.

The cloud of vape smoke vanished. She sat up, swinging both legs over the edge of the hammock. Suddenly she was wearing an expensive-looking black pantsuit, her feet shod in patent-leather ballet flats. "You'd offer such a thing?"

Smelling the burning forest outside, I swung the recliner into a more upright position. It wobbled, but I clung to the armrests to hold myself up. "Yes. The torc in exchange for— we'd have to negotiate exactly what. I haven't agreed yet. Something to protect the town."

"But why? You don't own your house. You don't particularly care for the springwater. You have a car. You could use the torc at a different wellspring. You're free to leave and start over somewhere else."

"Aren't you? You're a genie."

She brushed lint off her shoulder. "Yes, well. You see, I have a few geographical limitations at the moment."

"You're stuck here?"

"This store is my power and my prison. Like a lamp in the stories, I am rather... imprisoned." She lifted her chin proudly. "At the moment."

"How long is this moment going to be?" A moment in genie time might be a century. For me to negotiate safely, I needed to know what her limitations and motives were.

"There is a small matter of business that needs to be settled before I can depart." She touched the choker around her neck, then smoothed her hand over her hair with a sigh. "Unfortunately, it's unlikely to be resolved before that fire gets here."

"Your curse won't let you save your own life?"

"Life?" She laughed, kicking the ground to swing the hammock. "You humans have life. What I have is something else."

I looked over my shoulder toward the entrance, imagining flames licking at the first houses up in the hills. "All right," I asked, "will you continue to exist however it is you exist now?"

"What do you care?" she asked. "Am I your new project, like the changeling?"

Clutching the torc with one hand, I clambered out of the lawn chair and stood in front of her, my throat burning with smoke and anxiety. I could simply offer the torc to extinguish the fire, but she'd said something important. She was imprisoned because of unsettled business. Like me, in a way. I needed to prove who killed Bosko, not just put out this fire, or the Protectorate would come back and do it again, and in her reluctance to interfere, I couldn't count on her indefinitely. The torc was valuable, but it wasn't as if I was offering the ultimate price: my life.

Life. There had already been one life given. "Did you make a deal with Kurt Bosko?" I asked suddenly. "Was that why he died?"

"Is that what you *wish* to know?" she asked sweetly.

I quickly put the torc under my jacket. Holding her gaze, I unfastened a beaded bracelet and held it out to her.

She shook her head.

I clutched the bracelet in my fist. I wouldn't give her my beaded necklace, which held strands of my own hair and could give her power over me. The car had a few items she might value, but there was no time to run out and get them, especially without any guarantee she'd take them.

The copper ring. Raynor would be annoyed with me, but I had no choice. I slipped it off my finger and extended it on my palm. I needed to ask a better question than a simple yes or no. "Who—?"

She flung up a hand. "Speak carefully. I can't tell you about any fulfilled wish that has been paid for. That copper is quite nice, but it's not enough to loosen my tongue completely." Stroking her neck, her eyes held mine, unblinking and intense, as if she was trying to tell me something.

Maybe in a strange way we were on the same side. I just had to find a way to make it an equal exchange for her to be able to deal with me.

My mind raced, trying to function under the pressure. Percy could've made a wish for Bosko's death, then hidden it with his mind magic from probing. But if she'd done that for him, he must've offered something of great value. The opal ring?

No, Raynor had the ring.

Watching Jen's fingers play with her red choker as she sipped her beer, acting as if she had all the time in the world, the gears in my brain finally began to turn.

Click. A memory of a fairy house in the vineyard. The way Flor had stopped on the path for a moment as if she'd seen it too.

Click. The red hair bow Flor had worn on the night before Bosko's death, the same color as the velvet choker around Jen's neck today.

Click. If the genie had killed Bosko, Flor's alibi was irrelevant. And if Flor had better fairy sight than I did—she'd been studying fae for years in countries I'd never visited—she might have detected the jinn's presence at Cypress Hardware when she arrived.

And if she was demon printed like me and Raynor... She'd feared exposure. I didn't know why she'd risked working for a man she'd already witnessed using the ring to kill, but I believed she had. I'd been there when she saw Percy bring the ring and give it to Bosko. Right afterward, Bosko had sent her out to find him a meal, and she'd walked up and down Silverpool streets, unsure what to do. That was the panic I'd felt in her trail around town—not about the food, but about her career, maybe her life.

And then, outside the hot dog truck, she'd had an idea. She'd gone into Cypress and made a wish.

I remembered something the genie had said on my first nightly visit. *You witches are strangely nocturnal, aren't you?* Yes. Flor had visited her on the night before Bosko's murder. Why hadn't I considered that?

And something else the genie had said. *Every once in a while, a human figures out I'm here.*

Honestly, had the genie done something to my head to keep me from seeing the obvious? I set the ring on a patio table between us. "Did you kill Kurt Bosko to fulfill a wish made by Flora Werner, and what payment did she offer?"

"Are you sure you want to offer your treasure?" she asked. "I will be unable to tell you the truth about any wish that has been fulfilled and paid for. You might not know if it's the truth or not."

She was trying to scare me, but with Bosko dead, I could risk giving up the copper ring. "I repeat my question. I wish to know if you killed Bosko because of a wish Flor made, and what she promised to pay you in exchange."

Jen nodded once with visible satisfaction, then leaned forward to take the ring. "Yes. It was Florence Werner's wish that Protector Kurt Bosko be permanently unable to implicate her with having any so-called demon ancestry or damage her career in any way, forever and ever." She slipped the ring on her finger and admired it. "She assured me an unusual trinket would be in the room, one that didn't actually belong to him, and it could be mine. In a few days or weeks, his ownership would've been strong enough to make it his. But he'd only had it less than a day."

"She didn't ask you to kill him? Just that he be unable to implicate her?"

"At first, no. But when I suggested that the only 'permanent, forever and ever' cure for a human like that was death, she said nothing."

"But she never actually said 'kill'?"

"She knew what she was doing. I'm a genie. She made a wish." Jen stretched her arms wide. "Look around. My store fulfills the material needs of every human in this town. How do you think I manage that? I don't need to hear them say it in words. I don't interrogate people when they walk in the door. My customers come in with a wish in their heads. In fact, oftentimes they don't even know what it is they're looking for. But luckily, they also walk in with a method of payment." She made a graceful gesture toward the registers at the front. "It works beautifully."

I thought back to what she'd said earlier, about wishes that hadn't been paid for. "You're telling me this because you didn't get the ring," I said. "You're waiting to collect."

"In my eagerness to provide quality service, I killed him before I claimed the ring." Her lips pressed together. "It was not in the room as she'd promised. The debt remains unpaid."

"Why didn't you just… take it from the person who had it?" I thought it might've been Percy, but I wasn't sure. If he'd taken it, he'd returned it before Raynor looked through the trunk.

"She'd promised it would be in the room. It was not." Jen gave me an incredulous look. "I can't just steal things from one person to make another one happy. There are *rules*."

"Rules," I repeated. I didn't trust her rules. They seemed to result in people dying.

She scowled and tore the velvet band from her neck. "I never should've allowed her into the store, but the witch knew a few unusual words to summon me. She'd done her research."

"That's her specialty," I said.

"The price must be paid." She saluted me with the hand wearing the copper ring.

"But why did you risk killing a Protector when you fear exposure so much?" I asked. "You must've known killing Bosko would bring more Protectorate attention here."

"Once summoned, I'm not at liberty to refuse a good deal. The ring is quite valuable, especially to your kind. Extremely valuable." Her gaze dropped to the region of my jacket where I'd hidden the torc. "Like what you have there. So? Are we ready to make another deal?"

Chapter Thirty-Three

I put the torc on the table next to the yellow sticker advertising a sixty percent discount. Knowing what had happened to Bosko, I needed to be especially careful about how I worded my wish. Silverpool was in danger from a fire—but extinguishing it might only delay its destruction from some other method. Protecting it from all damage would be too risky, causing all kinds of unpredictable magic to be unleashed: the inability to enter or leave, for instance, or the death of anyone with dangerous thoughts.

"You said once you wanted your customers to be happy," I said. "I'm worried I might fall into a trap and wish for something I'd regret."

She shrugged. "I do my best," she said, throwing the red band next to the torc. "But remember what they say. Perfect is the enemy of the good."

Great. A genie quoting inspirational posters. But the smell of smoke was getting stronger, reminding me of how little time I had. "You've gotten to know people here pretty well. When you execute my wish, whatever I ask for is always going to be within the boundaries of the motives, values, and welfare of humans who live in this town." I took a deep breath, hoping that would limit any unintended damage. "My wish is to protect the town from unnatural, magical destruction, but that ordinary, limited damage is part of life and should proceed."

She stared at my mouth, hanging on every word. A faint crease formed between her eyebrows, warning me of a flaw in my request.

"Except for wildfire," I added. "Protect the town from that too, even if it's natural." Because at this stage, based on magical technicalities I could only imagine, the expansion of the fire set by the Protectorate could be dismissed as natural.

Her frown vanished. The corners of her lips curved up, her eyes sparkled, and her posture straightened as if pulled by a string. Casting aside her beer and vape pen, she jumped out of the hammock, picked up the torc, and faded into the shadows.

Then her voice came out of nowhere, enveloping me like vape smoke. "Don't forget," it whispered. "Trust *nobody*."

I froze, my heart pounding, afraid of what she might do. Had I put enough limitations on my request? Maybe I should've specified *which* humans she should consider when measuring motives, values, and welfare. Those who had settled in Silverpool weren't the most collectivist social butterflies on the planet. Were my quiet neighbors actually secret misanthropes who collectively, on average, desired the rest of us to explode in a puff of smoke, never to bother them again?

Speaking of smoke…

I hurried outside to see if there had been any change in the color of the sky.

Yes. It was a clear, bright blue from the tops of the trees along the ridge to the roofs and utility poles of downtown.

The air was clean, as crisp as the coast, and smelled of damp earth and evergreen trees.

Relief rushed through me. Something about fire was worse than any demon attack. It had no motive but to consume and destroy, growing more powerful with each inch it traveled.

But the genie hadn't stopped the exodus, only the fire, and the traffic along Main Street continued to flow smoothly, each car rolling at the same speed as before as if it were a freight train.

It was the witches who were leaving now, their belongings strapped on car roofs, into truck beds, and pulled behind in trailers. I saw the family that owned the taqueria in their catering van; the pink-haired witch in her nineties who I'd only seen online organizing food drives; the retired Protectorate agents with the B and B with private beach on the river. Everyone was leaving now, willing or not, just because Flor was ambitious, Bosko was a bigot, and Jen Bardak, who I liked more than either of them, was willing to let the world burn to obey her code of supernatural commerce.

Perhaps that was unfair; she'd said it was a curse. Perfect was the enemy of the good, even for the semi-immortal.

I got in my Jeep and headed for the winery, where I hoped Flor was with the rest of the agents. They wouldn't have evacuated until the last human had departed. They had to be upset the fire was out. Would Raynor, as the highest-ranking official, be blamed for the failure?

My trip to the winery was stalled by the flow of traffic; I had to cast a spell to force a gap big enough for me to slide between a red pickup and an unmarked white van, go over the bridge, avoid the suspicious gazes of the utility workers, and then turn left at the entrance to the winery.

The vineyard along the drive up to the house was overrun

with fae who had fled the fire, showing the estate had been sitting in a bubble of magical protection. Fairies danced and twirled in a cloud around the building holding the tasting room, wood dryads camped out along the barren vines, and a bridge fairy swam in the fountain, squirting water from his green, jagged-toothed mouth at the angry gargoyle, who in a show of impressive endurance, had escaped the house and crawled onto the top of a rose arbor.

I parked as far from the fountain as I could, then got out with my staff. As I recast the protective spells around my Jeep, I thought how Darius would've told me I should've left it at Cypress and walked. Thinking of him, I took out my phone to send him a text, then found he'd sent me several messages within the past ten minutes in increasing urgency.

I'm coming over, his last message said. *Tell the gnome to go easy on me.*

I'm at the winery, I wrote back. *Fire seems to be out.*

Even if I'd wanted to tell him my role in that one, the genie had made that impossible. Nice of him, though, to risk his life to come rescue me, even if he'd only been following orders.

As I turned away from the Jeep to walk to the main house, I saw a black Audi sedan parked between two black SUVs. Flor was here.

I had no way of proving she'd been responsible for Bosko's murder even if I'd been able to talk about the genie. But if I wanted to prevent the Protectorate from new draconian measures in Silverpool, I'd have to find a way to get her on the hook somehow.

The smallest fae—a yellow-and-green type, smaller than moths—fluttered in a cloud under the rose arbor leading to the fountain. The gargoyle was still there, flinging insults and magical firebombs at the bridge fairy. When one of his bombs missed the fairy in the fountain and struck a patch of dried grass, it burst into fire. At that moment Flor strode out from behind the house and, after putting out the fire with a quick extinguishing spell, aimed directly at the gargoyle and blasted him off the arbor. He fell to the ground in his natural state: a jade figurine. Nodding in satisfaction, Flor spun toward the fountain and hexed the bridge fairy too.

Her perfect aim confirmed she was able to see him as clearly as I did. My own ancestry was a mystery, but I accepted that somewhere in my family tree was a man or woman who had been demon possessed, leaving their mark on me. Did Flor know which ancestor of hers had been possessed? Was it a family secret she'd known about for years, or had it been the shock that sent her into a breakdown when we were at school?

The moment Flor's hex struck the bridge fairy, every fae in the region fled. The cloud of tiny fairies under the arbor dispersed for a second like an explosion before drawing back together and flying off to the trees. The bridge fairy, limping from Flor's hex, crawled out of the fountain and ran across the dry, exposed earth—a habitat bridge fae usually avoided at all costs.

The crunch of tires on gravel made me turn around.

I stared in shock at Birdie's RAV4 turning in to a parking spot just behind me. She saw me through the window and waved.

I strode over, angry because I was afraid. "What are you doing here?"

Smiling, she climbed out of the car. "I can't leave you to face this alone. What kind of friend would I be then?"

Birdie shouldn't be here. It was too dangerous. "I put a spell on the car," I said. "How did you break it?"

She patted the beaded chain around her neck that I'd made for her. "You're a good teacher."

Regretting our lessons, I looked into the Toyota. It was filled with belongings but not my dog. "Where's Random?"

"He's with Seth," she said. "Don't worry. He brought him to the beach until this blows over."

A black fairy the size of a monarch butterfly fluttered past my nose. I spun back to Flor, who was still standing by the fountain, rotating in place with her hands extended. Every fairy, dryad, and troll had disappeared. And if I couldn't see them, that meant they'd fled the area. Even the vineyard was bare of the larger fae I'd seen when I arrived.

What had she done to them? I thought back to the moment she'd struck the troll. She hadn't been aiming at them, but they'd fled in terror.

Terror. Maybe Flor wasn't just demon *stained*, but…

No. She never would've taken a job with Bosko if she was a demon, especially with the opal ring so close.

She'd studied around the world. She must've learned tricks and secrets of the fae that others didn't know. I was no expert myself, preferring instead the botanical arts, but she had a passion for them. She loved them enough to have been willing to kill Bosko, just to study them at Silverpool.

Flor lowered her hands and began walking toward me.

Chapter Thirty-Four

Gripping my staff, I turned to Birdie. "Go. It's not safe." I didn't think Flor would do anything—she didn't know her secret was blown—but I couldn't be sure.

Birdie shook her head, her expression serious now. "No way."

I spoke tightly in a low whisper. "Please, it'll be easier for me if you leave. I won't have to worry—"

"Alma?" Flor called out behind me. "Darius was looking for you." She continued to approach, pulling something out of the pocket of a silver-embedded jacket.

I put my hand on Birdie's arm, my breath coming faster. "At least go inside."

Ignoring me, Birdie looked over at Flor, her head tilting curiously. "Isn't that your friend?"

I thought of the genie's whisper: *trust nobody.* "Not anymore," I muttered. "People change."

"I don't think so," Birdie said. "You just get to know them better."

Flor walked under the arbor, touching up her hair bow,

which today was a bright green. The black-and-silver jacket, dark jeans, and black boots provided a sinister contrast to the preppy color. The item in her hand wasn't a weapon, but car keys. She aimed the fob at her Audi, which chirped.

She was leaving.

I realized that I might not have another chance to confront her. She'd traveled the world; she could be out of the country in hours, out of my reach. Without evidence, the Protectorate wouldn't waste time or resources chasing her down.

But with the genie's wish, I didn't need to prove Bosko's murder to the Protectorate anymore. I could let her go. Had she really murdered him, just making a wish?

Yes, I believed she had. She'd murdered a man and might do it again. The Protectorate needed to know.

For enough power to force a confession, I could tap into Birdie's natural power even if she didn't know the spell herself. And my house was just close enough to amplify the power of my staff.

Flor paused in front of us, just out of arm's length. "Why haven't you evacuated?" She studied Birdie, obviously non-Protectorate. "Everyone should be feeling it."

"I feel it," I said. "Though it's better in here. The winery is protected, right?"

Flor looked around at the sloping vineyard. "Just around the house. The fae were swarming, but they seem to have gone now."

"Seem to," I said.

"Maybe they noticed the forest wasn't on fire anymore," Birdie said cheerfully. "Boy, that was terrifying, wasn't it? I'm so glad you guys put it out."

Flor frowned at me. "It wasn't the Protectorate who put it out."

I used my staff to wrap me in a veil of truthfulness.

"Maybe New York changed its mind," I said. "Realized it was overkill."

Her probe rolled over me, prodding at the edges of my words, searching for deceit, but I'd made a suggestive statement that was too slippery to pin down.

"They sent Raynor up here to find out what happened," Flor said. "He's on his way now."

I glanced at the keys she was holding. "So why are you leaving?"

She flung up her hands and let out a loud, exasperated sigh. "They don't need me here anymore—can you believe that? Fired, basically. I'll be lucky if they give me my old job back. Bosko's death will haunt me forever. He never even made me an apprentice, but it won't matter. No other mage will want me, not in this country." Her voice was loaded with the self-pity she'd expressed after the murder, but now I knew better. She did feel sorry for herself, that was true, now more than ever—but only because she'd felt killing Bosko had been necessary for her own survival and she resented the consequences. And now she was already laying the groundwork for an excuse to leave the country.

"You should stay here and show them how dedicated you are," Birdie said with surprising career advice. I'd avoided talking about my years in the Protectorate, and she couldn't know much about it. "If you leave now, they'll think you're only looking out for yourself."

I caught Birdie's eye. Did she know something? I'd made a bad habit of underestimating her. "I agree," I said. "Especially with Raynor on the way. If he sees you here, helping out, he can put a word in for you."

And he could take her into custody, or at least prevent her from going too far.

Where was Darius? The two of us had made an awkward team because of conflicting values, but if we were working together, we could be impressive. If I had his help, I could hold Flor until Raynor arrived. But he wasn't here and hadn't replied to my text.

Birdie put her hand on my arm, and I felt a sudden surge of energy. It was unsteady and untrained, but I could sense it tapping into the ground under our feet, connecting to the staff, filling me with power. Her bonds to Silverpool, to me, and my staff, were paying off. She couldn't control her power, but I could draw it out of her.

And she could be a valid witness to Flor's confession. Two witches against one—the Protectorate would believe it. But we had to act now.

Pulling the staff closer to my body, I pushed its tip against the driveway. The aggregate concrete had exposed pebbles—granite, I sensed—which I might be able to use to make her talk.

Flor moved to step past us. "Raynor isn't going to put a word in for me unless you tell him to," she said. "And we both know that's not going to happen."

I tried to look sweet and innocent. "What do you mean? Why wouldn't I?"

She shot me a contemptuous look. "Please. You'll be glad to get rid of me."

That seemed like the perfect excuse to try to get her to stay. "Hey, don't leave on that note. We might not ever see each other again. It's bad luck to part on a dark word." I moved my staff to my left hand and held out my right, smiling. "Please?"

Eyes narrowing, she hesitated. Then, maybe because Birdie had begun to eat a granola bar she'd had in her pocket, Flor decided it was best to act normal. She put her car fob in her pocket and put her hand in mine.

I'd centralized every resource into my personal magical well: my body, my beads, the staff, the herbs and amulets in my jacket pockets, the granite in the driveway, my distant house, my nearby friend. Now every spark of my power was swirling around the words I formed in my mouth. It would travel through the air to Flor's ears, into her brain and heart and skin—and hopefully compel her to tell the truth.

"Were you responsible for Bosko's death?" I asked.

Flor's eyes widened. She tried to pull away, but I held her. The drain on my power began to tug at me physically, making my limbs tremble.

"Answer the question," I intoned in a low growl, my voice altered by the magic pouring through me.

"No!" Flor shouted. She touched the green bow in her hair, and a stabbing pain ran up my arm, forcing me to release her hand.

Next to me, Birdie cried out and flung up her hands. A second later, she remained that way, arms up and unmoving with her eyes glued open. I realized she'd been hexed.

Flor pointed at me. "What made you think that?"

The genie's lock on my speech prevented me from alluding to her, even to one who already knew of her existence. "Tell the truth," I said, and again my voice was unnaturally low.

She gaped at me. Although we no longer shared skin contact, I clung to the tenuous bond between us. While I watched, shaking as I held the spell, the whites of her eyes became bloodshot. Sweat beaded on her forehead. Her mouth twisted to one side, lips pressing hard together. She was about to break.

But then she jabbed a finger at me. "You tell *me*. How could I have done it?"

Her seemingly rhetorical question landed in my ears like a bomb. Vision flashing, I lost control of the spell I'd cast over her and staggered back a step. As nausea roiled my stomach, I felt my throat close up. The urge to speak became overpowering, but it was battered by the simultaneous requirement to remain silent.

The hex I'd cast upon her was now acting upon me—and the genie's magic stood in the way. *Speak*, my own spell commanded. *Don't speak*, insisted a very powerful, alien force.

I was being torn in opposite directions. Never before had I felt so much pain—psychic, emotional, physical, magical. How could I fight my own magic without destroying myself?

Chapter Thirty-Five

I flung aside the staff, afraid Flor was using it against me somehow. The pressure to speak lessened slightly.

But then Flor stepped closer, her bloodshot eyes blazing. She turned her arm and pulled up her sleeve, exposing a gold cuff bracelet that emitted a white glow that was too bright to look at directly.

Whatever it was, it was the thing that had reflected my spell.

She touched the green hair bow, and another blast, harder than the first, struck me between the eyes.

My vision failed. Gravity ceased for a moment, and then in another, slower moment, I was floating and floating, and then it pulled my cheek against the cold, rocky driveway. Pain shot through my skull.

Vision returned. Head on the ground, I was staring sideways at Flor's shoes. Exposed toes, pink nail polish. A silver toe ring with a tiny ruby setting. The world seemed oddly peaceful, and then I realized I'd gone deaf.

I found the energy to tilt my head just enough to look

up. Flor's arm was raised, hovering above my face. She was about to strike me again.

Her voice, the only thing I could hear, was the same low command as before. "How do you think I did it?"

Tell her, you must tell her, my own voice insisted. *Tell the truth. You must tell the truth.*

I felt my jaw lock. Then my lungs stopped pumping. Trying to keep up with the panic building in my mind, my heart began to race, then tripped, wavered uncertainly, began to slow.

My own magic was pushing me to speak, but I *couldn't* speak. I would die if I didn't make her stop.

Suddenly I felt Birdie's hand on my cheek. She'd managed to break away from Flor's hex. Sound roared back into my ears.

"Alma," she said softly.

The agony eased. She was giving me just enough power to protect myself.

But then Flor lunged forward and picked up my staff. Because the command to speak was coming from me, and I'd used the staff, it momentarily increased the pressure building in my chest.

Her reflection spell was throwing every spark of my power back at me.

"Let it go," Birdie said. "I've got this."

My vision faded to a dim haze. How could she break Flor if I couldn't? Maybe if Flor was locked onto me completely, she'd have nothing left to fight a hex from another witch. But if Birdie's confidence was misplaced, releasing my power would make me completely vulnerable to the blast that was already causing my organs to fail.

While I continued to hesitate, I felt Birdie paw at my neck, claw her fingers around my beaded necklace, and tear it off.

Then her hands fumbled at my wrists, where I'd wrapped more of my beads, and tore those off too. She was removing the amplifiers of my power, lowering the magic blazing through me.

My next breath came more easily. I was able to focus my gaze on Flor and watch her furious gaze land on Birdie. "How—?"

Each beat of my heart brought my strength back to me. I rolled over, scrambled to my feet, and put an arm around Birdie to join our forces. "We have to get her to talk," I said. "It's not enough to fight her off."

"She almost killed you," Birdie said, gasping. "Who cares if she talks?" She turned back to Flor, and I felt power rush into her.

Of all the times for Birdie to discover her deep, personal well of magic, this could be a good one—I was very glad to be alive—but only if she could control it.

"She has to confess," I said. "For justice." The word felt right in my mouth. Yes, that's what I wanted.

Birdie hesitated, plainly conflicted, but then she nodded and turned to Flor. "Do it," she said. "Now."

I didn't have my beads, but I had my own natural, inborn power. Linking it with Birdie's untamed energy, I pointed at Flor. "Were you responsible for Bosko's death?" The granite pebbles in the driveway had left a residue on my skin, enough to enhance my spell. "Answer me!"

Flor's eyes bugged out. Her mouth opened and closed like a baby bird. Then she broke. "Yes," she gasped. "He's dead because of"—she whimpered—"me. I did it. Me. I killed him."

"Why?" I asked. Demanding she tell me *how*, which would blame the genie, would only cause her to collapse the way I had.

"The opal ring was going to... expose me as..." She snapped her teeth together, but another combined blast from me and Birdie broke them apart. "De… de… demon stained. It would've ruined everything."

The next question was for my satisfaction, not the Protectorate's; what she'd admitted already should be enough to convict her. "Why did you take the job if you knew he might get the ring again?"

"I'm not a demon!" she cried, still trying to fight the spell commanding her to speak. She writhed in place, her shoulders rising and falling, her hips swaying. "I thought the ring only exposed demons, like your father's bride! I'm a human being, a witch. It's not my fault my ancestor was possessed!"

If I goaded her, she'd keep talking, and the more I got her to say, the more convincing her confession would be. "He would've fired you," I said. "Or worse. You never would've gotten what you'd always wanted. Power and prestige. What you think you deserve."

Her writhing became more violent. "I do deserve it! I do!" Her furious glare was hard to look at. "I deserve it more than *you*!"

As she spat the last word, a beam of energy shot out of her wrists and struck me in the foot. My leg immediately lost sensation, and agonizing pain shot up my spine. Next my neck locked into a spasm, and a blistering headache spread from the base of my skull over my ears to my eyes.

Again, I lost my sight. I began to collapse.

Birdie's arm around my waist broke my fall, but then she released me.

"No," I said. "Don't let go. You need me. You need my power."

But she didn't seem to hear me. Had I even spoken aloud? The pain in my head was building, putting unbearable pressure on my eye sockets. I lifted my hands to my face and held them over my closed eyes as if that would prevent them from exploding.

An electric storm crackled near Flor, then an explosion. What kind of power did that witch have anyway? As impaired as I was, I could feel magic throbbing in the air between us.

Then I heard Birdie's voice. "Stop it," she said. "Leave Alma alone."

Flor screamed. The electric crackling rose in pitch, increasing painful to hear and then silent as it rose up into registers beyond human hearing.

Silence. My headache faded away. I heard a thud, a woman crying, and my own ragged breath.

Chapter Thirty-Six

My cheek was pressed against the driveway again. I cracked one eyelid open, afraid of bringing on more pain, but the pressure behind them had ceased. I opened them all the way and saw Flor's body in a crumpled heap in front of me. Her arms were flung apart, her face gazing at the sky. It was similar to the posture Bosko had taken in his own death.

Death?

I scrambled to my feet. My body was weak, but nothing serious. The crying I'd heard was Birdie. She was squatting down, arms around her knees, rocking back and forth on her heels.

"I killed her," she was muttering. "I killed her. I killed her. I killed somebody. I'm a killer. I killed her…"

I touched her shoulder soothingly before hurrying over to Flor's body. The eyes were open. Lifeless. The bow was a sloping pile of cinders in her hair. Like my beads, her bow had focused her power.

Just to be sure, I touched the skin beneath her ear. No pulse.

"I killed her," Birdie continued to moan. "I killed her. I'm a killer."

I hurried back to her and put my arms around her. "We both did. It's not your fault. She had some kind of mirroring spell that made all the magic too hard to control. It reflected back on her. She'd tried to kill me, and it killed her instead."

"I told her to stop and used magic to make it really, really work," Birdie said. "I put everything I had into it. It was like there was this really deep thing inside me that just popped open and blasted her."

"It's not your fault," I said. "She almost killed me. She would've killed you too. It was self-defense."

"I didn't think I could kill her," she said. "How could I have the power to kill her?"

I hadn't felt enough power coming off Birdie to have seriously hurt Flor, but she'd found it somewhere. There was enough magic centralized around the winery to disrupt the normal rules of balance, restrictions, and order. The fae had gathered nearby, though Flor seemed to have driven them off, and the Protectorate witches had gathered to set fire to the town. The amount of energy swirling around had made a passionate duel between witches very dangerous.

Poor Birdie. She'd worked up the courage to look at the body and was now crying again silently, covering her mouth with both hands.

"It's not your fault," I repeated. "You saved us. Thank you. You saved my life."

I looked over at Flor, who had stiffed a genie. That debt was now paid. Had Jen Bardak intervened? Was she watching us now, quietly content with the deal's closure?

"She hated you," Birdie said. "Why?"

"I don't think she really—" I began.

"No, I felt it," Birdie said. "She wanted you to hurt. It annoyed me."

"Me too." Shuddering, I brushed a piece of dirt off my cheek. "We're going to have to go to San Francisco for questioning. It'll take a long time, maybe overnight. I guess it's a good thing Random is with Seth."

Scratching her neck, she turned to look behind us. "Somebody's coming."

A black SUV was coming up the drive. Behind the wheel, Darius saw the two of us and scowled. He was driving as if he'd love to run over something.

"Let me do the talking," I told Birdie quietly.

She said nothing, which I appreciated.

He parked, got out, and came over to us, his face reflecting the moment he noticed Flor lying on the ground near the arbor. He'd looked irritated before; now he looked enraged. Pointing at me, he pulled out his phone and hit a button without looking at it.

"Talk," he said, holding my gaze.

"Déjà vu," I muttered.

"I'm in no mood for jokes," he said. He typed something quickly into his phone, then put it away. "Your gnome friend held me captive for over an hour. Seemed to think I'd been the one to set the forest on fire."

"Did you?" I asked. "Following orders?"

Ignoring me, he crouched next to Flor's body. "What killed her?"

"I did," Birdie said.

In the middle of pulling steel disks out of his pocket to place around the body—an investigation boundary spell—he stopped and slowly turned to look at Birdie. "You?"

She nodded, starting to cry again. "I'm really sorry. I don't know how it happened."

"Flor was trying to kill us," I said. "We defended ourselves."

"Successfully, it looks like," Darius said.

"I've got a bit of a headache," I replied. "Thanks for asking."

Darius shot me a look and walked over to Birdie. His tone softened. "Hi, Birdie. We're going to have to take you to our office in San Francisco."

Birdie sniffed. "That's what Alma said."

"If it was self-defense, you'll be able to come back home fairly quickly," he said. "If not…"

"It *was*," I said. "Don't scare her."

"Why would she attack you?" he asked. "Old high school grudge?"

"She killed Bosko and I made her confess," I said.

To Darius's credit, his expression barely changed. "I see."

"Birdie witnessed it," I added.

Darius looked at Birdie again. "Then you might be in San Francisco for a while."

She nodded. "Will it hurt?"

"Of course not," I said.

Darius looked at me, raising an eyebrow.

"I won't let it," I said firmly.

Birdie adjusted her sweater and turned toward Darius's SUV. "As long as you leave Alma alone, I don't mind. Is that your car?"

Darius thrust out a hand. "Wait for Raynor. He'll be here in a few minutes."

I bent over to pick up my staff.

"Leave it," Darius said. "We'll need that as evidence."

I thought of Helen, who'd hoped to own it someday. Well, she'd have to settle for springwater. Which reminded me—I didn't have the torc anymore to give her that either. Like Flor, I'd acquired a debt I couldn't pay. But Helen would be more reasonable than Jen Bardak. Probably.

"The Protectorate has no reason to bury the wellspring or close the town now," I told Darius. "You've got to tell everybody that. Tell the other agents or anyone out there trying to set the fire again."

Darius nodded, and I wondered if this was this how the genie would grant my wish. Through the fruits of my own labor.

Darius picked up my staff and studied it for a moment, hefting it up and down, probing its magic, tapping it with his fingers. Then he looked at me. "Your gnome won't let fire come within miles of this town. Didn't you know?"

Willy? I shook my head, hoping I looked as bewildered as I felt.

"How did you think the fire just disappeared?" he asked. "With all the smoke, too? Even if Cal Fire had flown in on helicopters and doused it with chemicals, the air would be smoky for hours at least."

The genie's hold on me froze my jaw shut. I shook my head again, adding a shrug.

"I saw him do it. He had me pinned to the ground like Gulliver, lecturing me about the crimes of my kind, how he 'wouldn't be tolerating it.'" Darius tapped my staff on the ground. "When the sky cleared, he danced around me to gloat."

If it weren't for the genie's power over me, I would've laughed. But because she must've wanted Willy to get credit for extinguishing the wildfire, my face was frozen in a serious, even apologetic expression.

"I'm sorry if he hurt you," I said. "I'll talk to him."

Mollified, he shook his head and put the staff down near the body. "It's not your fault," he said. "He was defending himself."

"Just like we were," Birdie said.

At that moment, a caravan of black SUVs came up the drive.

"Tell it to them," Darius said, returning to the body to finish the boundary spell.

Chapter Thirty-Seven

We were interrogated at the Diamond Street office in San Francisco for sixteen hours. Me in one room, Birdie in another. An Emerald mage from New York supervised the questioning while Raynor looked on.

I told them what I knew. Flor hadn't known the opal ring might expose her demon mark until she was stuck in Silverpool with the one man who was driven to destroy anyone like her. Her history of impatient ambition was well-known among the hiring team at the Protectorate—they had years of job applications, letters, and personal entreaties for promotions and apprentice opportunities—and it was easy for everyone to believe she'd kill to protect herself. Among the lofty, powerful witches who questioned her were the same priorities. They would've done the same thing, although nobody could say so.

But they couldn't figure out how she'd killed him. Most of the hours of questioning I went through were about Flor's powers—could she levitate? Apparate? When we'd been in school, had there been a visiting teacher who had taught her something Shadowed, illegal, foreign?

I said no. I had no idea how she'd done it. But when I'd confronted her, she'd attacked me with powers I didn't know she'd had and almost killed me. With Birdie's help, we fought back, and she died. We hadn't meant to kill her, but she'd been using reflection spells of some kind. They noticed the four tattooed arcs around my left wrist but dismissed them as youthful vanity. They didn't realize that one of them had only appeared within the past day.

The genie's magic hid my secrets, made my lies effortless, and the mages' ability to detect them, impossible. They believed me completely.

Near dawn on Saturday, they reunited me with Birdie in the downstairs lobby, originally a living room and now a reception area. She looked tired but cheerful, and rushed over to greet me with a hug.

"That wasn't so bad," she said. "I didn't like the drink they gave me, though. It tasted like ashes, but spicy. Nasty."

"That's a truth potion," I said, giving the Flint watching us a hostile glare. He wore all gray and was in charge of making visitors feel small and powerless. Until he got the word, we wouldn't be able to leave. "How much of it did they give you?"

"Just one glass. That was bad enough."

They'd given me three. "I'd kill for a chocolate milkshake right now," I said.

The Flint's eyebrows went up.

"I'd kill and kill and kill," I said, showing him my incisors.

"Should you be doing that?" Birdie asked. "They seem kind of jumpy around here."

I sighed and sat on the maroon velvet sofa, which

reminded me of the genie, the hair bow she'd taken from Flor, and the recently emptied position of Protector in my beloved home town.

"They're done with us for now," I said. "Somebody is going to get stuck with driving us home. They're just arguing about who that's going to be."

I was hoping for Darius, who had given Raynor and the mages his report about my interfering gnome. I was afraid they were going to overreact as they did to all nonhuman beings who had the audacity to interfere in Protectorate affairs, especially near a wellspring, but I'd been unable to offer an alternative explanation for how the fire had been extinguished.

Percy walked into the living room and handed the Flint a piece of paper. "They're being released to me," he said. Then he waved a hand at us and walked to the front door. "Let's go. It's a long drive."

We jumped up and followed him outside. Next door on her stoop stood Helen, who pretended to be busy pruning the vining roses. It reminded me that although they'd given me my beaded necklace and bracelet, they still hadn't returned my staff, and I'd have to begin complaining to Raynor about it—after I was safely home and the town was officially off the chopping block.

Percy led us up around a corner and up a steep hill to his car, parked perpendicular to the road like the other vehicles. I got in the front seat, Birdie in the back.

"I'm going to sleep the whole way home," she said. "Hope you don't mind. I'm dead on my feet."

Percy backed out into traffic, a car honked and swerved around us, and he continued driving. "Speaking of dead," he said, not looking at me, "Flor is."

"Yes."

"Thanks to you," he said.

"Don't blame her, it was my fault," Birdie said. "I don't know what happened. I didn't know my own strength, I guess."

"You should work on that," he said.

His sour mood surprised me. "I didn't know you liked Flor," I said.

"I don't approve of killing." He swerved right on Diamond Street and hit the gas. The street rose sharply to a plateau for a block, then careened down again at Twenty-First into the Castro.

In the back seat, Birdie yelped and grabbed the handle above the window. Looking at her in the rearview mirror, Percy seemed to regret his aggressive driving and pumped the brakes.

When we'd slowed to a normal speed, I said, "We don't either. Especially not one of my oldest, dearest friends." Being interrogated by the Protectorate had put me in a lying mood.

He glanced at me. "I forgot about that." At the next stop sign, he cleared his throat and said, "Sorry."

I had the feeling I'd witnessed the worst of Percy's temper, and he was already back to his self-effacing, self-doubting self.

A perfect time to ask a few questions.

"Did you steal the ring?" I asked abruptly.

He braked, sped up, swerved around a cyclist. "Excuse me?"

"The opal ring. You stole it. Right?"

"The item entrusted to me on November the twenty-eighth should've been found in the room with Protector Bosko's corpse," he said.

"But before that, it was with you," I said. "Without your master's permission."

He pressed his lips together and began casting a spell that tugged at my thoughts like a catchy tune. Even with me prepared for it, his mind magic was strong enough to make me suddenly obsess about eating a burrito.

"Stop that," I said, throwing up a blocking spell, although I still craved the burrito. Food was much better in San Francisco than what I could get up in Silverpool. "They're done questioning me. I didn't tell them what you did. I just want to hear it from you."

He looked in the rearview mirror again. Although I'd blocked his spell from my mind, I hadn't protected Birdie. She'd fallen asleep with her head tilted back and her mouth half-open.

"I couldn't let him kill again," Percy said in a low voice. "I knew he'd use the ring as an excuse to go after perfectly decent, law-abiding, kindhearted…"

I waited a second before interjecting, "Demons?"

He gripped the steering wheel, and I had the impression he was frustrated he couldn't zap my brain to stop the threatening questions. "Individuals," he said. "Of all kinds."

"But then you put it back when you saw he'd been killed. You knew it would get you in trouble."

"I'd already lost my guts, just taking it for a few hours. All my adult life, I'd been working toward the moment I would finally have the courage to kill him. But year after year, I just couldn't do it. I told myself it was because I didn't want to lower myself to his level, but deep down I knew the truth: I was a coward." He maneuvered the car up and down the crowded four-lane route along Divisadero Street. "Then he got that ring and killed your father's bride. She was so beautiful. Your dad was happy. Who are we to interfere? To kill her in the middle of a sacred Circle? I tried to steal the ring after that. I knew he'd use it to track down and murder as many beings as he could and be rewarded for it, too. But

Raynor wisely locked it up. Bosko needed to find an excuse to get it again, so he took the Silverpool job. I doubt he would've stayed a year, but he'd get the opal, make it his, and find a way to keep it."

I was touched by his compassion for my father and Vera. He was the only Protectorate witch I'd ever met who shared my disapproval of knee-jerk demon killing.

"I tried to just… *not* bring it to him," Percy continued. "I almost threw it off the Golden Gate Bridge. But…" He pounded the steering wheel. "I couldn't do it. Even though I'd already met Flor and knew her secret—it was at the top of her mind, and I read it in her. I tried to warn her, but she wouldn't listen. I told her to find another job, that Bosko would be a terrible master to her. I didn't tell her why I knew it would be dangerous—"

"That you knew she was demon marked," I said.

"Yes, I didn't want her to worry about me knowing her secret," he said.

"I think you're lucky to be alive," I said. "If she'd known you knew she was demon marked, she might've killed you too."

"I don't believe that," he said. "She was sweet. Whatever she did to Bosko was in self-defense."

"The bow looked sweet, but it nearly killed me," I said. She'd fooled a lot of people over the years with her preppy little-girl look.

"So you say." He turned left onto Lombard, and we headed to the Golden Gate Bridge.

"That night, though, you did finally take the ring," I said.

"I realized he'd destroy her the second he shook her hand," he said. "I made him send her instead of me for takeout and then gave him more springwater than I usually let him have. One reason he keeps me around—kept me around, that is—was my ability to hold his addiction in check most of the time. I could stop the cravings. But some-times he had me turn that off and let him have a bender."

"When his guard was down, you took the ring," I said.

He nodded. "I took it with me to the moon party with my girlfriend. It was on the beach, and the setting and the enchantments of the party would put it completely out of tracking range."

Even the genie hadn't been able to find it, I thought.

"But then," he continued, "I changed my mind again. I convinced myself they would find me, give it back to him, and I'd lose the chance to get my real revenge."

"But he was dead," I said.

He nodded. "I put it back in the trunk and went for a drive, not sure if I should come back. Obviously I did. I've been terrified they'd find me out."

"You're safe," I said. "They know Flor—"

"I'm always safe," he spat out. "It's pathetic. Flor knew him for less than a week and took care of him. Bam. Just like that. The witch was dead. He'll never kill again. No thanks to me."

"She would've killed you too," I said. "She was just as much a monster as he—"

"I don't believe it. You're just rationalizing it so you don't feel guilty about killing her."

Even if it was me instead of Birdie who had killed Flor, I didn't think I'd feel guilty about it. Sad and angry, yes. Guilty? No. She'd almost killed me. I'd been about to run down the bright tunnel and discover the mysteries of the afterlife. "Her death was unintentional," I said. "I wish she were alive so she could face justice for what she did."

"The Protectorate doesn't care about justice," he said. "It's rotten to the core. I've resigned and am only driving up there again to get my stuff. My girlfriend and I are going to open a school in Oregon. A nice one for witch kids of all backgrounds. You won't need an old name or a lot of Protectorate connections to be treated well."

We were driving over the Golden Gate Bridge, the morning traffic heavy on the other side of the divider. The orange-gold beams of the bridge arched over our heads, heavy with fairies of all sizes, some naked, some dressed in furs or flowers, scattering into the air as we approached.

"Sounds really nice," I said. "I wish you well."

He patted the steering wheel, glancing nervously at me. "You aren't going to tell anyone what you know?"

"Know what?" I asked, eyes wide.

He frowned, shaking his head. "You're not what people say you are."

"Which people?"

"You know. At the Protectorate. They said you were too weak to kill demons. That you only got the job because of your last name."

"That's not all wrong," I said.

"You want people to think that. But it's not true. Flor is dead. Silverpool is saved. You could've had me sent to the Mojave, but you didn't—which you were sure to let me know." He pulled out a pair of sunglasses and put them on. "You lied through your teeth for sixteen hours to the most powerful Emerald mage in the Protectorate, who didn't realize it, and now you're headed back to a town with a wellspring that, once again, has no Protector."

"What did I lie about?" I asked.

"I don't know, but I could taste the omission in every word you spoke. They didn't feel it, but I did."

Had he felt the genie's lock on my tongue? I tried to sway him from his conviction that I had a secret. "It's true I never killed a demon," I said. "And it's true the Protectorate recruited me because I was a Bellrose."

He shook his head, staring at the road. "You might be a

Bright witch, but I hope I never see you again," he said. "You're scary."

Scary? Me?

I turned my head away, looking out the window at the tendrils of fog shimmering in the warm light of dawn.

I liked the sound of that.

Chapter Thirty-Eight

The evacuation spell in Silverpool had ceased by the time we arrived, but from the scarcity of cars on the highway into town, it seemed people were slow to realize they could return. It would take time for everyone to forget why they'd left, and Raynor had assured me they'd reach out and lure back those who needed help remembering, like the Souters.

At my request, Percy drove directly to the winery, where my Jeep was still parked near Birdie's RAV4.

"I guess this is goodbye," Percy said, opening his door.

I reached back and shook Birdie's knee. "Wake up. We're home."

It actually had been her home for a little while after she'd inherited it from Tristan, but she'd never moved in.

She stretched, yawned, and looked around. "Where are we?"

"The winery," I said, smiling at her sleepy face. "Your car is here from the other day."

"I can go now?" she asked.

"Free as a bird," I said. "I'll see you later. I want to get something inside. Will you be all right on your own?"

Birdie got out of the car. "This is where I killed her," she said, staring at the spot under the arbor.

"And where she almost killed me," I said.

With an unhappy grunt, Percy strode away from us to the house. With a shudder, Birdie turned around and walked to her car, reaching into her purse for her keys. "I'm glad we don't have to leave Silverpool," she said. "I kind of like it here."

Her understatement made me laugh. "Yes, me too," I said.

She yawned, got in her car, and drove away, waving. I waited until she was out of sight to go over to the tasting room. It was a Saturday, and in spite of the near destruction of the town the day before, it seemed to be open.

I walked inside and stopped when I saw the man in the apron behind the counter.

Darius.

"Is this my fault?" I asked, walking over.

He pushed a menu at me. "Probably. Raynor says I'm in charge of getting the town back to normal. New York doesn't want any of the other agents thinking too hard about what happened here. They're doing a combination of memory hexing and reassignments to cover up the incident."

I shook my head, disgusted with the Protectorate's aggressive tactics. "If any of those poor Flints come here and ask me, I'm not going to lie. I'll help them remember—even the times I was rough on them. Nobody should have their brain altered just for a job."

He tapped the menu and pushed it closer. "Raynor refused to help them, for what it's worth. They didn't like that at all."

I smiled, imagining how shocked the Emeralds must've

been to have Raynor, the famously tough demon hunter, take the side of his subordinates instead of his superiors.

I glanced over the list of wines, then up at the chalkboard, which usually listed the daily offering of crackers, cheese, olives, and chocolate, but today was wiped clean.

"No food?" I asked. I still hadn't gotten over that burrito fantasy.

Darius reached under the counter and handed over a half-eaten energy bar. "You can finish my breakfast for me."

I was hungry enough to accept it. "I'd like the most expensive bottle you have," I said, taking a bite. "Something rare."

"They don't have price tags. I'm just here for show."

I looked over the menu, flipped through it for the highest number, and showed him the name. "That one. Please."

He started to argue but stopped himself. "What do I care? You deserve it." He disappeared into the back for several minutes, then returned with two bottles. "One bottle isn't going to last you very long."

I reached into my pocket. "Do you know how to work the register?"

He waved that off. "Forget it."

"Thank you, but actually, I have to pay. At least for one of the bottles." I pushed my credit card at him. "If you don't know how to run it up, I can show you—"

He took the card. "I know how. I just thought you deserved an unofficial thank-you from the town of Silverpool." He scanned the bottle and swiped my card. "But you're too goody-goody for that. An Incurable Inability to break the rules."

I ignored his goading, took the bottles, and smiled at him as I turned to go. "Come by later and we can share one of these," I said. "I'll tell Willy to leave you alone."

"I'd rather drink a goblin's bathwater out of an old boot,"

he said. "No offense, but that gnome is a menace. I'm not going anywhere near your house ever again."

I saluted him with the bottles and went out to my Jeep, grinning.

Jen Bardak seemed as if she'd developed a taste for human luxuries. I drove to Cypress Hardware, noticed the coffee kiosk and hot dog truck were back in business, and went inside with one of the bottles.

I set it on the table near the hammock, then sat down in the tilting lawn chair from our previous meeting. Perhaps after the holidays, I'd have enough extra cash to buy it for myself.

"What now?" Jen asked behind me. "This is dangerous for both of us, you must know."

I rocked the chair up and down, imagining where I'd put it in my backyard. Maybe Willy would enjoy it too.

"I just have one question," I said. "I hope you like wine."

She was already holding it, stroking the glass. "Tristan said this was his best year."

"Will you accept it as payment for answering my question?"

Nodding, she perched on the edge of a vinyl-cushioned ottoman and waited for me to say aloud what was already in my mind.

"When was the first time Flor visited Cypress Hardware?" I asked.

"The week before your father's wedding," she said.

It all fell into place. Flor was not only responsible for Bosko's death, but for Vera's too. She'd wished to work in Silverpool as an apprentice to the new Protector, whoever he or she would be. Had she come to reunite with me, her old classmate, and see if I could put a word in for her? Or had she just come to see the fae, who had always fascinated her because of her special ability to see them? Either way, she'd come to Silverpool and ended up at Cypress Hardware, which was the only major retailer in town. Maybe she'd had a hot dog. Maybe she'd used the bathroom. But she'd sensed the genie's magic and made her wish.

"What did she pay you then?" I asked.

The genie stroked the red velvet choker around her neck. "It's cut from a very old piece of cloth," she said. "Almost as old as I am."

I nodded. It had been loaded with power like all those hair bows she'd worn.

That wish of hers had led to a series of odd coincidences: her invitation to my father's wedding, even though we hadn't been friends for ages; Bosko's arrival in San Francisco just as the opal ring had become available for borrowing; Bosko's presence at the wedding after he got the ring; Vera's existence as the bride. The series of events allowed Flor to step forward and prove her merit to Bosko, who gave her the job in Silverpool.

Her ambition had actually killed two people—Bosko and Vera. One of them happened to be a demon.

I climbed out of the chair and moved to leave. "Thanks. I'll try not to visit you again."

She stood up, holding the bottle. "This is worth more than those little questions," she said. "May I offer you a piece of advice?"

Chapter Thirty-Nine

I hesitated. Maybe she was having second thoughts about letting me walk around with her secret. "Is that a trick?" I asked.

She shook her head. "No. I'm incapable of lying." She looked around her store. "At least in here."

I debated the wisdom of taking her offer for another moment, but of course I wanted to know whatever she had to tell me. "If it is freely given with no further burden upon me, then yes, I'd like to hear it."

She cradled the bottle against her waist. "Trust no one."

I waited for more, disappointed. "That's it?"

She nodded.

"Thanks," I said. "I suppose it's always good to have my life choices reaffirmed."

Out from behind her, Random ran up between the aisles, dragging a leash. A clerk—I was relieved to see Samantha again, looking healthy—was chasing after him.

Random galloped over to me and jumped up to kiss me. Samantha, short of breath, asked, "Isn't that your dog?"

"Yes, how'd he get here?"

"He turned up during the fire," Samantha said. "I tried to call the number on his collar, but the phones were out. Jen and I fed him. Kept him safe. He's a sweetie."

I nuzzled Random's neck, soothing him as best I could, but he was frantic to be reunited. Thanking them both, I took the leash, distracted by Random's continuing wriggling, jumping, and whining, and went out to my car. I was going to feel a lot better once my belongings, my dog, and myself were back safe at home.

I wondered if Seth was still angry with me. Or if I'd ever see him again. Had he left Random to roam free, or had something else separated them?

Speaking of Seth—was that him at the coffee kiosk in the parking lot? No, it was a different guy. Good-looking, though, and talking to... Oh, it was Birdie. They both had coffee cups and were laughing about something. The day was sunny, the air smelled like clean, damp forest, no hint of smoke. The cars along Main Street were flowing inward, toward home—and without magic to control them, they were moving inefficiently, natural and human.

Birdie's laugh floated across the parking lot, and I smiled to hear it. She'd been through a lot this year. Just in the past twenty-four hours, she'd been interrogated by a series of suspicious, amulet-waving mages and managers at the Protectorate—but she looked great. Happy.

I was feeling cheerful too. Maybe life would finally settle down for both of us for a while. She could open her bookstore, use her inheritance to keep it afloat in the absence of actual profits, develop that well of magic she'd discovered inside herself, and maybe date that guy she was flirting with. As I drew closer, I recognized him from Cypress. The garden center. I liked men who appreciated plants. It was rare in the witch world.

"Hi," I said, walking up to them with Random dragging

behind me on the leash. He seemed to want to go to the Jeep, which was in the other direction. Eager to get home like I was. "Caffeine. Good idea."

Birdie smiled at me. "Hi."

The guy saluted me with his coffee. "Hi." He was movie-star handsome, dark and tall with a body that must've been made in the gym. Lifting perennials wouldn't do all that.

I looked behind me at Random, who continued to hang back, his posture rigid, his nose aimed homeward. "I was going to buy a banana muffin, but I think Random wants to get home."

Birdie gestured at the guy. "Jack works at Cypress." Her tone was warm and friendly, but something made me think she wasn't that into him. Usually Birdie couldn't stop talking around a good-looking guy. Actually, she couldn't stop talking around anyone.

I stopped thinking about my banana muffin and looked at her. Had the Protectorate left some kind of antianxiety spell on her, something to loosen her up? Because even if she wasn't interested in Jack for herself, she'd at least be nervous for my sake, chatting nonstop to make a connection between us.

Trust no one.

I turned a more critical eye on Jack. The Protectorate had agents all over town—surely another demon hadn't slipped in and possessed another Cypress employee? A quick probe of him didn't show anything sinister like I'd felt with Samantha last week.

Trust no one.

Random tugged at the leash. Samantha had found him running loose.

But that would mean…

For the first time in weeks, I turned my magic senses on Birdie, my friend. My best friend.

"You look so tired." She reached out and squeezed my arm. "I think you should go home. Get in bed. Sleep."

I didn't detect anything dangerous in her; in fact, she felt as warm and loving as ever, even more so. Her concern was sincere. She did feel older and more settled, as if the traumas we'd been through had made her stronger. Wiser. But something nagged at me.

"Let's go for a walk along the river," I said. "You up for that? Random seems restless, and I won't be going out again for a while."

"Sure, I love to walk." She waved at Jack, who hadn't been able to keep his eyes off her. "See you around."

"Bye, Birdie," he said, then laughed. "Bye-bye, Birdie. Right. See you. I hope."

I stared at him for another second—had Birdie made *him* nervous?—and then followed Birdie to the path behind Cypress.

My heart began to beat faster. It was a heavily wooded trail that led up and down the bank above the beach. In the winter, after weeks of rain, the river would rise dangerously high, flooding lower-altitude businesses and closing streets with slow-moving currents, potholes, and floating debris.

But we hadn't had a big winter storm yet, and the path was still dry, lined with fairy houses and tufts of yellow grasses that Random usually enjoyed sniffing, but today…

Today he was ignoring them completely. He trotted at my heels, tripping me every few feet as his body got between my legs on the narrow path. I barely missed stepping on a fairy house made of fennel stalks and poison oak leaves, which would've been bad for both of us, when I realized the tiny houses were empty. It was a sunny day in December, and the rains were about to come and bring the glory that was the wellspring—fairies from all over the west coast should've been gathering in growing numbers along the river.

But it was deserted. Squirrels and birds scampered among the brush, but the fae were missing. There was no river fairy. No dryads or flower fairies. I remembered the confrontation with Flor at the winery when all of them had suddenly fled.

My heart began pounding harder. I looked up into the trees, really focusing now, searching for the tiny fae that were so numerous and semitransparent, like gnats or dust motes, that even I forgot they were there.

There. Up ahead in the trees—a flash, a sparkling cloud, flying away. Retreating.

I stopped walking, my breath caught in my chest. Which of my companions was it—Random or Birdie? Or was it someone else nearby, such as Jake or Samantha?

One of them was possessed, and I'd been too trusting to see it.

Just that morning on the Golden Gate Bridge, I'd watched the fairies fly away from us as the car approached. Thinking like a human being, I'd taken their flight for granted—birds, if they were fast enough, fled from cars to survive.

But fairies didn't have to unless there was a supernatural threat.

It had to be Birdie. She was a single step ahead of me, seeming to be as happy as I'd ever seen her, Bright and alive, inhaling the fresh air, laughing at the head-bobbing quail that ran across the path in front of us.

The demon was not the one who had possessed Samantha, because that one had been so sour, Shadowed, and angry, I'd felt him instantly. This one was pleasant, even kind. She was glad to be alive. Her affection for me was real, as if she'd known me—

I stopped walking. Random was only too glad to let Birdie—whoever she was—continue on without us.

Did I have enough power to confront her? I did have my

beads around my neck, but when the Protectorate had confiscated them, they'd cast investigation spells over them that had diluted their power. I'd have to make new strands from fresh wood, but for right now I'd have to rely on the emergency bracelets I'd had in the Jeep, a pair I'd put on before visiting the genie.

I unhooked Random's leash. He'd be safer somewhere else. Maybe he'd run back to Cypress, and Samantha could take care of him again. Random was the best dog, but he wasn't a warrior. It was my job to rescue him, not the other way around.

I tapped Random's tail with my foot, encouraging him to leave; he immediately ran back the way we'd come.

This demon had known me before. That's why I hadn't noticed her invasion into Birdie's body. Although I'd only met her on two occasions, they had been unforgettable moments for me. For her as well, given she'd been killed at the last one, which even for demons had to be a memorable event.

"Vera," I said.

Birdie's body kept walking, but a twitch in her shoulders told me she'd heard what I'd said.

"Vera," I said more loudly. I was angry now, thinking of poor Birdie trapped inside her own mind while another being controlled her body.

How could I have missed the signs? I knew better than any witch how possessing spirits weren't always as sinister as was assumed. This one was charming and kind, and had managed to convince my cynical father it was time to get married. And even after seeing her as a charred demon corpse on their wedding day, he'd been hoping to see her again and give it another try.

Vera, it seemed, had liked the idea as well, because she was sticking around. Sooner or later she'd get back to my father and start over again. Ugh. The thought of Birdie's body with my father made my stomach turn.

My connection to Birdie must've made her vulnerable to Vera's spirit after she'd been pushed out of her previous body at the wedding. As Vera had died, she'd reached out to me and held my hand. Unbeknownst to me, I'd had a spiritual hitchhiker for a while.

That was why I must've been so sick after the wedding. The genie had exorcised her when I'd wished for good health. But then she'd found Birdie, who'd helped me recover from the wedding. No good deed went unpunished. Knowing me was dangerous.

How long had it taken Vera to move into Birdie? After she'd put the necklace in the Cypress employee lounge, after she'd been in my house...

Right. The trip to the beach. She'd brought Random back—too clean, I realized now—and hadn't come inside. She'd never come inside my house after that.

"Talk to me," I said, this time putting a magic command in my voice. The bracelets had a silver chain beneath the beads and would have more impact on her than wood alone.

Birdie's figure stopped and turned around. She was still smiling in a warm, affectionate way at me.

"Alma," she said, holding out her hands.

I crossed my wrists over each other. "Get out of Birdie right now."

Frown. "But it's perfect. She loves you."

"And I love her," I said. "I can't let you take her body."

"You'll understand once I explain," she said. "Alma. There's so much I want to tell you."

I braced my feet on the ground and gathered my power into my chest, expecting her to attack me any moment. She was still smiling, but her impressive social skills had kept her true spirit hidden from my father and from me for a very long time. I couldn't underestimate her. My training had prepared me for a cornered demon to immediately strike to kill.

"Leave Birdie's body," I said. "There's no time to talk more."

Her face brightened. "That's just it! We didn't have time, but we do now. After twenty-six years, we finally have time." She reached her arms out. "You have no idea how much I've missed you."

Chapter Forty

A deep, dark pit opened up inside my belly. I stared at the mouth, Birdie's mouth, making words that weren't hers.

Twenty… six…

I was going to be sick.

"All I want is to love and protect you. That's all I ever wanted. But the body that gave me you wasn't strong enough to survive your birth." She shook her head, her expression sad. "I knew the risks, but I thought she was young enough to make it. When it perished—"

My voice sliced through the air like a silver knife aimed at a demon's heart. *"It?"*

"The body," she said, tilting her head as if confused by my sharp tone. "When it—"

"She," I said, breathing heavily. *"She.* She died. Not you."

"It was like a death. I lost you, my baby. My daughter."

Seeing Birdie's lips form the words that I'd ached to hear my entire life was too much. I cast three sharp spells around myself to block out the sight and sound of the monster in front of me for a moment.

This demon had been inside the body of my mother when I was born. She'd returned to marry my father, and claimed to love me.

I couldn't breathe. It was too much. I needed to get away.

No, no, I had to stay. She was killing my best friend. It didn't matter if Birdie's body survived another ninety years—the spirit that made her *Birdie* couldn't survive much more of this. It might already be too late.

But my mother. She was my mother. What was she? How many lives had she known? Had she sprung into existence a century ago, or a millennium?

What was her name?

What was I?

There wasn't time. She would lie anyway; tell me just what I wanted to hear.

I broke apart the bubble I'd locked myself in and struck without hesitating. "Get out of her," I said, turning all my anger into the spell.

She flicked it away with a small wave. "I didn't choose your friend's body at first. I really didn't want to do that. The first one was a horrible person who hurt children—I didn't enjoy taking her shape, but it was necessary, and did do some good, even if the witch killer ruined it so quickly. Your father found her appealing, which was necessary." She held up two hands, fingers spread, and I felt something lock up inside me. "With your help, I was able to escape before the silver weakened me too badly. After your birth, it was fifteen years before I could roam the earth again. This time I only needed a few days."

I tried to make my mouth form words—to tell her I'd hate her for this, she had to free Birdie, I'd never forgive her —but I couldn't move.

"You brought me to Silverpool, which is such a nice place," she continued. "A wellspring, so many fairies, the beach just down the road. And I found your best friend. A lovely girl. So sweet. Both of us want the best for you, so it was easy to settle in."

Settle? I screamed inwardly.

"You must have so many questions," she said. "Your dad didn't remember much about our first time together—I'd had to tweak his brain a little bit, but men like that don't fight too hard to forget their own pain. What did he tell you about me? There must've been something. Was it my laugh? My singing? No matter what body I share, I find a way to bring the miracle of music into it."

She was asking me questions, but I couldn't answer. She'd frozen me. If I stopped struggling, maybe she'd think she'd won, and her ego would insist she give me a chance to talk about her.

I turned my mind inward and found a center of calm so I could let go of the compulsion to resist. I wondered if Birdie was having to do the same thing. Cold anger gave me strength. I would free her. I would.

Vera—I couldn't call her Birdie—watched me approvingly. "Oh good. You're starting to relax. I can't wait until we can really get to know each other."

Not going to happen. My anger was now a glacier of calm inside me, clarifying my energy into a single beam of power, stronger than any Protectorate silver dagger.

My relaxation had deceived her. Smiling, she brushed her —Birdie's—hair out of her eyes and looked up at the sky. "There's still a little sun today. Maybe we could grab some takeout at the deli and have a picnic." She made a very human, self-deprecating face. "It's still hard for me to be inside Birdie's apartment. I've been sleeping downstairs in the office. Eventually her spells will wear off—"

As I'd hoped, she'd loosened her hold on me as she'd

talked, and now I took the opportunity to strike her between the eyes with a ray of energy.

Her eyes popped open. "Oh," she gasped.

I sliced through her hold on me and erected a stronger barrier. "Leave Birdie's body," I said. "Now."

Her brow furrowed. "But I don't want to."

"You have to," I said, regaining my muscle control. I curled my toes inside my shoes, remembering to stretch my wards to my feet, and crossed my hands to hold the beads on each wrist. "I won't give you what you want. I won't be your daughter."

I felt her spirit touch me again, but this time I struck fast enough.

Her head snapped back. "Oh," she said again.

I struck again; she stumbled backward. Then she took two more steps away from me on the path.

Keeping my feet planted where they were, unwilling to risk physical contact by following her, I tried to remember how I'd felt when I'd exorcised the demon from Samantha. A sweeping, gathering, lifting, and dumping. As if I were cleaning the kitchen floor with a broom and dustpan. Lots of bits and pieces of her were all over the place—inside Birdie's skin, floating around her head, in the air between us, seeping into the soil—and I had to find it and bring it into a manageable density.

She was a spirit; physical form was unnatural for her. Her primary instinct was to scatter, float, disperse, and so to push her out of Birdie, I could leverage the innate tendencies of her kind. It wasn't normal for her to take Birdie's body. Forces bigger, older, and more powerful than mine wanted her to get out.

"But I *know* you want to know me," she whispered. "It's here. I can feel it." She touched Birdie's chest, but my own heart squeezed.

And then memories washed over me. School gatherings, holidays, mealtimes, breakups, celebrations—all alone, or with Malcolm, wondering who she was. Who I was.

The pressure in my heart became more intense, interfering with my breathing. My ribs creaked. Love as pure as anything I'd ever felt before surged into my body. It was too much, too strong, a tsunami of emotion that made my knees buckle. I heard myself cry out. As I fell to the ground, I reached out to break my fall, severing my connection to my beads, and forgot what I was fighting for. Didn't I want to just let go and enjoy the wave? Drown in this love I'd wanted my entire life?

I rolled onto my back, feeling a sharp rock under my shoulder blade but not caring about the pain. The blue sky was vast and Bright. Really, there wasn't anything to worry about. All troubles were temporary. Life was so short. The eternal experience for all beings was spirit, energy, and love. It didn't matter if little ones suffered, even died.

Idly I noticed the sky was only half-blue. Dark clouds were pushing in from the northwest. It was getting colder, too, and I smelled moisture in the air. Rain was coming. The fairies loved this time of year, coming from as far as Alaska or Baja to celebrate in Silverpool. Dryads in brown dresses. Goblins in red or green. Flower fae in bright colors or naked, shimmering and semitransparent. Ancient enemies would stop fighting for the solstice until the earth turned again and again, weeks passed, the wellspring dried up, and they fought or fled again.

"Go," I told the spirit inside me—because Vera had left Birdie, as I'd insisted, but had then taken up residence inside myself. The loneliness I'd tasted every day of my life was gone, and I'd never forget the pure wholeness I was feeling now. But the price would be my life, and I wanted to live. "You gave me life. Don't take it away."

My words were a whisper, but she was inside me, sharing them with me as I spoke, and she heard them well. I knew she did; I felt her as well as she felt me.

And then she began to slip away. It hurt—it hurt so much—and then the pain was gone. Only joy remained.

My vision came back into focus. I was lying on the ground, staring at the blackening sky. Time had passed, and no more blue sky remained. Hearing a groan, I pushed myself up and scrambled over to Birdie's body.

<h1 style="text-align:center">Chapter Forty-One</h1>

Birdie was alive, but her eyes were closed.

I gathered her in my arms and pulled her halfway into my lap. "I'm so sorry," I said. "I'm so sorry. I should've seen her earlier. I'm so sorry."

There had been warning signs. Random hadn't liked her. She'd refused to come to my house. She'd refused to go up with me into her new home, which she was so proud of. She'd stopped talking compulsively all the time and hadn't been nervous around people, even during the hours of Protectorate interrogation.

But really, I should've realized something was wrong when she'd offered me coffee.

Not to mention how she'd killed Flor. It must've been easy for her—a little human trying to hurt her "daughter." But I'd thought Birdie had somehow suddenly developed the ruthlessness to kill another human being. Her true nature would've been to disarm Flor, strike her down and break the spell—not snuff her out. Other witches or other humans would've killed, certainly—but not Birdie. She was too sweet.

The kind of person vulnerable to a well-meaning demon possession.

"Birdie?" I asked, over and over. "Talk to me. It's me, Alma."

"Let me try," a voice said behind me.

I looked up. "Seth!" He wore heavy fleece and hiking boots, and his hair was messy and unwashed.

"I didn't abandon you on purpose," he said, kneeling next to me. "I hope you know that. She stuck me in the woods. Here, let me hold her."

I let him put his arm around Birdie's shoulders. He sat cross-legged in the dirt as raindrops began to fall on all of us.

"Where did you go?" I asked, wiping rain from my cheeks. Some of it might have been tears mixed with rain. I was so glad to see him. If anyone could help Birdie, it would be a changeling.

"That spirit in Birdie kept me away from you." Shaking his head, he put his palm over Birdie's forehead. "She was an old one. Strong. Kicked me out of Silverpool on Thursday night after we last saw each other."

"We argued," I said.

"She must not have liked that." He stroked Birdie's hair and hummed a tune I could barely hear, in a high register like a mosquito, beautiful but sad.

I wiped more tears away. "Will she be all right?"

Nodding, he continued to hum. I looked up at the sky and let the rain pelt me in the face. I'd have to make it up to her. Would the bookstore need a clerk? Vacuuming? A free beaded necklace with every purchase?

She had to be all right. I'd never forgive myself.

"Let's bring her to your place," he said.

"Won't that hurt you?" I asked.

"I'll manage."

Together we lifted Birdie, who was able to get her feet

under herself, a good sign, although we had to help her walk. I held her head against mine and made soothing noises all the way to the Cypress parking lot. Random ran out from behind some cars and paraded along with us.

"Coward," I told him affectionately.

"He's no dummy," Seth said. "Let's put her in my car. Yours is a hoarder's paradise."

"I was evacuating!"

"I've seen your garage. It always looks like that." The back door of the little blue rental car flew open, and we eased her inside. Even empty, she barely fit. The interior smelled like lily of the valley.

"I'll meet you there," I said, running over to my Jeep with Random.

Five minutes later, we carried her into my house. Her eyes had fluttered open but weren't focusing on anything; she kept asking if the nice lady found her keys.

"She was so nice," Birdie said. "Did she find them? Nice lady. I hope she found her keys. Do you know if she found her keys? She was really nice."

"Yes," I told her, fluffing up pillows on the couch before helping her to lie down. "She found her keys. She's gone now."

With a sigh, Birdie smiled and let her head fall back onto a pillow. "That's good. She was a nice lady."

"So you said." I looked at Seth, who rolled his eyes. "It's time to wake up now, Birdie. You've been sleeping."

While Seth stayed with her, I hurried into the kitchen and poured a small glass of wellspring water from a bottle I'd left on the counter for Willy while I was gone. With Seth holding her upright, I cupped her cheek and helped her drink it. Most of it dribbled onto her chest and the couch, but enough went down her throat to do its magic.

Her eyes popped open. "Did that lady find her keys?"

Seth stifled a laugh. Avoiding his eyes so I wouldn't laugh too, I put my hand on Birdie's shoulder and felt the warm, true energy of her spirit running through her body.

"She sure did," I said. "She's gone now."

"Oh, that's too bad." Birdie took the glass and finished it by herself, every drop going in her mouth. Then she inhaled deeply, looked around with bright eyes, and smiled. "She was really nice."

Epilogue

irdie didn't remember anything other than a powerful impression of a very, very nice woman who'd lost her keys. Even a week later, she was still forgetting what I'd told her and would ask again if the woman had found them. It was as if her brain had been caught in a maze, kept busy in an altruistic quest so she wouldn't notice her body had been completely hijacked.

For a week after Vera had left her body, she stayed with me at my house; I wouldn't let her leave the property boundary, and I even discouraged her from going outside. Vera's spirit was out there, probably nearby, looking for somewhere to land. I'd felt the intensity of her love and believed she would always be nearby if she could, watching me, waiting for another opening. All my life I'd wanted a mom; now I had a stalker.

Although I couldn't shake the feeling she was out there watching me, I took Random for his second walk of the day on Saturday afternoon, a week after Birdie and I had returned from San Francisco. Sunset came before five, and the light was already fading; winter was in the air. Under my puffy coat, the newest tattoo on my arm was still sore to the touch. What was causing them? How many more would I get? I'd have to find a witch who studied skin spells to help me determine precisely what was happening.

As I walked down the street, Seth flashed into existence at the end of his driveway. "Good evening," he said, bending over to pet Random, who was more in love with him than ever.

"I wish you'd stop doing that." My heart was pounding from the surprise. "I don't need any more excitement."

He grinned. "I'm so flattered to know I excite you."

I rolled my eyes. Since he'd regained his fae powers, he'd resumed the incessant flirting. I pretended to be annoyed but was secretly pleased he was feeling better. Mopey, springwater-addicted Seth had been a downer.

"I've been thinking about Vera," he said, falling into step beside me.

"Not this again," I said. He'd been trying to convince me to forgive—or at least understand—her. To my surprise, although he'd been so critical of his mother's decision decades ago to steal the body he now possessed, Seth had a more sympathetic view of Vera.

"She loves you," he said.

"Whatever that monster thinks she feels, it doesn't matter." I was still furious and was rethinking my philosophical opposition to demon killing. I thought she deserved it, though I knew I couldn't ever stab her myself. "She almost killed Birdie."

"She could've wiped Birdie out completely," he said. "But she didn't. She kept her relatively safe and sane, which isn't easy. I wouldn't be able to do it. I think she would've moved out as soon as she'd found a more justifiable victim."

"Moved out? People aren't apartments."

With a shrug, he moved Random's leash to his other

hand. When Seth was around, the leash was just a formality; he had an invisible power over my dog that made me jealous. "Being born into physical form is a privilege you've never had to consider—"

I grabbed Random's leash. "Are you saying I need to check my privilege before I give demons a hard time for possessing people?"

The corner of his lip curved upward, but he shook his head and said seriously, "I don't think she's a demon."

I stopped walking and stared at him. "But—" I'd seen Vera's husk at the wedding. I'd thought only demons burned up like that. "Do you mean… she's a changeling? Like you?"

He recoiled. "Brightness no. She's nothing like me. Can't you tell?"

"Give me a break. The subtleties of spirits possessing humans are a little hard for a mere mortal to grasp."

"That's what the Protectorate should be teaching," he said, "instead of how to slide silver blades into people."

"Possessed people," I said.

"We're not all the same."

"Don't lecture me," I said. "I might be the only witch on the planet who agrees with that. And maybe Percy." The apprentice had sent me a text from the southern Oregon coast, suggesting I drive up someday to check out the carnivorous plant preserve he'd found.

"You're right," he said. "I apologize. You have an unusual openness of mind for a Protectorate witch."

I sniffed. "Thank you."

"I'm sure, in time, you'll be ready to accept the obvious," he continued.

I didn't like the sound of that. "You can't mean…"

He looked up at the sky, then slowly back down at me. "I can almost hear the harps playing, can't you?"

"No," I said. "You can't honestly believe, after what she

did, after how Birdie suffered, the way she was willing to… She can't be a…"

"She might not be an angel anymore, but I think she started out in that job."

My mind reeled. "She killed Flor!"

"And it really upset her, you said. She was forced into it."

"Angels can't kill people," I said. "Flor hadn't even killed anyone directly. She'd just—" My teeth clamped shut.

Demon's balls. I kept forgetting. Even though Seth must know about the genie, I couldn't mention her without my mouth freezing up. If I fought it, I'd pass out. I had to turn my attention to Random, who was sniffing the stop sign at the bottom of the hill, and wait for the urge to talk about Jen Bardak to pass.

"Flor had almost killed *you*, her daughter," Seth said. "That was what pushed her over the line."

"The woman who gave birth to me was not Vera," I said. "A human woman was my mother. I'll never know her. Vera was a bystander, a thief."

"You're the daughter of both the human woman and the possessing spirit. Vera is a thief like your father. I bet she really does love him."

"You're crazy," I said. "You're so far gone in the human experience, you're giving human motives to supernatural monsters."

"Who better to make that call," he asked, "than another monster?"

I strode across Main Street and walked onto the bridge. The river was beneath us, the winery up ahead in the hills. "I'm not part angel," I said. "I can't even sing."

"I thought you'd be curious to know the truth about yourself. But maybe it's too soon." He paused in the middle of the bridge and braced his elbows on the railing, looking upriver. The rows of grapevines in the hills were visible through a gap in the trees. "I'm going to be leaving for a little while. I came by to say goodbye."

Now that he was free to travel, I hadn't expected him to stay as long as he had. "Where are you going?" I tried to keep my curiosity—and disappointment—out of my voice. Since he'd regained his health, he'd also regained the personality he'd had when we'd first met, and it made me uneasy. He wasn't harmless anymore.

"Don't know. Everywhere and nowhere." He looked up at the winery. "It's time." He squatted down and scratched Random roughly, making him shake his leg and writhe in ecstasy.

"When do you think you'll be back?" I asked.

He looked up at me and grinned. "Already missing me?"

I felt my heart pounding. "Birdie will ask." He'd always been too charming. Too good-looking. Too... important. "Take care of yourself."

"If I don't, you might track me down and do it for me," he said.

"I'm done with taking care of you," I said.

"Too bad." He stood up, glanced over my shoulder at the winery again. "Really is getting late. I'll be in touch."

I turned my head to see what he was looking at, but it was just the trees and vineyard. When I turned back, he was gone. I cast out my senses, feeling for his spirit, coming up as empty as always.

"Can't you even say goodbye?" I yelled into the empty air.

Behind me, I heard Raynor say, "I just got here."

Random stopped sniffing the ground where Seth had stood and pulled at the leash to greet the newcomer, who had just stepped onto the bridge from the other side.

Raynor wore unusually casual clothes—fleece and denim, as if he were an outdoorsy man just enjoying the weekend. A wool beanie covered his bald head, and he'd started to let his beard grow out. He looked like a superhero in street clothes, pretending to be a normie but not quite pulling it off.

We hadn't spoken since my interrogation after Flor's death. Even then, he'd kept his distance, letting the New York mages handle the questioning. If the spit of his I'd saved held any power, I hadn't had the chance to use it.

I'd hoped he'd finally decided to leave me and Silverpool alone. Not because I'd convinced him with my actions but because I'd made that deal with a genie. The torc had to have been worth some period of safety.

"What are you doing here?" I asked.

He approached, patted Random, and braced his elbows on the bridge railing the same place Seth had done. "Can't you guess?"

My stomach tensed. Were they going to set the town on fire again? Bury Cypress? Dam the river? Had a smarter witch paid the genie a higher price for a better wish?

"No," I said. "Just tell me. Please."

He looked over at the winery, his expression unreadable. "I'm the new Protector of Silverpool."

Books by Gretchen Galway

SONOMA WITCHES (Paranormal Mystery)

Dead Witch on a Bridge (Sonoma Witches #1)

Hex at a House Party (Sonoma Witches #2)

A Spell to Die For (Sonoma Witches #3)

Charmed to Death (Sonoma Witches #4)

Murder by Magic (Sonoma Witches #5)

Hexed in Show (Sonoma Witches #6)

Dead Witch in the Library (Sonoma Witches #7)

The Sonoma Witches Series Box Set: First Three Novels (Sonoma Witches Books 1-3)

OAKLAND HILLS SERIES (Romance)

Love Handles (Oakland Hills #1)

This Time Next Door (Oakland Hills #2)

Not Quite Perfect (Oakland Hills #3)

This Changes Everything (Oakland Hills #4)

Quick Takes (Oakland Hills Stories Boxed Set)

Going For Broke (Oakland Hills #5)

Going Wild (Oakland Hills #6)

Oakland Hills Romantic Comedy Boxed Set (Books 1-3)

RESORT TO LOVE SERIES (Romance)

The Supermodel's Best Friend (Resort to Love #1)

Diving In (Resort to Love #2)

About the Author

GRETCHEN GALWAY is a *USA Today* bestselling author who writes mystery, fantasy, and romance. She lives in Sonoma County, California.

For more information:
www.gretchengalway.com